Praise for *From Jim Crow to CEO: The Willie E. Artis Story*

"Most stories out of Flint are not for the faint of heart. It's a once-great city that has been whipsawed by global economic trends, political malfeasance, and de-industrialization. Yet the underlying spirit of the city somehow endures, and that spirit is captured in the story of Willie Artis. On one level, it's an in-depth portrait of an entrepreneur. But to call this a business book would be selling it short. It's really the story of someone succeeding at life in a place all too often defined by failure." —**Gordon Young**, author of *Teardown: Memoir of a Vanishing City*

"I had the opportunity and pleasure to meet Willie in the early 1980s when I and others participated in the automotive industry's supply base. Willie was extremely supportive and outspoken relative to these specialized programs from which we all received significant benefits. Willie was well respected by management and willingly shared his expertise with other minority suppliers. We should all be thankful for his commitment, dedication, and support!"
—**Dave Bing**, Bing Youth Institute and former Mayor of Detroit

"When you read Willie Artis's story of how he persevered through Jim Crow's school of very hard knocks in the South to become founder and CEO of a successful manufacturing business in Michigan, you will be astounded by the number of rungs he climbed despite all of the weight on his shoulders from racism and discrimination. The way Willie kept moving will keep you turning the page to find out what's next. In this fascinating first-person account of his life, you will come to know his friends, family and co-workers like they are your own—except Willie's include B.B. King and President Obama. This is a remarkable memoir covering a chapter in American history of which too few people pay any attention. The era of segregation, as Willie reminds us, may return if our past is forgotten. With a touch of southern charm, Beale Street hustle, Chicago smarts, and Vehicle City muscle, Willie's account of how he lived up to his own high standards, learned from his mistakes, based his decisions on merit, and changed his corner of corporate America and his local community, offers numerous lessons for today's entrepreneurs, business managers, civic leaders and anyone aspiring to a good life and a better world." —**Dayne Walling**, former Mayor of Flint and Rhodes Scholar

"Willie Artis and I have been friends for over 30 years and I have always admired his business success. I am proud that his achievements have been recognized nationally and locally. Although Willie has retired, the company continues to grow as a multimillion-dollar enterprise. His story is a must-read." —**Harcourt G. Harris, M.D.**, former Chairman, Omnicare

"Willie's story is one of perseverance and vision. The lessons of his ability to succeed in business are a great read and certainly helped me to be the businesswoman I am today. Entrepreneurs young and old will find Willie's experiences to be thought provoking and perhaps a spark to a new idea of their own. I hope that all readers get to know Willie as well as I do and find his story to be as inspirational as he is in real life." —**Jane Worthing**, President and CEO, The Genesee Group, Inc.

"Willie E. Artis is a personification of the American Dream. I have known Willie for over 40 years. He had a vision for his company, unbounded energy, terrific talent, a lack of fear and almost no money. He was determined to succeed and, against all odds, he did so, overcoming recession and a number of significant challenges. Willie was always the leader, encouraging and inspiring his employees and making sure that they and their families were well taken care of. He was determined that his company would be a minority company in more than just ownership and he has recruited, trained, and empowered a majority of minority workers from the very beginning. Willie E. Artis, for all of his success, is still a warm and loving man who has friends in every walk of life, of every color and every strata. The benefits of his creation continue for others, bettering and empowering their lives. I have always been proud to say that Willie is my friend." —**Bernard L. McAra, BA, JD**, Master in Taxation

"It is rare in life to meet a person of strong character who stays true to his word while surmounting obstacles that are only accomplished by tremendous fortitude, talent and strength. Willie E. Artis is the epitome of that man of character who worked tirelessly through the years to build a successful business while facing a multitude of odds. One can only imagine what he must have felt and experienced, as he faced the trials of being a young visionary and a person of color with an entrepreneurial spirit. As a tenacious businessman, Willie has lived through the hard days and transformed what was thought to be a non-traditional business with a non-traditional leader at the helm, into a textbook testimony. He comes out on the other side as a true success. Today, he shares his journey as he leaves a rich legacy for all to marvel and enjoy." —**Lennetta Bradley Coney**, President, Foundation for Mott Community College

"The Willie E. Artis personal story allows us to focus on his experience from the inside. It shows his factual and human path to becoming a successful businessman. He uses his powerful story to illustrate how to be competitive in a tough business environment. Best of all, he shows us how he comes through to the other side, a healthy, stronger person." —**Veronica Artis**, Wife and Business Partner

"It is *honest*! Business memoirs celebrate success, and Willie's story is full of exceptional success. But this story also celebrates the mistakes as terrific opportunities to learn! Willie's story is that of a gentleman, with the grit and the fire in the belly that it takes to succeed in a tough, challenging, racist business world, who does it with integrity, true to one's values. Willie obviously takes joy in the accomplishments of others. His life lessons—as retold in this memoir—present that beacon of hope that young people and those who come from disadvantaged beginnings need to look to as the example of how to accomplish their dreams. Willie's story removes all the excuses we use for not pressing ahead. Willie's focus was never on fixing the blame but total focus on fixing the problems. I found his retelling of growing up under Jim Crow to be a valuable window into a past that we must continually work to never repeat. I have known Willie for decades as a start-up entrepreneur, as a successful business owner, as a community leader in Flint, as a friend and, most importantly, as a gentleman. With Willie, values and integrity rule and his life story illustrates the power of this foundation."
—**Linda S. Holloway**, former regional CPA firm President, hospital system VP and Flint community leader

FROM JIM CROW TO CEO:
THE WILLIE E. ARTIS STORY

WILLIE E. ARTIS
as told to David L. Stanley

AUXmedia, a Division of Aquarius Press
Detroit, Michigan

From Jim Crow to CEO: The Willie E. Artis Story

Cover design: Aquarius Press
Front cover photo of Author: Willie E. Artis Estate
Book jacket photo of Author: Willie E. Artis Estate
Back cover portrait: Aran Kessler Imaging
Interior photos: Willie E. Artis Estate

ISBN 978-1-7330898-5-2
LCCN 2019950618

AUXmedia LLC, in association with Aquarius Press
www.AUXmedia.studio
www.ArtisCEO.net

Printed in the United States of America

In loving memory of my parents, James and Violet Artis, who provided me with core values that helped me to succeed in life.

Contents

Acknowledgments

In 2011, my wife, Veronica Artis, strongly suggested that I think about writing the story of my life. She said, "Your accomplishments should be in a book. Perhaps it could help some other black person. They'll read it and realize that he or she could set a higher goal for him or herself."

I would like to thank Veronica for her assistance in this book. Veronica has provided me with memories and wisdom from our 25 years together as owners of our company. We worked very hard to make our business a success. I could not have done this alone.

I want to thank Jane Worthing for her willingness to step up and become the owner of the company I founded in 1978. Jane has been, and still is, the one loyal friend who would allow us to retire in comfort. Under the leadership of Jane and her executive staff, the company continues to function at a high level.

I want to thank my 88-year-old sister, Jessie Wooten. Jessie provided me with so much family historical knowledge. I was fortunate that Jessie's memories of our childhood were still sharp and clear.

I would like to thank David Stanley. We started on this project in the spring of 2016. We have worked closely together on this book, and I am grateful for his insights and his help.

—*Willie E. Artis*

Preface

How does a black kid from Memphis, Tennessee, born into poverty, with Jim Crow and segregation as a way of life and the law of the land, do something extraordinary with his life? What pieces must fall into place? How does a young black kid find the mentors and lessons that will teach him to build a multimillion-dollar corporation?

The odds against him were astronomical, and the circumstances were dire. The larger society conspired against his success. Yet, here is the story of the man who beat down those odds to claim his place at the table.

This is the life story of a black man born and raised in the Deep South in 1934. This is not a story told as you may see in the movies. This black man does not have a college degree. He struggled to get through high school because he was more interested at that time in hard work, not education. Yet he knew that education was very important but so was hard work to reach his potential.

His parents were not able to give him money. Every dollar his father earned fed his family. Fortunately for this young man, his parents did recognize the value of a good education. Along with two of his siblings, he was sent to a parochial school. Of course, in the Deep South, even this effort was a difficult task. In 1940, Memphis was the nation's 32nd largest city in the U.S. with a population of just under 300,000 people. In the pre-war era, Memphis was evenly split between black and white populations.

Yet, there were only two Catholic schools in Memphis that black children could attend. Because of Jim Crow law, the teachers at both Catholic schools were white nuns and the students were all black. However, his parents were determined to help their children achieve, in every possible way, regardless of their financial status.

As a young black man, he taught himself how to earn a living. He looked at those nearest to him who were successful and made a decision that would shape his life. He decided to surround himself with people who were smarter than him, more successful, more powerful. Today, we'd call it mentorship. Back then, we called it the school of hard knocks.

In the early 1950s, the young man left the Deep South for better opportunities in Chicago. He left his first job in Chicago because his co-workers engaged in a battle to organize a labor union for the hourly employees. He would not walk in a picket line. Yet, at his very next job, he became deeply involved in the union.

The young man's second job was a union shop. All hourly employees were required to join the union. Several months into his new job, his co-workers encouraged him to represent them as a union official. He agreed to do so and was elected. This early vote of confidence gave the young man the assurance that he was responsible, trustworthy, and honorable.

More importantly, his new position allowed him to attend college in Ohio. With the union's sponsorship, he took college classes in union management and organization.

Despite his growing influence, the young man was slapped in the face: Black people did not work in management. The better jobs always went to white employees who were managers. Black men and women worked only in the hourly ranks. Even in the North, racism was the norm.

The young man was raised in a poor home with four siblings and wonderful parents. The father told him as he grew up that hard work and honesty were always rewarded. While he never doubted his parents' wisdom, the facts were clear; as a black man, it was very difficult to get ahead. Years later, he would discover that his father was absolutely correct: *Work hard, remain honest, and you will create your own opportunities.*

The black kid from Memphis was a dreamer. He would never be satisfied to be a non-achiever, a punch-in punch-out, Monday through Friday worker. He was never satisfied with his earnings. He had to discover a better way of life. He did not know how to become a better earner, but he knew the secret was out there. He held one thought in his mind as gospel, his father's words: *Work hard and you will make things better.*

The young man wanted, *needed,* to climb the ladder. He was not a person to change jobs frequently. He wanted stability. He wanted to be promoted where he was currently employed. He wanted to be recognized for his skill and dedication. Yet, because the company did not promote black employees, his hard work was not rewarded.

A highly motivated dreamer is a powerful person. Although he craved greater earning power and a better life, the young man never thought of a business life. This young black man had no idea that a business life was waiting for him in later years.

In the 1950s, a young black man could not see himself as an entrepreneur. He did not create business plans. Never in his wildest imagination did he envision a company of his own. In Korean War-era America, young black people did not—dared not—think that far ahead in life.

When this story first began to take shape on paper in 2013, this black kid from Memphis was 79 years old. He had homes in two states and a net worth over 13 million dollars. This book is not intended to dramatize his achievements as a businessperson. It shows how wealth can be achieved with a blessing from God, a little luck, a lot of hard work, and the proper use of your God-given talent. Furthermore, it helped to have parents who were willing to provide the best guidance they could offer. Despite the abomination of racial segregation, Jim Crow, and hard times, this kid made it.

When this black kid thinks of what he has achieved over many years, there is only one piece missing. He wanted to provide material things to his parents. They passed on too early in his business life to take advantage of his business success. His parents never owned an automobile. He wanted desperately to purchase a new home and car for those most responsible for his success. Imagine that—they either rode the bus or walked where they wanted to go.

This black kid always felt his parents deserved more than what they had achieved in life. He had the financial ability to provide them with things they never had and the opportunity to have a better and more gentle life. The mother always wanted more than what the father could give her. The father gave her as much of the money he earned as life would allow. She never complained. They agreed; the children came first.

The kid's father was always the last person to eat. When he came home from work, he'd always ask, "Have the children had their dinner?" His wife would say gracefully, "Yes honey, the kids have eaten." Only then, would he would eat.

When this black kid came of age, Jim Crow was the law of the land. A black man could go to jail for any number of violations; drinking from the wrong fountain, using the wrong rest room, sitting in the wrong seat in a theater or at a lunch counter, being accused of merely looking at a white woman. For a black person, the American dream was a pipe dream.

This black man always wanted more but did not know how to get it.

I am that black man. My name is Willie Eldrage Artis. I live in Flint, Michigan, and this is my story.

Chapter 1
The Early Years

My mother, Violet Artis, was born in Farrow, Mississippi in 1900. Farrow does not exist today. Our mother had very little education. Our grandfather, Robert Morris, my mother's father, insisted that she was needed to help on the farm. In our Grandpa's opinion, there were functions that could be performed by a small child that would be helpful to the family working on a farm in the south; a farm they did not own.

My grandparents were sharecroppers. Sharecropping was the way Jim Crow law kept black people in poverty after slavery was outlawed. Sharecroppers were forced to sign agreements that ensured they'd continue in debt to the landowners. It looked good on the outside; the landowners supplied land and seed, tools and a mule. However, since the farmers were forced to do business with the plantation store on credit and were entitled to only a small portion of the crop proceeds, sharecropping ensured that the farmer stayed under the landowner's thumb. Children were family, sure, but just like adults, they were labor.

A child of five was expected to pick cotton. The child would drag a bag as big as a calf up and down the rows, plucking cotton bolls from plants and placing them in the bag. A small child would feed the chickens, if the family was lucky enough to own any. They were also expected to gather cow dung from the main farms to burn as fuel.

In the rural South of my mother's childhood, nearly 40% of

all children died before adulthood. Children of that era were loved, necessary, and sadly, too often expendable.

My father's name was James Artis. James and Violet were older when they married. Daddy was 42. Mama was 30. Typical of the time, they immediately had children. In total, Mama bore nine children. Again, as was usual for the times in the South among black people, she lost four children at birth. Those that survived were Louvenia, Howard, Robert, Jessie, and the baby. Me, Willie Artis.

In the early 1920s, Mama told our father that she had to get out of Mississippi. After a lengthy discussion, my parents agreed that St. Louis made good sense. They decided that Daddy should head to St. Louis by way of Memphis. As my Mother had relatives there, this would give my father a home base for a while; he could find a little work, save some money, and then continue to St. Louis.

My father left for St. Louis in 1928. It was a big day. Black people did not travel far in the South in the Jim Crow era. As planned, Daddy stopped in Memphis. My mother's Uncle George met Daddy at the station. Uncle George convinced him to stay and look for real work.

Just like today, family looked after family. Daddy stayed with them until he found a good job. It took him several weeks, but he finally settled into place at Jones Lumber as a carpenter and glass cutter. Living with family, he could set a few dollars aside. With that bit of a nest egg, he sent for my mother and my older sister Louvenia. Still, my parents really wanted to move to St. Louis.

It is 300 miles from the Southside of Memphis to St. Louis. Given the economics of the Jim Crow era, it may have well been 3,000 miles. My parents never saved enough money to reach their destination. Therefore, my parents decided to remain in Memphis and raise the family.

My mother had saved some money from her days of work while living in Mississippi. As an adult, Mama worked on her father's farm for pay. When Mama made it to Memphis, our parents rented a large house in south Memphis. The house had many rooms and my mother decided to turn this house into a boarding house and rent the rooms to earn additional income for the family.

She rented only to single working men. No job? No room. In return, she would provide one meal per day to the renters. Momma grew what she could in her garden; beans, potatoes, greens. What she couldn't grow, she got at the market. Between Mama's room and board, and Daddy's pay from the lumber company, the small family got by.

Within several years, between the money my mother earned and my father's hard work, the family bought their own house. They found a small home in the Klondike section of town. It was no small feat for a black family in that era to own their own home.

Klondike was the black part of town. No white people. Not just by choice, but by law. Jim Crow laws barred integrated neighborhoods. The only white people we saw were women picking up laundry from a neighbor. Mrs. Cooper, a true entrepreneur in her own right, had a linen laundry business in the rear of her home. She made a financial contribution to her family. White women from other neighborhoods would bring in their dirty linen and pick up clean linen on a weekly basis from Mrs. Cooper. Imagine, a black woman in the 1920s and 1930s had her own business.

Chapter 2
I Was Blessed with Great Parents

I say with no doubt in my voice that my parents were the greatest people in the world. Our home was poor, my parents were poor, yet Mama and Daddy always took care of each other and they took care of the children.

A large part of that was that I had a father who had integrity and self-respect. He was law-abiding. He was honest. He loved my mother. We always knew where our father was. Daddy was either at church, at work, or at home. In the mornings, there was no fooling around. Daddy got up, got dressed, and went to work. Most importantly, Daddy made sure we knew that he was going to work. From as far back as I can remember, Daddy instilled upon us a work ethic.

Our mother did not work outside the home. Well, she did work for about six weeks doing housework for a white family. But the day I set our house on fire while putting paper into the oil stove was the day she stopped working. The fire didn't cause a lot of damage, but it was scary enough that my father stopped our mother from working at all. Our father was always adamant about supporting his family. Daddy believed he could support his family without our mother cleaning a house for white people for very little pay. Mama never worked again in her life.

Although we were born and raised in the South and governed by Jim Crow law, we were a happy family. Our father was totally committed to his family. We were poor, but we didn't know it.

Our parents had extraordinary family values with strong core principles. There was no lying in our house. No stealing. No fudging. Things were right, or they were wrong. The rules were clear. The punishments were clear, quick, and just.

During the Depression, Mama always found a way to feed us. Like many women in that era, she was a master of pulling a meal out of nothing. She could cook a meal from scraps and shreds in her kitchen. Friday dinner was always great because that was payday for Daddy. He would purchase two large bags of groceries on his way home from work. I would watch for him to come down the street so I could run and meet him to help carry the bags.

There was never a Christmas that we did not have a tree and toys. In 1944, when I was 10, the height of the war, my father purchased a new bicycle for me. Although I was not big enough to ride it without falling off, I managed to learn how to ride my new bike. In those days, bicycles only came in one size. I had to push my bike three doors down the street, get up on the front porch of our neighbor and jump on the bike to ride. I performed this routine for several days until I could reach the pedals sufficiently enough to keep from falling. How he managed to find and buy a boy's bicycle at the peak of World War II remains a family mystery.

I never met any of Daddy's relatives. Our father had brothers, sisters, and other relatives living in Alabama. When Daddy left for Mississippi, he never communicated with any of his relatives for the balance of his life. In an era of cell phones and email and even U.S. Mail, it's hard to imagine how difficult communication was in the Deep South of the Depression and WWII eras.

As our family grew, my parents decided to sell the boarding house. Mama and Daddy realized that the children needed care and feeding more than Mama's boarders did.

In 1929, our parents purchased a three-room house. Still under the crushing weight of Jim Crow, they had to buy a house in a "Blacks-Only" neighborhood. Two of my brothers and sisters were born in that original home. Over the years, my father—a carpenter—added several rooms to the house. Originally, we had an outdoor toilet located behind the house. The first thing Daddy built was an indoor bathroom. Over the years of my childhood, the original three rooms increased to seven.

The house became sufficient in size to accommodate not only Daddy's children, but his seven grandchildren as well. My sister Jessie had four children and my brother Robert had three children. After Robert's wife passed away in their adopted hometown of Chicago, he sent his three children to live with our parents.

By this time, I had moved out and made my way to Chicago as well. Jessie had steady work, yet she continued to live at home with our parents. Her husband, an unreliable man, was in and out of her life as their children grew up. Still the dependable breadwinner, it was Daddy's paycheck that supported his daughter and her children.

"Teenage Years"

Chapter 3
My Early Childhood

I lived in a neighborhood where there was absolutely no serious crime or drugs. As kids, we might have a fist fight. The next day, maybe even the same day, we would be hugging each other and playing marbles in a vacant field. No one stayed mad for very long. At night, doors were not locked. The screen door would be hooked to keep the wind from blowing it open. Everyone on Annie Street knew each other. Further out from Annie Street, people on neighboring streets knew each other and we knew them. A real upside was 99% of the kids had both parents while growing up.

Children went to school; some went to public school and others attended one of the two Catholic schools for black children. Parents looked after other people's kids. Big kids looked out for little ones. Black folks in those days looked out for each other. We were a neighborhood. When times are tough, it really does take a village.

Although we played together as kids, we did not know the last names of most of the children we grew up with. We only knew the last names of a few kids. We always addressed each other by a first name or a nickname, so last names were not necessary. One kid might be "Turtle, over at the blue house." Another might be, "You know, Curtis, lives over on the corner."

It was a quiet neighborhood. Occasionally, we would see a police car. White police officers liked to drive with their windows down during the summer months and stare at the black children playing in the streets. I don't know what they were thinking about. We played ball and chased each other around. The girls played hopscotch and dolls and jumped rope. *Little dirt-poor kids, what else would they be doing?*

I don't know how my parents managed, but Mama and Daddy kept all us kids happy. My mother was not an educated woman. She did raise five children and seven grandchildren in her home on a seriously limited income in the middle of the most repressive times. It was work. Hard work.

Mama learned hard work early. As I mentioned, she was taken out of school in Mississippi to help Grandpa, her father, on the farm. In the first years of the 20th century, life in the deep South for black people hadn't changed much since Reconstruction. Work hard. Keep your head down around white people. Don't speak to whites unless spoken to and then always with a "Yassuh" or "Yes'm." With all those harsh lessons, Mama learned to read people and gained a life's worth of common sense. I was fortunate enough that she passed that on to me. Mama died from cancer in November of 1972, at the age of 72.

Mama was a militant. I wouldn't hear that word until the 1950s and 1960s, and she never knew it, but she was a trailblazer. During my mother's lifetime, she was a strong and enduring presence. We may have been legally required to live under Jim Crow law, but we didn't have to like it. For Mama, being able to shop in a white clothing store yet forbidden to try on hats or clothing angered her to no end. We'd hear her say through clenched teeth, "Like my dollars ain't as good as those white folks' dollars."

Mama did not realize how aggressive she really was. She absolutely resented the fact that if she wanted a new pair of shoes or a new hat to wear to church, she had to buy them without trying them on. Our mother would openly level criticism at her relatives and friends when they purchased clothing from certain department stores that would not allow black people to try on their purchases.

There were a few department stores that would allow black people to try on their purchases before paying for them. They were not located in the downtown shopping area where the high and mighty of Memphis—those fancy white folks who didn't like to mix with black folks—always shopped with their racist noses in the air. But Mama knew about voting with her wallet. She would only shop at the stores outside of downtown where she could try on the goods.

Mama's brother, Uncle Henry, worked for a food company. He delivered flour and food supplies to grocery stores outside of Memphis. One day, while he was loading his truck with bags of flour, he had a disagreement with his supervisor which spilled over into an altercation. The supervisor, a white man, slapped my Uncle Henry. My uncle hit the supervisor with his fist and knocked him down.

Uncle Henry was arrested and jailed. He was sentenced to six months in what was called a "workhouse." A workhouse is a southern genteel way of saying "prison." This situation caused a great deal of pain for my mother. Mama had to explain to our grandfather what happened to his son. She informed him that Henry had hit a white man. In Memphis, during Jim Crow, a black man could *never* hit a white man—this was against the law, regardless of the reason. It always meant jail. And jail always meant beatings by cops and guards.

One Sunday morning, my brother and a friend were walking. The police stopped their patrol car, got out and one asked,

"Where you two niggers going?"

My brother said, "We're not going anyplace, sir. Just walking towards home."

"Get in the car," the cop said. "We think you two guys broke into the ice cream factory last night."

The cops put them in handcuffs, took them to a secluded place and beat the hell out of them.

The cops dragged their bloody bodies back into the car and drove to our home. They hauled my brother's still-cuffed body up our front steps like a sack of cotton. The police entered our home without knocking. They barged right in, hauled my brother in with them, and dumped his body on the floor. One cop stood on my brother's chest.

Mama began to scream. The other racist cop told my mother to shut up and he unsnapped his gun. When Mama started screaming, I ran out the back door to the church. I knew Daddy was teaching Sunday school. My father immediately left church for home. My father walked in his front door and went directly to the cops. My father was a strong man. Quiet, but his strength radiated outwards.

"What has my son done to cause you to arrest him?" Daddy asked.

One cop gave him the ice cream story.

The other said, "We're going to take this boy (my brother) back to the car and talk to them."

My brother's friend was in the backseat of the police car. They'd already been to his home where they intimidated his family as well.

Daddy knew that "talk to them" was code for "beat the crap out of them again." My father, with his quiet dignity, managed to convince the cops to let the boys go. He saved both from another savage, brutal beating.

My father found out later that the ice cream factory never had a break-in. The two cops wanted to stop two black guys and create a situation for them and their families. Jim Crow law allowed them to do so. It was commonplace for a cop to grab a black man or teen, cuff him, drag him somewhere, and beat him to a bloody pulp. Maybe the cop would then dump him back in their front yard. Maybe he just left the bloody man in a field to find a way home with shattered bones.

Daddy lived for stability. My father did not change jobs. He was employed by one lumber company for over 60 years. He lived to see projects through to completion. After Mama and Daddy moved to Memphis, he attended Booker T. Washington night school and finished the 11th grade.

My father lived for his integrity. He created such a sense of trust that if he had a late lumber delivery, he could bring the lumber truck home with him. The white owner trusted Daddy, and only Daddy, with that privilege.

Daddy was a great man, a wonderful teacher, role model, and father. After he finally retired, I wanted to do something for him in his old age. Every year, I would fly him from Memphis to my home in Flint for a vacation.

In 1973, I flew Daddy into Flint on his first plane ride. I buzzed down to Memphis and we flew together to my home. Daddy was captivated by flight. I loved to watch him those first few flights. He was thrilled just to be on the inside of a plane. When it was time for take-off, Daddy would stare out the window, fascinated to see the ground leave us below. His eyes would get big. I could feel his heart swell.

Once back on the ground, Daddy would tell anyone—strangers, friends, waitresses in a diner—"My son had me fly on this big bird." He was so proud of me, that I knew my way around this world. After a few times of flying on a plane to Flint for visits, I stopped accompanying him. He'd still be excited to tell me about the flight.

"Oh, son, I was on a 737 this time," Daddy would say. "We had a little turbulence right after take-off."

In 1975, we went to Ohio's Cedar Point Amusement park for a few days. Right on the shore of Lake Erie, we stayed at a local motel and I made sure that Daddy had his own room. One morning, we were preparing to go to breakfast and his room was being cleaned. While we walked to the restaurant, my father leaned over and said to me,

"Son, never in my life did I ever think I would have a white maid to clean up behind me."

In 1977, we visited the city of Windsor in Ontario, Canada. Windsor, just across the Detroit River from Detroit itself, is a geographic oddity. To get into Windsor, you drive almost due south via the tunnel that connects the two cities.

My father had never seen or experienced the procedures of going through Customs. He was a little shocked at the requirements: "Driver's license. Are you bringing anything into Canada? How long are you staying? What is the purpose of your visit?"

Daddy didn't realize that the Detroit-Windsor crossing (via the tunnel under the Detroit River and the Ambassador Bridge over the river) is the busiest US-Canada crossing in the United States. Tens of thousands of people cross each way every day for work, and even in the 1970s, billions of dollars in trade went back and forth.

I also took Daddy to Niagara Falls on the Canadian side. More than four million cubic feet of water rolls over the top of Niagara Falls every minute. The three falls that make up Niagara are the most powerful waterfalls in the world. Daddy and I donned the tourist raincoats and walked near the base of the falls.

As we walked, we saw tourists riding onboard the *Maid of the Mist*, a 65-foot, 65-ton ship that carries 210 passengers. She's powered by twin 250-horsepower diesels to get her passengers as close as possible to the base of the 165-foot falls.

"Daddy," I said. "You want to go for a boat ride?"

He stared at me long and hard, his eyes flicking back and

forth between me, the top of the falls, and the *Maid of the Mist*. I recognized that look. It was the one he used on me when he was just flabbergasted at something dumb I had done as a kid.

"Not today, son," he said. "Not today."

It is with both pride and humility that I can say that I am successful. Over the last 35 years of my business life, by any measure, I have accumulated substantial assets. Yet, I missed out on two things. I desperately wanted to purchase my parents a comfortable new home in Memphis. I also wanted to give them something they never had, a brand new car with all the accessories. Sadly, they passed away before I could achieve this most important goal. I couldn't begin to repay them for all they did, but a new home with air conditioning and a loaded car would have made their later years more comfortable.

When Daddy passed away in September 1981, he was 92 years old. My older brother Howard became a father figure to us. Howard lived in Milwaukee, Wisconsin. He owned a car that was not in good condition.

I decided to remedy that situation. I bought Howard two nice cars, Chevrolets, both fully loaded, all the options. He loved those cars. I think it was not only that they were very nice, but that his brother had accomplished enough with his life that he could afford to give his brother a couple of expensive vehicles. My brother Howard drove to church until his health deteriorated to the point that prevented him from driving.

When I was 13 years of age, my father taught me to drive. I learned on an old truck that belonged to the lumberyard where Daddy worked. It had a stick shift and as a skinny kid, it was difficult for me to move the gear. Back in the days before synchronized manual transmissions, shifting gears was hard work. I'd have to jump on the clutch pedal with both feet, all my weight, to get it to engage. Sometimes I'd have to take both hands off the wheel and yank that floor-mounted lever around. With no power-steering, it took a lot of arm strength to turn that big truck steering wheel, too. Trying to manage all three actions was tough, but Daddy stuck with me until he was confident in my skills as a driver. He had to. Back in the 1940s in Memphis, there was no such thing as driver education in schools for black folks.

One night, I got into the truck and pretended that I was driving. I pushed and tugged at that big ole' steering wheel, stomped on the pedals, pulled on the shift lever, just like a real truck driver. I left the gear in this big lumber truck in neutral position and went to bed. Around three a.m., the truck rolled down our driveway, sped right across the street and slammed into a light pole. The light pole flew back about six inches. The noise from that impact was so loud it woke up the neighbors. The neighbors were so frightened, they thought the world was coming to an end. Lights exploded. Power went out. It was a little bit of chaos.

I never got out of bed. I stayed hidden beneath the covers. After my foolishness wrapped Daddy's work truck around a pole, there was no way I wanted to face my father at three a.m. in the morning.

Chapter 4
The Teachers were White...
The Students were Black

All the teachers at the Catholic high school I attended were white nuns. The priests were also white. The nuns were great people. They were tough and knew how to discipline students. Believe me, I had my share of discipline. Some of it was deserved. Some of it was me being in the wrong place. But I got away with some things, too, so in the end, it all evened out.

The nuns were of a religious sect that gave their entire lives to the poor. They could not teach at a wealthy parish. Nuns from a different sect taught at the "Whites Only" Catholic schools in town.

While two of my older siblings, Louvenia and Howard, attended public schools, my parents soon learned that their other three children, Robert (we called him Boots), Jessie, and Willie would receive a better education in the Catholic system. But Jim Crow law prevailed, even within the Catholic faith of the time.

There were only two Catholic churches in Memphis for black worship. If a white man wanted to openly attend one of those churches, he was out of luck. A few older white people lived in our neighborhood and they had to sneak into our church. They'd sit in the back pews for Mass. We would have welcomed them, but I'm sure they felt they didn't belong. Besides, in the eyes of the law, it was illegal for them to worship with us. The folks who wrote the Jim Crow laws must have skipped the all the parts of the Bible about love and inclusion and equality in the eyes of the Lord.

Memphis did not lack for "whites only" Catholic schools and

churches. I never saw the inside of them.

During my boyhood in the 1940s, there were a few black priests and nuns in the Catholic religion. Ninety-nine percent of them were in Louisiana. One year, a black priest named Father Turk was invited to come to our school for a short visit. He went to each room along with our parish priest, Father Coyne, to talk to the students.

Although none of us had ever seen a black priest in our life, it was obvious to all of us that this black priest was real. What an eye-opener! We never imagined such a thing in Memphis. A black priest. To us, a bunch of black Catholic kids, the idea of a black man conducting Mass was like a man from outer space doing Mass. We were dumbfounded that this man had such dignity and grace with the Lord. We were told that there would be a High Mass on Sunday and that Father Turk would be the officiant.

Because we had never seen a black priest, some of the students were wondering if he could speak Latin. I was fortunate enough to be selected as one of the altar boys to serve that Sunday's High Mass. This allowed me to be near to him. Just to be near Father Turk's presence was an inspiration. He was kind to all the altar boys, and you could feel the love from him.

People from other neighborhoods in Memphis, even non-Catholics, came to Mass that day. A black priest was that much of a rarity. His visit was even covered in the local newspapers. People were standing outside on the sidewalk because they could not get into the church to see this black priest. He left the next day to return to his home in Louisiana. We talked about his visit for months. On the other hand, I never saw a black nun until I left Memphis for Chicago.

Chapter 5
School Sports and Jackie Robinson

My high school did not have a sports program. However, the other black Catholic high school did have a football team. Some of the kids from my school could play football there. There were five public high schools in Memphis for black children. Jim Crow prevented white and black people from playing sports together.

Remember, Jackie Robinson wouldn't break the color line in major league baseball with the Brooklyn Dodgers until 1947 when I was thirteen. Moreover, he couldn't stay with the rest of his team during spring training at Vero Beach, Florida. The Southern hotels, and many hotels in the North, barred him from their premises or made him enter through the back door or kitchen.

It all started with Branch Rickey. In Memphis, all the black men in our community knew about Branch Rickey. Rickey was a great athlete himself as well as a sports genius. He played pro football before there was an NFL. He played major league baseball. He invented baseball's farm system and the batting helmet. Not only did he sign the first black man, he also signed the first true Hispanic star, Roberto Clemente.

A graduate of Ohio Wesleyan University, Rickey was a man of great Christian faith, but he was also a smart businessman. Jackie Robinson was signed to a Brooklyn Dodgers contract for three main reasons. One, the Mexican League was signing a lot of U.S. talent. Some terrific white ballplayers signed with Mexican teams and Rickey could see that when black men started signing for good money in Mexico, major league baseball would be in trouble.

Two, Rickey knew talent. He saw the men of the Negro Leagues play. He knew how good those men were and he wanted that talent for his team. Some of the greatest players in the history of baseball never played an inning in the Major Leagues.

Three, he had a conscience. As a Christian, a coach, a college graduate, and as a man, Rickey hated slavery, Jim Crow, and all forms of discrimination. He most famously said, "I may not be able to do something about racism in every field, but I can sure do something about it in baseball."

The older black men of Memphis knew all this about Branch Rickey and they made damned sure the younger men knew about him, too. In many newspaper articles of the day, Rickey was often referred to as the "Mahatma of the Brooklyn Dodgers." But we were baseball fans before Jackie's signing. Baseball truly was the national pastime back then.

When I was a teenager, there were only 16 teams in the Major Leagues; eight in each league. No divisions, no playoffs. The American League pennant winner and the National League leader faced off in the World Series. No team was located further west than St. Louis. St. Louis and Washington were the furthest south. But there was plenty of minor league ball.

We had two teams in Memphis. The Memphis Chicks were in the Chicago White Sox system. Naturally, being attached to a major league team, the Chicks were also an all-white team. The Chicks, short for Chickasaws, had some fine players. Luke Appling, one of baseball's all-time great hitters, played for the Chicks. Another guy, Pete Gray, was a real story. He lost his arm as a kid and still made it up to the St. Louis Browns for a season toward the end of WWII.

What a great irony. The Chickasaws were a Native American nation. Under Jim Crow, Native Americans were classified as "Colored." In short, they were treated as harshly as black people.

Yet, the "Whites-Only" team was named after them.

Our guys were the Memphis Red Sox. They were owned by the Martin brothers, two black men in Memphis. The brothers were dentists and loved baseball. They were very influential men in the Memphis area. They invested in real estate and made sure all their kids went to college. In fact, Dr. J.B. Martin IV is a dentist today in Virginia. The Martin brothers were smart businessmen, too, the first Negro Leagues team to own their own stadium.

White and black teams never played each other during the regular season. But back then, teams would barnstorm, get on trains and buses, and travel the country playing a couple of games every day or so at these country fields. They'd charge a nickel or dime admission, split up the proceeds, and give the local fans a treat. Remember, most ballplayers back then were not educated men, and pro baseball did not pay well. The guys needed the money.

When the teams barnstormed in northern states, Jim Crow was not in force. The white and black teams would play each other. White people knew how good the Negro Leaguers were. Yogi Berra once said the best catcher he ever saw play was Negro Leaguer Josh Gibson. Black pitching great Satchel Paige, who played in both the Negro Leagues and MLB, said the fastest player ever was Cool Papa Bell.

"Nobody, my friend, nobody, is as fast as the Cool Papa," Satch said.

The marginal players in the Major Leagues were terrified of the black stars. They knew that if the color line was broken, many of them would lose their jobs to the Negro League stars. They were right. The Negro Leaguers were that good.

When Jackie was signed, everything baseball became about the Dodgers for the black fan. Every black man, boy, and woman instantly became a Dodger fan. Jackie was not an unknown. He had starred with the Kansas City Monarchs in the Negro Leagues. He'd been through Memphis. We'd seen him. Jackie played his first white league professional year with Brooklyn's minor league team in Montreal. With the Montreal Royals, he hit .349, led the team to League's title, and became a superstar. Jack Roosevelt Robinson was good, but he was far from the best player in the Negro Leagues. Still, he was such a leader, a sparkplug, as we said, everyone in the black community knew he'd be headed to Brooklyn soon.

If Jackie wasn't the best player in the Negro Leagues, who was? That probably went to Josh Gibson. He was fast. He hit for power and average. He was the best catcher in white and black baseball at the time with an amazing arm.

But Josh had a temper. He blew up. He blew up fast and hard. The first black man in the Major Leagues had to be good, sure, but he needed to be a man of dignity and respect. If the first black man fell into all those terrible lies about us—that we were uncontrolled, that we solved all our problems with fights and knives and drink, that we couldn't handle pressure—it would be years before another baseball general manager dared to sign a black player.

Jackie was the right man. He was tough enough and smart enough to not lose his cool. He'd been through Hell in the service. Robinson was a lieutenant in the Army. Based at the time in Kansas, he had an injured ankle. He boarded a military bus and refused to move to the rear when told to do so by the driver. He was arrested by military police. Court-martial proceedings for a wide range of trumped-up charges were brought against him. He was acquitted by an all-white panel of nine officers.

When Jackie got called up to the big club in Brooklyn, he knew what he was up against. Branch Rickey made it clear that the entire Brooklyn Dodgers organization was behind him, provided he could keep his cool. Jackie suffered the worst public displays of hatred that were possible. He was beaned by pitchers. In one game, he played first base. As he stretched to receive a throw from the infield, the batter deliberately stomped on Jackie's ankle in an attempt to break his leg. Jackie needed stitches. Opposing players would throw bananas at him. Others hung stuffed monkeys in nooses from the roof of their dugouts. Somehow, Jackie kept his cool. He played great ball.

Jackie was our guy. My brothers, uncles, my Dad, every man at church—all became massive Dodger fans. It is hard for people today to understand how big a deal Jackie in the Majors was. Bigger than big. He was the biggest deal. Ministers preached about him. We'd pray for him in church. You'd think people would be talking about church and God, yet it would turn out to be about church and Jackie. It was all anyone talked about.

Our Jackie.

"Did Jackie get a hit today?"

"Did Jackie steal a base today?"

"The Dodgers still in first place?"

He wasn't the first famous athletic Robinson, by the way. Jackie's older brother, Mack, ran the 200 meters in the Berlin Olympics of 1936, the "Hitler Olympics." He finished second, just behind Jesse Owens. Yes, two black men stood atop the medal podium that day.

We all wanted to be like Jackie. When we played ball in the streets, we'd all want to be Jackie Robinson. We'd have these big arguments over who'd get to be Jackie in our street ball games. It got a little better the next year. Larry Doby was signed by the Cleveland Indians of the American League, so we now had two black heroes.

He was a great player, an excellent hitter and equally brave guy, but Larry Doby was not the sparkplug that Jackie was. Doby was signed just a few months after Jackie, but Doby was a quiet man, and being the second black player, he didn't draw the same amount of attention as Jackie. Doby went straight from the Negro Leagues to the American League, that's how good a hitter he was. He hit .326 in his third year in the Majors and ended his career with a fine .283 average. He was also the first black man to win a World Series when the Indians beat the Boston Braves in 1948. Jackie and the Dodgers wouldn't take the Series until 1955.

The year after Jackie's Major League debut, 1948, the Dodgers signed another black man, catcher Roy Campanella. He was brought up the year after Jackie made the Big Leagues. Winner of three MVP awards, Roy would become one of the greatest catchers in history.

Roy Campanella. The name alone made us scratch our heads. It made us think, *A black guy with an Italian name? How does that happen?* Being from Jim Crow Memphis, it never occurred to us that an Italian man and a black woman might have a baby.

It is not possible to state how influential Jackie Robinson was to me. As a young kid, I always wanted to be an athlete. I would read professional football magazines and 99% of the players were white. I had great admiration for the few black players like Kenny Washington and Marion Motley listed in the magazines. I would purchase a sports magazine just to see the photographs of black athletes.

We always felt that one day there would be more black athletes in the NFL. Just one year before Jackie broke baseball's color line, the color line was broken in the NFL. The racism didn't seem as bad in the NFL as in the Major Leagues. Maybe it was because there were far fewer Southerners in the NFL. Who was one of the first guys to integrate the NFL? Kenny Washington, Jackie Robinson's All-American teammate on the UCLA football team. Yes, Jackie starred on the football team, too. In fact, many considered football to be Jackie's best sport. Jackie also won an NCAA title in track and field, the 1940 long jump. He also starred on the UCLA basketball team.

How talented an athlete is that? Four varsity sports, with a letter in each; Jackie Robinson was the first UCLA athlete with enough talent to do so.

The NBA wasn't integrated until five years later, in 1951. Basketball wasn't on our radar in Memphis at all. Not the NBA, not college, not the Harlem Globetrotters. We played a little football in the streets and the park, but our interests were all about Jackie and the Dodgers, and to a lesser extent, Larry Doby and the Indians.

When I realized that athletics would not be my future, Jackie's strength and courage and the way he demanded respect from everyone, white and black, was always an inspiration. I was lucky that I rarely faced either such ugly hate or huge amounts of discrimination. But whenever I did, I always found strength inside by reminding myself that whatever was happening to me, far worse had happened to Jackie Robinson.

Chapter 6
A Game of Dice

Because we were altar boys, someone had the bright idea that we should attend novena. A novena is a series of prayers that are said for nine straight days, usually as a prayer of petition, but sometimes as a prayer of thanksgiving. We could serve mass and that would make Father Coyne happy because he would have altar boys in church on Wednesday nights. After praying that evening's novena, we decided to sneak into the basement in our school and shoot dice.

All of us thought this was a great idea. However, Father Coyne wondered why he had altar boys so eager to serve at novena during the middle of the week. We may have been altar boys, but we were no angels. We were thirteen-year-old boys.

After one novena service, Father decided to follow us. He waited at the top of the basement stairs until he could hear us talking. The window screens from Father Coyne's house would be removed during the winter months and placed in the basement of the school. We placed a couple of screens on the floor and shot dice on them. It wasn't exactly the felt tables you'd find in Las Vegas in the 1950s, but it worked for us.

Father Coyne opened the door at the top of the stairs and came down the stairs two at a time. I'd never heard a priest curse before. He has a stick in his hand and it was swinging at all of us. It hit all of us, too. We were so scared we couldn't move. We just took it. He, quite literally, beat the hell out of us.

Father was livid. His face was bright red with rage.

"Now you've done it!" he shouted. "You made me use the Lord's name in vain. I'm going to kill all of you. But first I'm gonna beat the daylights out of each and every one of you! You used my novena because you wanted to gamble. I've never been so mad in all my life. I'm gonna beat you so bad, you're gonna hurt for weeks."

He beat us. He beat us bad. We deserved it. He also punished us. Father Coyne made us wash those same screens after school every day for one month. Every time we scrubbed those screens, we thought about that beating and why we'd gotten it. Believe me, we never played dice on Father Coyne's window screens again. We shot dice in alleys like all the other kids after that.

Every six weeks, we would receive our report cards. Father Coyne would come to each classroom to pass out the report cards and make his comments to the class regarding how well we were performing. He would review each report card, address each student, and let them know their grades. Father had no problem embarrassing a student in front of the entire class about poor grades.

Father Coyne once embarrassed me in front of everyone.

"Willie Artis," he said to me in front of all my classmates and the nun, "why do you have failing grades in math? If you don't improve, I'm going to sit down with your parents and tell your father to take a stick to your rear end. You are too smart to allow poor grades to show up on your report card."

When he finished with me, he went after another kid.

My math grade went up.

Chapter 7
My First Job and the Jim Crow Rules

When we were young, all of us worked during the summer months and after school. We worked in grocery stores, bowling alleys, restaurant drive-ins and delivered milk to earn money. This was war time. Money was scarce. I first worked at a bowling alley as a pinsetter.

Jim Crow ruled, even at bowling alleys. All bowling facilities were "Whites Only." No black people could bowl. Black employees were barred from the front door. We were invisible.

During those times, there were no automatic pinsetters. Black male kids were the pinsetters. White people would bowl and knock the pins over. Black kids would pick them up and place them into a rack. We'd lower the rack and that would enable the pins to stand in formation. Some kids were strong enough to work two bowling lanes and they made more money. A little kid back then, I could only handle one lane. If we set the pins quickly for the bowlers after the league was over they would throw money down the lanes to us for tips.

They would throw. Money. Down the bowling lane.

How insulting. Demeaning.

They wouldn't touch us. They didn't even want to see their money touch our hands.

Invisible.

We were poor people, but we didn't grasp the depths of our poverty or situation. Jim Crow and segregation were at the highest point. We did not know or understand the real meaning of Jim Crow. It wasn't until later that I learned that Jim Crow was designed to keep black people enslaved. I would hear my father discussing this law with his church members. It appeared to me that, although fully unfair and inhumane, this was our reluctantly accepted way of life. What choice did we have? White people made the rules. White people enforced the rules. Beatings, jail, and worse were the fate of any black person who stood up to Jim Crow.

Chapter 8
I Learn About the Nazis

During the early 1940s, I often heard my father discussing the war with church members and neighbors. They would say, "How come these Nazis are killing all those Jews and nothing's being done about it?" We were the United States. We stood for all the right things. This seemed to be wrong, but no one in the government seemed to care.

I often wondered how my father and his friends were able to discuss the war. They knew what was taking place in Germany, the slaughter ignored by all the leaders of other countries, including ours. At the time, I did not realize that our local grocery stores were owned by Jewish people. Because the storekeepers still had relatives living in Germany and Poland and Austria, they could inform their customers of what was taking place in Europe.

Because I attended a Catholic school, prayer was required every morning before class began. We would pray to our Lord and ask Him for His blessing. We would also ask God to bless the Pope. Nothing was ever said in our classroom regarding the Nazis exterminating Jewish people in Germany. Never. Not one word.

Later in life, I became an avid reader of European history. I paid particular attention to World War II. I needed to enlighten myself. *How could any country make a concentrated effort to completely annihilate an entire race of people without world leaders making every effort to stop the slaughter?* I wondered.

I discovered the exterminations occurred mostly in occupied

Poland where the majority of the extermination camps were built. I wondered how world leaders—the Prime Minister of England, the Pope, and our own president—could not be aware of what was taking place. Many requests were made by Jewish people to bomb the railroads, the method used for transporting them to the extermination camps. The Allies turned a blind eye.

Why?

In my early adult years, I began to compare the Holocaust to slavery and Jim Crow. I quickly determined there was no comparison. The Nazis believed they were a master race and all other people were subordinate to them.

In contrast, slave owners regarded enslaved people as property. Slave owners did not kill the enslaved because they were free labor which allowed southern owners to live a rich life. At the height of the slave trade, there were four million enslaved people in America.

Living under Jim Crow law in Memphis, I learned about millions of people of a different race and religion who were being slaughtered in Poland by the Nazis. It is still difficult for me to comprehend the silence by world leaders at that time in our history. Racism is a terrible disease.

After the war, I would hear my father discuss the extreme chaos throughout Europe. He and his church friends heard that Nazis were escaping Germany to South America through the Catholic Church underground. As a twelve-year-old kid, I knew this information was coming from the Jewish grocery store owners with relatives still living in Europe. As I grew older, I learned, through reading about Nazi-hunters like Simon Wiesenthal, that this was true.

My Catholic Church helped Nazis escape justice.

Chapter 9
A Butcher at an Early Age

I worked at two grocery stores during the summer and after school. Both shops were owned by Jewish families. One store was in my neighborhood. On Friday evenings and Saturday mornings—when most black people shopped—the owner and his family had a bucket full of *bullshit* ready to hand out to each and every one of his black customers. A lot of talking and chit-chat went on continuously. Much like a street magician or card hustler's banter, this bullshit served as a distraction so the customers would not realize they were being overcharged. Yet, this family owned the grocery store for many years.

The family made a tremendous amount of money as the owner of a neighborhood grocery store. They also built apartment buildings across the street from the store and rented to all black people. They themselves lived in one of the few all-white neighborhoods that would accept Jewish people as neighbors.

I began working at the neighborhood store at a very young age, ten years old. My parents purchased their groceries from this same store. Occasionally, I would go to the store with them and help carry the groceries back home. Because so many black women in our neighborhood worked as cleaning and laundry ladies in the white neighborhoods, they knew how much groceries should cost. It was common knowledge that the black customers were being cheated by the white storeowners, but there was nothing anyone could do about it. Even if a black man had enough money to open a grocery, it was just about impossible for him to get white wholesalers to sell to him.

On Thursdays, the store owners would hire young black kids to place their advertising handbills on porches throughout the neighborhood. I asked my parents if I could approach the store owner about passing handbills after school. My parents allowed me to approach Mr. Joe, the manager. I met with Mr. Joe, who I thought was the owner, and asked to be hired.

Mr. Joe said, "I see you with your parents when they are buying groceries, but how old are you?"

"I'm twelve," I said.

That was not correct, but I didn't think Mr. Joe would hire a ten-year-old kid.

"Are your parents aware of what you want to do?" he asked.

"My parents said I could talk to you about the handbills," I answered.

"Well, I don't know," said Mr. Joe. "Why don't you come around next Thursday? I'll give you a tryout. You know this takes several hours, right? You do a good job, pass out all the handbills, don't throw any away, I'll pay you fifty cents. You know some kids dump the handbills in a ditch and say they were all placed on the porches? You do that, I won't hire you again. You got that, boy?"

As I grew a little older, I asked Mr. Joe if I could work inside the store during the summer and after school during the winter. He put me to work inside the store stocking shelves and delivering groceries on my Christmas present, a bicycle. I took pride in being the neatest shelf stocker and the fastest delivery boy I could be.

Mr. Joe must have noticed. Soon afterward, he gave me more responsibility in the store; I decided I wanted to move to the meat counter and learn to cut meat. Mr. Joe put me to work with the butcher, Eddie. I was thirteen. This was quite a step up. The war had just ended, meat was still in short supply, and a good meat cutter had to be very accurate with his knives. No waste was tolerated.

Eddie was a very skilled butcher and knew every part of a cow. Although Eddie was a good person, he was an alcoholic. On his sober, good days, Eddie was a good teacher and I learned how to cut the best parts of all types of meat. Like most local butchers, not only did we cut meat, we were also expected to know how to cook and serve it, too. Back then, butchers were like a food magazine or TV cooking show.

Payday was Saturday. Eddie would almost always miss work on Mondays because he would get so drunk over the weekend. This worked to my advantage, as I was the only butcher on a Monday. Without Eddie to help, I got very good at meat cutting. However, I was never as good as Eddie. When he was sober, he was the best, but I was a good butcher at that time in my life. Not just for a kid, but for anyone in the business. Because of me, the store made good money, and customers could get a good deal.

I've always been a friendly, easy-going guy and so customers became friendly towards me. They would ask me to wait on them. Just a kid butcher behind the counter, but I had regulars. They knew they'd get a square deal from me. Since I was good for the store, I got regular raises from the owners. I was making grown-up money. It felt great to be able to give some of my earnings to my mother to help with the household. For a kid born during the Depression to make enough to help support the family was a big deal in those times.

The grocery store was started by a Jewish immigrant from Germany in the late 1930s. He got out of Germany just in time. The owner had one son and two daughters. His son's name was Sam. One daughter, Rose, was a schoolteacher. The other daughter, Tillie, was married to Mr. Joe.

Like most stores during that time, the staff was a family affair. Sam, Tillie, and son-in-law Mr. Joe were in the store every day, all day. With a family-owned business, the best way to look out for the family's money is to have family look after the money. That's a message I learned early on and carried with me when I started to run my own businesses.

Mr. Joe was a very sharp guy. The owner watched his son Sam in the store all throughout Sam's youth. He flat-out did not measure up to Mr. Joe's skills. During the time Mr. Joe courted Tillie, the owner watched him at work very closely. After much thought, he decided that Mr. Joe would manage the store. The founder told his family that when he died, all family members working at the store would work for Joe.

Sam never took to the idea of being forced to work for his brother-in-law. I remember Sam and Mr. Joe arguing. I remember anger and bad words. It was not a good situation and it would get worse.

When the owner passed away, his will stated that his son-in-law, Mr. Joe, would inherit all responsibility. The store was his to run; hire and fire, make store policy, and make all financial decisions. To paraphrase the words of President Truman, "The Buck Stopped There." But Sam? Sam was just another employee.

After the provisions of the will were enforced, Sam spent most his time being angry and mean. Never a good worker, he was now a bad seed. He would frequently complain to customers and employees and just about anyone whose ear he could grab about his father leaving everything to that "bald headed son-of-a-bitch." That would be Mr. Joe.

Sam's complaints were always the same, and they were always loud.

"Joe's not even a blood relative!"

"Joe's got his hands all over the money!"

"I can't even sign a check and I was my father's only son!"

"I don't know, you have to talk to that bald-headed son-of-a-bitch in charge!"

Mr. Joe was a master at handling money. He knew how take money and use it to make more money. During the early years, the owner realized that Joe was not only the hardest worker, but the smartest guy in the family.

One of the first things Mr. Joe did was very smart. He invested the store's earnings into real estate. At an early age, I was being shown how to build a business.

It was Mr. Joe who took a small neighborhood grocery store and built it into a major business enterprise. Not only did I work for this Jewish family at a very young age, I saw them become wealthy from selling food to black people in a black neighborhood. They knew how to make money and they were very good at it.

Under Mr. Joe, the family store left behind the cheating of customers that I mentioned earlier. The new tactic was simple: *Sell a good product at a fair price*. I applied that tactic in my business life: I sold a great product at a fair price. I never imagined that this experience at a very young age would play a huge role in the success of my business life thirty years later.

Mr. Joe was a master at making financial decisions that were of great benefit to his family and their business. Joe also understood that smart, hard work was the key to success. As a young man, just starting out with the store, Mr. Joe also had a newspaper route. He delivered the morning *Memphis Commercial Appeal* throughout the neighborhood. After he delivered all his newspapers, he would come to work at the grocery. It was that extra money that was his profit.

The grocery store was in a mid-sized building and a drug store was next door. One of Mr. Joe's first purchases was the drug store. He hired contractors to knock out the wall that separated the two stores and this created more space for the grocery.

Not much later, Mr. Joe's son, Phillip, graduated from college with a pharmaceutical degree. After the building was enlarged, Mr. Joe set up a pharmacy for his son and they created a drugstore. With that move, Mr. Joe taught me two lessons:

1. *Always look forward.*
2. *Real estate matters.*

When I first went into business for myself, I leased a building for three years. With Mr. Joe's lesson in mind, I knew that I would soon want to own my own facility. Everything I did in those first three years was designed to get me into my own building. I got there ahead of my plan. When I signed the papers for my own building, I thought about Mr. Joe and I sent him a silent "thank you" for his lesson. When I sold my company, I owned three large buildings.

All told, my buildings covered 270,000 square feet. That's about six football fields worth of building. My buildings sat on 20 acres of land and were valued at $8.5 million dollars. That was a very valuable lesson Mr. Joe taught me, don't you think?

Mr. Joe and his family got on well with black people, but it was still Memphis and Jim Crow was still law. When beer or soda was delivered to the grocery store, there would always be two men on the delivery trucks, one black and one white. The white man would come into the store and take the order. The black man would load and unload the heavy crates of glass bottles. There were never two black men or two white men riding on a delivery truck; always one of each. When the delivery was complete, the white man drove the truck and the black man rode in the passenger seat or stood on the rear step in the back of the truck. Always. This was standard procedure under the Jim Crow system in the South. If there was heavy lifting, it was done by black men. The effects of slavery lingered long after the laws were changed.

The other grocery where I worked during the summer months was not located in my neighborhood. I did jobs that didn't bring me in contact with the customers. You see, this store was in a "Whites-Only" neighborhood. I could deliver groceries (always taking them to the back door), put up stock, take out the trash, but I could not help the customers. Invisible, still.

Of course, the customer base was all-white. The owner, a Jewish man, grew impatient and unhappy with his demanding customer base. Customers would call the store and ask what was on sale. They would buy only the sale items and always wanted the groceries delivered. The owner would complain, but only to himself; he was always muttering under his breath.

Several years later, that owner decided that he could make more money in the grocery business if he relocated his store to a black neighborhood. He made this decision because he knew black people paid more for their groceries. He knew he could price-gouge like crazy with no fear of reprisal. Further, he also knew there were no major chain grocery stores in Memphis located in black neighborhoods. Both Jim Crow and just plain prejudice against black people made this so. White grocery managers didn't want to come to work in black neighborhoods. Black people couldn't move up the ladder into management.

That fact remains true to this day, and many poor black neighborhoods are "food deserts" with scant produce and second-rate meat and dairy items. Instead of healthy foods, the shelves are stocked with high-fat, high-sugar foods. Stores in food deserts charge more than stores in affluent white areas for exactly the same items. It's a terrible circumstance for the people who need good nutrition the most.

After that boss moved his store, he ordered products that black people liked to eat. Black people have always liked what we call "soul food" today: Greens, chitlins, and neckbones. It wasn't fancy food. Most of what we now call soul food was the garbage that the white folks considered beneath them. Soul food was the food of dirt-poor black folks.

The store owner did so well with black customers that he did not even want white ones. Since white people could go to any grocery, there was plenty of competition to drive prices down. White people wanted free delivery, and that ate into the proceeds. There was very little profit in a white customer base for a neighborhood grocery store. I followed the store owner to the new building and helped him prepare the store in an all-black neighborhood because I could work after school and continue to make money for myself.

Chapter 10
Public Transportation: Ridin' with Jim Crow

What I did know—and was very aware of—was where to sit on a public bus. It wasn't like I was taught this, it was just something all black kids absorbed in the South. Remember, I was born in 1934. It would be 21 years, December of 1955, until an exhausted Rosa Parks would refuse to give up her seat in the colored section on a crowded Birmingham bus to a white passenger. When I got on the bus, I entered at the front door and took a seat in the back of the bus. I would always exit at the rear door. Black people were not allowed to exit the front door. We entered the front door because we paid the bus driver to ride. I also knew that I could not sit in front of a white person. Never.

To sit in front of a white person was against the law. White people would enter the bus and occupy the front seats. If the front seats were full, they would work their way to the back and occupy those seats as well. When black people got on the bus and there were no available seats in the back, they would have to stand. If a white person exited the bus and a seat became available, but white people were sitting behind the empty seat, we continued to stand. If you dared to sit in front of a white person, you'd be thrown off the bus. Unless you were arrested. Or beaten by the cops. Or all three.

That was Jim Crow. Every law that governed interactions between white and black people was designed to make us remember that black people were less than human. There were "Whites-Only" taxi cabs. In Memphis, black people could not ride in Yellow cabs.

If you got caught violating Jim Crow, you'd spend a few days in jail; possibly a week if you were deemed particularly "uppity." You'd likely also be beaten with the cop's night stick in the bargain.

There were a couple of black-owned cab companies. However, if you were black, it was very difficult to be picked up at home by cab. Most black cabs operated on Beale Street, where black people congregated. In that case, you might be able to get driven home.

Beale Street was not very long, only a couple of miles, and it ran from the Mississippi over to East Street. Back then, it was filled with clubs and restaurants that black people liked. It was "our" street.

Beale St. was important to music. Riley King, the guitarist, got so famous playing on Beale Street that he became known as the "Beale Street Blues Boy." Fans called him "B.B.", short for "Blues Boy." B.B. King—you've probably heard of him.

During the late 1960s and 1970s, the Beale Street area turned bad. It's since recovered, and it's busier now than it ever was. Fortunately, Beale Street's restaurants and clubs are now filled with people of all colors.

Jim Crow was the river that ran through our lives; black people on one bank, white people on the other. There were no black public bus drivers. We did not have black police officers. There were no black people working in banks. Black managers did not run factories because there was no such thing as a black manager. Black people did not work in sales at department stores. Any place where a white customer might have to deal with a black person as an equal just didn't exist.

Because of Jim Crow, there were separate drinking water fountains, separate eating areas, separate restrooms—all with signs clearly marked for "Colored Only" and for "Whites Only." They were often located in the same department store where both races could purchase goods. Just as it happened to my mother, black people were not allowed to try on garments, hats or other items purchased at downtown department stores. You could buy a suit or a dress or hat from those stores—our money was gladly accepted—but there'd be Hell to pay if a black man's hair touched the inside of a hat that a white man might later purchase.

As a child growing up in Memphis, I was completely ignorant of the real meaning of Jim Crow. I was never inclined to think of a different way of life. I did not realize that the black people's health was destroyed by segregation. We could not be treated in white hospitals. Few white doctors would make house calls to black neighborhoods. We relied as much on old wives' tales and superstitions as we did on medical knowledge for many ills. The city hospitals that would treat us were often filled with disease and germs. You might go in for a simple operation and die from a totally unrelated infection. Pediatrics for black infants didn't exist—twice as many black babies died as white babies during that time. Black mothers routinely died in childbirth. Despite the widespread use of insulin, undiagnosed and/or untreated diabetes killed many black people far before their expected lifespan. We were expendable.

It wasn't until I was in my twenties that I discovered how Jim Crow was founded and became an institution. This demeaning, degrading, and infamous law was started as the result of a white actor named Thomas Dartmouth Rice in 1828. This actor, dressed in clown clothing and black face, became an act in a minstrel show in New York. Rice's character was that of a black-faced fool. By holding up our people to ridicule and contempt, he became a success with white audiences and was often imitated by others. The character was named "Jim Crow."

Because of the "singing, dancing, grinning fools," the character evolved into a caricature of black people. The southern states chose to use this caricature to further their racist cause and made Jim Crow the law of the land. Black people like me were born into and raised under this law without any recourse or any opportunity to make a change. We existed and lived with a law that had a devastating effect on all black people living in the South.

Uneducated black people had no idea how to fight a law that mandated segregation. These laws were upheld by the courts. Jim Crow was America's version of South Africa's Apartheid. The systems were in existence at the same time. I'm sure the caretakers of these two systems communicated with each other frequently.

As strange as it may seem, growing up in the Deep South, I never experienced any blatant or cruel forms of racism. I was never called the "n" word by a white person to my face. I never heard a white person use the "n" word within my hearing. I heard "n" used every day by black people when talking to each other. Although I worked in many different environments among white people while working after school, I was never made to feel uncomfortable. I worked in bowling alleys, drive-ins, and grocery stores. I mowed lawns. I did anything legal to make money as a kid because we were poor people.

I did hear my father refer to Jim Crow as "a wrong, a sin" against black people. I cannot explain why I was never called the "n" word by a white person. I was always treated as just another black kid doing whatever I was hired to do.

There were days when I would skip school and catch a truck loaded with black people going to Arkansas to chop cotton for three dollars per day. That's about forty bucks today. I was only thirteen or fourteen. I would bring the money home and give it to my mother.

"How did you get all this money?" she would ask.

I'd lie.

"I did some work for a man after school."

The first couple times she believed me. Later, she discovered that I was not in school and was instead catching a cotton truck to Arkansas. My parents put a stop to that activity right away.

I've always been a hard worker. I believe my work ethic and attitude had plenty to do with how I was treated as a kid in a segregated community. Because I showed respect for others of all colors and ages, I was generally treated with respect. I just treated everyone the way I wanted to be treated.

Further, my calm demeanor as an adult allowed me to succeed in the world of business. Later in this book, I will talk about my success in business and the comfortable way of life my company created for me and my family. I was never a fool. I was never an "Uncle Tom," "Yassuh-ing" to the white man. In the business world, I always carried myself with a certain amount of calm and dignity. I rarely lost my temper. As a result, I was always treated with respect and dignity.

While providing products and services to the automotive industry, I made many friends. Furthermore, as an employee and a business owner, I never experienced a single incident that could cause any discomfort because of what a person said to me about my race. If any negative comments were made about me, it was never made directly to me in over fifty years of working with different industries.

The most important industry in my business life wanted good suppliers to provide products and services to them. They were willing to work with minority suppliers to make them competitive and produce a quality product. I became a better businessperson and a better supplier as a direct result of how we were treated by this great customer. They wanted us to succeed. They did not accept poor quality and demanded that we be competitive with on-time delivery. This extraordinary forty-year relationship with my largest customer continues. For that, I am extremely grateful.

Chapter 11
This is the Army, Mr. Artis

When I was sixteen years old—in 1950—I decided to join the Army. The Korean War ramped up with North Korea's invasion of South Korea on June 25, 1950 and I wanted to serve. Of course, I was underage. I bumped up my age, signed my mother's name, and the recruiting officer believed me. My joining up was my brother Robert's fault. Remember, we called him Boots.

Boots was in the Air Force. He came home on leave with two of his USAF buddies. Oh, they looked so slick in their uniforms. I loved my brother anyway and wanted to be just like him. These men were great fun to have in the house. They were worldly and sophisticated. They wore their hats tipped over one eye. Slick.

They were airmen. I wanted in. Bad.

At the time, a young man had to be eighteen to join the military, but if his parents would sign off, a seventeen-year-old was acceptable. I took myself down the street to the military recruiter.

"How old are you, son?"

"I'm seventeen, sir."

I gulped.

"Seventeen?"

"Yes, sir."

I gulped again. I knew I was lying. I'm pretty certain he knew I was lying.

I was tall for my age.

"Son, you'll need to take this test."

I was nervous. I did not do well. I did not qualify for the Air Force. However, I did do well enough to qualify for the Army.

"Son, you take this paperwork home, have your mother or father read it, get a signature, and I will be glad to sign you up for our nation's military."

I took that paperwork right home and explained to Momma that it being war time, a sixteen-year-old boy could join the military. That was Lie #1. I told Momma that I'd be headed to basic training for a while, and that I'd serve at posts around the U.S. That was Lie #2. Later that night, I forged Momma's signature. That was Lie #3. Three lies. I don't believe that I had lied three times to my parents in my sixteen years' lifetime before that evening.

My parents were not thrilled but they were not unhappy, either. They saw how well the Air Force and Boots got along. They realized that I was proud to follow in my brother's footsteps.

Several weeks before my enlistment, my best friend Johnny Rhodes pulled the same stunt at his house. He forged his mother's name and joined up. His service ended in a heroic death. He died a hero, manning a machine gun to provide cover as his unit retreated. I was both gutted and proud to have been his friend.

I trained at Fort Pickett, near Richmond, VA. Fort Pickett was named for the Confederate Army general famed for Pickett's Charge. Today, the fort is a National Guard training center. At Pickett, I learned to be a soldier—how to march, fire a weapon, survive—all the basic skills of the frontline soldier. I was too young to realize what the Army had in store for my unit. My black unit.

The U.S. Army was still segregated. President Truman signed the Desegregation Act, Executive Order 9981, in 1948, but it took time before some companies, especially in the U.S. South, became fully integrated. There were four companies in our battalion. Two were all-white. Two were all-black. From the captains on down, we were a black unit. All the lieutenants in our black half of the battalion were named Singleton. They were all from Georgia. None were related. Unless you consider some slaveowner 80 years earlier.

When I finished the first portion of basic training, I was shipped to California. Although I didn't know it, this was a sure sign I was headed to Korea. I was granted a furlough before I finished my training. On the bus ride home, I stopped and bought corporal stripes at a store and stuck them on my uniform. Technically, I was still a recruit. I wasn't even an official private yet. It takes about 16 months of service to advance from recruit to corporal. I had those bars on when I got off the bus in Memphis and everyone knew I was full of it.

I had just a few days of leave. My parents still thought everything was on the up and up. Boots came home on furlough while I was on the way back to California. He straightened Momma and Daddy right out.

"He's in the Army. The real Army, ground troops, infantry. They are training him as a foot soldier. He's going to go to Korea as an infantryman and he will be killed. They are shooting and killing frontline soldiers. I don't care where he told you about where he'd serve. Eldrage will get killed."

Mom turned into a raving maniac. She was on the phone to the Army, to the recruiters, to the base. I was in deep trouble. Remember my three lies? There was also a fourth problem. I was the baby of the family.

I was barely off the bus in California when I was called into the Major's office. He was responsible for the entire battalion. That's 800 men under his command. I knew I was in trouble and I was scared to death I was headed to the stockade. He was, thankfully, a kind man.

"We know you are not here legally. We've been in contact with your parents, your recruiter, and the higher-ups here at camp. I am honored that you would go to such lengths to serve in the military. However, you cannot stay. When you are of legal age, please consider joining us legally. I've reviewed your file and I'm pleased and proud to grant you an honorable discharge for the six months you served well. You will now get on a bus and return home to Memphis and your family."

To this day, when I hear of young soldiers killed in a war zone, I flash back to that Major who saved my life.

When I got home, my mother and father were both very angry and very proud. Of course, they were thrilled to have me home. Things were chilly between Boots and me for a few days. He let me stew a little, then he sat me down and explained why he had to rat me out.

He knew the truth about infantry in Korea. In the three years of the Korean War, the U.S. Army reported 110,00 casualties. I'd have been one of them. Black infantry platoons suffered fatalities far out of proportion to their numbers in the war. In short, black troops were machine gun fodder. And my brother knew it.

The next time I left home, I was 18. I left for good and went to Chicago. In the meantime, I re-enrolled in school and got back to making a little money.

Chapter 12
Back to Work, Back to School

I grew up with a kid who lived across the street. His family owned a push lawn mower. On Saturdays and after school during the summer months, we would push the mower to areas where white people lived, knock on the back door. Whoever answered the door was asked the same question: "Can we cut your grass?"

Before we knocked on the door, we looked at the size of the lawn and had a price in mind. This was an early lesson in pricing and estimates and negotiation. If they said yes, they always asked us the same question: "How much do you charge?"

Some folks wanted to negotiate. As black kids in a white neighborhood with a push mower, we didn't have any leverage, no negotiating power. Most of the time, we cut the grass for the amount they were willing to pay. Because my family did not own a lawn mower, at the end of the day, the kid that owned the mower received more money than me. After all, it was his lawn mower. Another lesson: *Owning the manufacturing process has its advantages.*

Brown vs. Board of Education of Topeka, Kansas, the desegregation of schools, came down in 1954. My last years in high school were still under Jim Crow. We did not understand why our Catholic schools were segregated. As children, Jim Crow was, sadly, just the way things were. It was unquestioned. Schools were either all-white or all-black. In either case, the priests and nuns were white. In my family, while not Catholic, three of us went to Catholic schools. My parents realized early on the quality of a

Catholic education outstripped what was available to us in a poor, blacks-only school district. Two of us became practicing Catholics and practiced the faith for a lifetime.

We were raised as God-fearing children. Our father was a deeply religious man and a church deacon. He also taught Sunday school. Daddy enjoyed church; the faith and fellowship and community. As for me, after my time in school, I moved away from Catholicism and did not practice any religion as a young man. I did not see faith or God serving a useful purpose in my life.

One thing I did know as an older teen: I did not want to live in Memphis. I didn't know what I wanted to do. I didn't know where I wanted to live. I just knew two things for certain: I wanted to make some money, and I wanted out of Memphis and the South. It didn't take a genius to realize that while life in the North without my family would be difficult, life in the South for a young black man was a dead end.

Chapter 13
Sweet Home Chicago

In the mid-1950s, I moved to Chicago to work and finish school. My brother already lived in Chicago, so he helped me get a job with his employer. The job paid $1.05 per hour. The average wage back then was around $1.60 an hour. That's around $9.50 an hour in today's money; for a kid living with his brother, I was making good money. Plus, I was happy to be back at work.

The additional educational piece did not materialize the way I planned; a lack of money was the reason. A couple of my high school classmates went on to college because their parents could afford to pay their tuition. I really wanted to go to college, even community college, but I was not that fortunate. I knew that a college degree would put real money in my pocket far sooner than without that degree. I did manage to attend Wilson Community College and take classes, but I came up short of a two-year associate's degree.

During this time in my life, I fathered a child at age 19. I had very little input or involvement with the child. To this day, that is a major regret in my life. Where that child is, how, he or she has done in life, any grandchildren...that's all a sad mystery to me.

At the first manufacturing plant where I was employed, the hourly employees became unhappy with management and tried to organize a labor union. Because I had not been with the company long, I sat on the sidelines and watched the posturing and angling and negotiating on both sides. I saw there was truth and deception on both sides. I learned how difficult it was to organize company employees into a union. After two weeks of walking a picket line, I could see that this was a dead-end situation. By 21, I had learned that strikes did no good for either side. It was years before I would hear the phrase "negotiate in good faith" but by 1956, I knew that principled negotiation was the answer to labor-management disputes. I decided to look for employment elsewhere.

When I left the company, one of the employees wanted to travel with me to look for a job. I discovered he lacked an education. He had problems reading and writing. He could not even complete the simplest application. He asked me to write it for him and I agreed. We visited several plants to no avail.

At one plant that manufactured corrugated cardboard products, the personnel manager waited until we were almost out of the door and called me back.

"Hey, Willie!" he said. "If you were alone, I'd hire you right now on the spot. Why don't you try looking for a job by yourself?"

This was great advice. Life-changing. *Be careful of your associates. Choose wisely.* You'll be judged on those you hang out with. It might not be fair, but it's reality. Only then did I realize why we were not getting any offers. We may have been friendly, this young man and I, but nobody wanted to hire someone who could not read and write. Another lesson learned: *If you haven't the time and discipline to master the basic skills of life, how can anyone put you to work?*

At that time, employment was great in Chicago. I did not want to go back to my old job where I'd still have to walk in a picket line. I took a job as a cab driver to earn some short-term money. I wanted to get back to a manufacturing plant where I could create a better opportunity for myself, make some real money. Driving a cab in Chicago was a low rent job, not something I intended to do for long. I hated driving a cab. However, by that time I'd found my own place and the rent had to be paid. This is the only time in my working life that I absolutely despised what I was doing to make money.

Chapter 14
Lying to Get a Job

I returned to the corrugated plant on the west side of Chicago we had visited previously. This time, I went alone. During my interview with the personnel manager, he asked if I had been there before.

I said, "No, sir, this is my first visit."

This was the first lie I told him.

The second lie occurred when he asked me about my experience working in a corrugated plant. I told him I had worked in a corrugated plant previously and I was experienced.

"That's great, I'm going to hire you," he said.

As we walked through the plant, he introduced me to a foreman and instructed him to finish the tour. I had never seen machines as mammoth as these. I did not know the name of the machines but pretended that I did. Truly, I had no clue. I knew with time, I would learn, but at that point in time, I was in trouble.

I would look at the name plate on a machine and say to the foreman, "Wow, this a great looking printer!"

"Now, that's a slotter!"

"I've never seen such a big taper."

When we reached the corrugator, I was overwhelmed with the size of the machine. It was the biggest machine I'd ever seen. I saw the name plate and said, "My God, I've been here before. This corrugator is absolutely magnificent. I know how these work!"

That was the last lie I told that day. I went to work for Chicago's Town Corrugated Products the next day. Owned by Sam Bernstein, Town Corrugated was one of the largest corrugated manufacturers in the Chicagoland area. Much to my chagrin, the first place they put me was on the dry end of the corrugator. I had the worst job on the machine. Because I did not know how to handle paper, my hands were bloody from paper cuts. After a few days, I did learn how to handle paper without being cut. Remember, OSHA (Occupational Safety and Health Administration) didn't get started until the 1970s. No gloves, no safety equipment, no rules.

A corrugator is a large machine, made up of a series of smaller machines. It combines the two outer facing sheets, called the liners, with the wavy inner layers known as the corrugating medium. It first puts the waves in the medium, sandwiches it between the liners, and glues it all together. It then cuts the corrugated material to size and delivers it to the box-making machines. It's an impressive machine, and each is about the size of a good-sized pickup truck.

I soon learned how to operate different pieces of corrugated machinery. I was intrigued and fascinated with the manufacturing process of corrugated products. It was a learning curve that I soon mastered. I love to be around manufacturing, and in particular, cardboard products. For me, it was something amazing to see raw paper products go in one side of the factory and to see the huge industrial heavy duty boxes come out the other.

To manufacture corrugated products, you need to have knowledge of fractions. The entire manufacturing process was fractional in all shapes and sizes. I wasn't too bad with math in school, especially after Father Coyne beat my ass in front the class and threatened to talk to my parents. Things do have a way of working out later in life.

I learned how rolls of paper are turned into corrugated boxes. I was fascinated to the point where I decided to work in other sections of the plant. I wanted to learn how to operate different pieces of corrugated machinery. I became a master of the printer-slotter, the machine that prints the logos and wordage on the boxes. Occasionally, customers would visit the plant and watch me print their corrugated orders. One of Town Corrugated's major customers was Del Monte Foods. Their design required elaborate printing and expertise in the manufacturing process. I developed that expertise. As a machine operator instead of a helper, I was paid more money. I worked hard and improved my skills. I achieved a better income. I had a much better life in Chicago than I did while living in Memphis.

Over the years, I became fully proficient in all aspects of corrugated product manufacturing. On this job, I learned engineering. I learned how to create a great product. I learned to see what worked and how to spot flaws in design and process. Nowadays, they call it *kaizen*, the act of continuous improvement. We didn't speak any Japanese in that plant, that's for sure, but we sure practiced *kaizen*. We made damn good boxes.

I felt that if I continued to master the manufacturing process of corrugated material, I would advance up the company's ladder. As my responsibilities would increase, so would my job security and my earnings. I was mistaken. I was never promoted. I would never be promoted. I was black.

Chapter 15
I Become a Union Man

I was employed at Town Corrugated for six years. During this time, I learned how to produce corrugated products by working on many different machines. Because I could master a new machine quickly, I became a very valuable employee. There were only a few of us who could be shifted around the plant from job to job in emergencies and not have the production line back up. Yet, as I mentioned, I was never promoted. Something was wrong.

I decided to act—I became a union official. The plant had been organized for several years. My co-workers could see I knew my way around the plant, even though I was young. Thanks to Mr. Joe's instruction back at the Memphis grocery, I also had a good head for numbers and business. More importantly, I was on a mission. I needed to know why a qualified black man couldn't get promoted. I needed to solve that problem.

My union brothers and sisters elected me as financial secretary. Since the overwhelming majority of the rank and file were black, these people were really my brothers and sisters. Toward the end of my time with Town, I was honored to serve as union president.

My time as a union leader was a turning point. I learned how unions function and managed their membership. I learned to lead workers. I learned how to put the needs of the group into perspective for the good of all. Although I didn't realize it at the time, I also learned what was important to the working guy. I believe that one of the reasons I had so few problems when I ran my own firm was because I had experienced first-hand all the difficulties of the working guy on the line.

Our union local sent me to Gambier College in Gambier, Ohio for sessions on union organization and contract negotiations. Our instructor was a professor who taught both corporate and union management. He taught us how to manage the rank and file. He made sure that his class clearly understood that confrontation with management was the integral reason for a union's existence. To believe that union leaders are truly on the side of the working guy, the rank and file must see that the union will always go to bat for them against management.

Our professor told us the following. I remember it to this to this day.

"Tough talk with management is how we must function, expand, and grow as a union. To be successful, the rank and file must respect you and you must continue to convey to them that you will always represent them against management. You must always convince them of this. They must believe that you represent them only. You cannot ever agree with management. Ever. Even if management is correct. You must always find something wrong with how the company is managed. To stay in the union business, this is how you must operate. Remember, the union is a company and your job in the company is to serve your members."

Harsh words, maybe, but true words. Most companies are heartless. They exist to make a product and generate a profit. Most company managers clearly understand how things work with unions. At contract time, they know it is necessary for the company's negotiating team to give up something. In negotiations, you show strength, for sure, but you must allow the other guy to show his strength. It was all about the ability of union negotiators to go back and sell the contract to the union members to get them to ratify an agreement. In a way, you're like dance partners. On second thought, more like sparring partners.

Chapter 16
A Bitter Fight with Management

On cold winter mornings in Chicago, the hourly employees at our plant would buy coffee and donuts from a peddler. The peddler, a Polish immigrant nearly fresh off the boat, would park his truck outside of the plant's gates. His coffee was always hot, and his donuts were always fresh. Best of all, it was great for the hourly employees because he allowed us to purchase on credit.

This created a problem for Town Corrugated. The plant manager felt that we should purchase food from their vending machines. The vending machine coffee was always weak, and the donuts were always stale. Of course, company management received kickbacks from the vending company. We all know Rule Number 1: *Follow the Money.*

The plant manager informed me that if the hourly employees continued to buy from the peddler's truck, he would report the peddler to the health department. This was not a good thing for the union employees. Weak coffee and stale donuts were no way to start the day.

Plus, we liked the guy. He was one of us, a working guy trying to make a buck. We could not do anything to help the peddler. Even if the peddler moved his truck away from the plant's front door, the manager said that he would still call the health department.

I called a special union meeting to inform our membership of the situation. I also informed the peddler that he should leave or he would have a problem. It was my responsibility to explain to the peddler what was taking place. This broke my heart because the peddler was an immigrant.

The more I thought about it, the more I realized that immigrants went through Hell, just like a black kid growing up in the Jim Crow South. Everyone liked the guy; he was really a good person. The union employees did not always have ready money. His credit plan was a big help toward the end of a pay period. As soon as our members got paid, their first stop was always to pay off their tabs with the coffee guy. We were that close. The union membership became sad and angry to hear about this terrible story.

Because of the position taken by the plant manager on this issue, I decided to make sure the plant manager realized that he had done a disservice to our union members. I also decided I would institute a plan of retribution that would teach this manager a good lesson, one he would never forget.

The next weekend, I called our chief steward Hal Williams and our vice-president Ken Avery over to my home. We spent the entire weekend writing grievances against the company for everything possible. I had gone to several members and asked them if they had any complaints with their foreman or if they had been wronged in any way. If I did not get enough problems from the members, I decided, I would create situations myself.

When we finished writing, we had a total of 40 grievances. We decided to serve all the grievances at the same time. This was a backbreaking pile of paperwork. Legally, the manager was required to handle them immediately. The manager was furious at us but had no recourse other than to deal with the problems. He requested that we take the grievances back and he would negotiate with us. I refused because I wanted to punish this manager. His plan was intended to inconvenience my members, drive a good man out of work, and line the pockets of management. His anger at us was matched by our disgust with him.

The plant manager went completely out of his mind. I could not tell him the real reason we filed 40 grievances all at once. I merely told him that we were tired of being mistreated by his management team. Fact is, this was not true. As a rule, management at this plant was reasonable with my members.

As a result, Town's owner, Sam Bernstein, removed the plant manager from his position. He was transferred to a lower level job where he could not be involved with our union membership. Although I could never inform him of the true reason we kicked his ass, on behalf of the peddler, I felt some form of vengeance had taken place.

I continued my employment at this company without any chance of greater earning power. The handwriting was clear. Looking back, I did not know or understand what I was looking for in life. I would sometime ask myself, *"What is it you really want to do?"* I realized that opportunities for increased wages and more responsibility in a factory environment were not present for black people.

I was just beginning to realize that I had to create my own opportunities. The problem was, as a young man, I did not know how. I wanted to learn how to make real money. I did everything possible to be around other people who earned more money than I did.

However, they were all white people. Often, I thought about the two Jewish-owned grocery stores back in Memphis where I once worked. I knew how they conducted their business with their customers to gain financial wealth. They were willing to cheat people. I had no interest in trying to manipulate anyone. My upbringing would not allow me to become involved in anything that was against the core values instilled in us by our parents.

At that time, Ken Avery and I were the smartest two guys in the plant, but we could not achieve a level of income commensurate with our skills and knowledge. We knew that we had more to offer management than the supervisors they had in place.

Further, we knew that our skin color prevented us from

advancement with this company. Not long after the coffee and donuts incident, Ken Avery was given an opportunity to work as a group leader and was paid five cents per hour more.

Five cents. Two bucks a week. What an insult.

That was not even "hot dog and Coke" money. In today's terms, that's a $16 per week raise. Two combo meals at Wendy's.

Yet, this was looked upon as a good break for him in the eyes of the black employees. How sad was the state of things that a two dollar-a-week raise was celebrated as a big deal? Ken remained in the union and could only pass on the orders given to him by his white foreman. Ken was ten times smarter than his supervisor. His white supervisor.

I left Town Corrugated in 1964. Ken left the company a few years after and he became the manager of a competing corrugated company on the outskirts of Chicago. Years later, I visited Chicago and went to see Ken. It was great to see him function as a plant manager. He certainly had the talent for the job and he was a great friend. By this time, I was getting comfortable with my own company. When we looked back at our time together, we were both saddened and glad. Saddened by what we had to endure, and glad that changing times and our own hard work brought us some success. We were brothers-in-arms.

But back in Chicago, as we fought with management for the rights of our black union brothers and sisters. Never in my wildest imagination did I see myself in the corner office of my own corrugated plant, the founder of a firm that did business with one of the largest and most powerful manufacturing corporations in the world.

Chapter 17
Chicago–Life is Good,
but the Labor Strife Continues

The years I lived in Chicago were much different than the years spent in Memphis. There was segregation but a different type. People were segregated by ethnicity and geography. Very few black and white people lived in the same neighborhood. As a matter of fact, most white neighborhoods were segregated by ethnic groups. The Poles all lived in one part of town. The Italians claimed another area. The Irish had their own neighborhood, and so did the Germans. Most people living in Chicago did not mix between ethnic groups. Each neighborhood was a small enclave onto itself, with its own *de facto* mayor and culture and codes.

Black people lived on the south and west sides. Most white people lived on the north side and downtown. During the time I lived in Chicago, very little socializing between black and white people took place. Segregation may no longer have been legal in Chicago but just because laws are changed doesn't mean that behavior changes.

Town Corrugated Products employed a measly handful of white people in the plant. Black employees totaled approximately 99%. All managers were white. The owner of the company, Sam Bernstein, was Jewish. In my experience of that time, many Jewish people felt strongly about racial equality. However, Bernstein was as deeply prejudiced towards black people as most other white people living in Chicago at that time.

In the best of times, union-management contract negotiations are difficult. With the Civil Rights Movement gaining steam, our meetings were always on the boil. Negotiating a big contract is tough. There is a lot of posturing and storming around and flexing that finally ends up in the give and take of honest negotiation.

When the tough final meetings were underway, Bernstein would enter the office. Both Management and Union had been hard at work to get a good, fair contract and this asshat would always jump into the middle of things without any firsthand knowledge of what his management team and our union team had been striving for during those 18-20 hour days in the conference room.

His song and dance always began with the same story. Bernstein would recount to the union committee of how poor he had been. He would tell us about his childhood. He would talk about the time when he came home from school and all the furniture was sitting on the sidewalk because his family had been evicted from their house.

Without saying all the words directly to him out of respect, I said enough to make sure that Sam Bernstein understood our position. I wanted him to understand that the union didn't give a damn about his childhood or his family. We didn't care where his family's furniture was sitting.

Simply, I informed Mr. Bernstein that the employees had authorized a strike and a work stoppage would occur unless we could negotiate a fair contract. I had absolutely no difficulty informing the owner of our position. Bernstein's hiring policy was obvious to everyone in the plant: me, the stewards, the rank and file—black people worked in the plant and white people worked in the office and as managers.

Right after World War II, Big Bill Broonzy sang about it:

> *If you is white, you's alright,*
> *if you's brown, stick around,*
> *but if you's black, hmm, hmm, brother,*
> *get back, get back, get back.*

I believed this was a company policy from the beginning of its existence. The owner decided his workforce would consist of black hourly employees. The exceptions were for maintenance and the corrugator machine operator. Naturally, these "white worker" positions were the highest pay rates for hourly employees.

All management personnel were white. In all my years with Town Corrugated, there was one white hourly employee. No one could figure out why this one white person was hired to work in the plant. Until this day, I still don't know why.

One summer afternoon as people were leaving the plant, a female employee was walking to her car. She saw a car approach her and she ran back towards the plant. The plant had one entrance at the front of the building. The front entrance had two doors: One door to let you into the foyer and a second door where you had to wait for a receptionist to buzz you into the front lobby. When she started to run back towards the building, she was halfway to her car. As she turned to run, a man jumped out of his car and began firing a gun at her. Dozens of employees were walking along the sidewalk when he began to shoot at this woman.

People dove underneath cars to protect themselves from the shooter. He turned out to be her boyfriend. She could not open the door and was shot to death.

Our receptionist completely froze. She was so stunned, she decided to retire from the company. During the early Sixties in Chicago, there was not a great deal of crime. You could walk the streets at night without fear or harm. Parts of Chicago are still safe. Others are some of the deadliest urban streets in America.

Chapter 18
I Love the Blues

During the cold winter months, we would visit Chicago's "Jew Town." The section was on Halsted, between Roosevelt Road and Maxwell Street. It was called "Jew Town" because many years ago, the open-air Maxwell Street Market was almost entirely filled with Jewish peddlers. After a night of fun and drinking, even with below-zero weather, we would visit "Jew Town" because we wanted to eat Polish sausages from an outdoor open eatery. You could sit on a stool and stay warm because the heat from cooking grill kept you warm.

We hung out in "Jew Town" during the summer months, too. I lived to hear the blues back then. Still do. Entertainers performed on street corners. You could hear Little Walter entertaining on a corner, playing his guitar and harmonica. Street musicians, buskers, they would flip their hats upside down on the ground for contributions from folks passing by. In those days, just to name a few, I saw Howlin' Wolf, Muddy Waters, Magic Sam, Otis Rush, and Freddy King.

I always loved the blues and guitars. In Chicago, I would hit all the night clubs and bars to hear the blues being played. There were many great musicians living and playing music in Chicago. Some were discovered and went on to become world renowned.

The famous made recordings and appeared on stages and theaters around the world. A few made real money. Sadly, most of them ended up broke. They were like many athletes of that time, particularly prize fighters, who did not know how to handle their money. Uneducated and trusting and powerless, they would accept a new car rather than cash money because their record company told them it was a good deal. To be perfectly honest, they had no idea what was best for them. I would visit taverns, the "joints" as we called them, where the blues was played every weekend. The west and south sides of Chicago were filled with musicians.

I was fortunate enough to meet several of them. I met a singer named Joe Williams when he was singing at a local night club on West Madison Ave. On Saturday nights, I would visit this nightclub to hear Joe. He was just a local guy with a great voice. He was the singer at this club until Count Basie visited the club and heard Joe sing. The rest is history.

I always wanted to play the guitar but never took the time to learn. I like to think I made up for it with my passion for the blues. Little Walter, the greatest harmonica player the world ever heard, was killed in a street fight at the age of 37. Magic Sam died of a heart attack the age of 30. I saw them both. In the 1950s and early 1960s, Chicago was the Blues Capital of the World.

Chapter 19
A New Life in Michigan, the Racism Follows

While working at Town Corrugated in Chicago, I met a lovely lady, Cecelia, who also worked there. We began to see each other on a regular basis. I'd managed to put a fair amount of money aside and I was looking to settle down. However, that would soon become problematic. While I sorted out my future, Cecelia decided to move to Michigan and live with her brother.

Before I left Chicago in 1964, I had a conversation with Glen Horton, an executive at Town Corrugated. Over the negotiating table, he and I had developed a mutual respect that occasionally took on aspects of friendship. I knew he was honest and trustworthy. I let him know that I was thinking about moving to Michigan.

"Any place in particular?" Horton asked.

"Maybe Saginaw," I said. "I hear there's good work going on there. And you know, I hear it's a good place for black folks, too."

"You should think about Flint," Mr. Horton answered. "The two cities are only thirty miles apart, there's lots going on in Flint, it's a good factory town.

"Even better, I know of a company that could use your experience and expertise. These people I know own a plant in Flint, but they're having employee problems. The folks on the floor they have, I hear, just do not know what they they're doing. Not enough corrugated knowledge, you know. They just do not know the corrugated process. I hear they've struggled for five years. I know you could really help them. If you're interested, I'm happy to make a call for you. Whaddaya think? How's Flint sound now?"

Horton gave me the name of the company, Best Box Corrugated, and I rode a bus for six hours from Chicago to Flint for my interview.

In the early 1960s, Flint was a boom town. General Motors was founded in Flint on September 16, 1908. By the time I arrived in Flint, the city was home to factories for Buick, Chevrolet, GMC trucks, Fisher Body, and AC Delco. The 1960 Flint census tells us that Flint had 196,940 people within city limits. What the census doesn't tell us is that nearly 90,000 of those people were directly employed by GM companies. Of the rest of Flint's residents, tens of thousands of those were indirectly dependent on GM for their work; physicians, lawyers, stockbrokers, waiters, store clerks and newsboys all relied on the largesse of GM for their incomes.

The hiring people were impressed with my expertise. I had been well-trained at Town Corrugated in Chicago. When you add in that I took it upon myself to become a corrugated expert, there was no doubt that I knew my stuff. The hiring manager told me that the company was desperate for experienced people and they'd like to hire me immediately.

However, I had to wait a week because the vice president who had final say-so on the plant hiring was on vacation. When I walked the floors as part of my interview, it was clear the people working for Best Box Corrugated had very little knowledge or experience in corrugated manufacturing. That included the manager. With my years of experience and my expertise with corrugated product manufacturing, I was what they needed. I knew it. More importantly, they knew it.

I returned one week later for an interview with the VP for personnel. Before the manager hired me, he gave me a test.

"Can you read a tape measure for me?" He asked.

"Sure, of course I can," I said.

Read a tape measure? I thought to myself. *What's this guy up to? You can't be in manufacturing as long as I have and not know how to read a damn tape. Is this a joke?*

I kept that thought to myself.

"Okay, here's a tape. Tell me the exact size of this wooden block on my desk," he said.

He's not joking, I thought. *Better play it straight.*

"That's four and nine-sixteenths inches, sir," I said.

"Good to hear you say that," he said. "Just had another fella in here looking for work. Asked him the same question. Know what he told me?"

"No, sir, I do not."

"Guy looks at me and says, 'Lemme see, it's, um, four inches, okay, and a half, and oh, another little mark.' Can you believe that? Wants to work in my plant and he can't read a tape. Whaddaya think of that?"

"I think he should know how to read fractions on a tape, sir."

To this day, I really do not know if he told this story to me as a joke, because I was black, or if it was a true story. I was hired the same day.

I decided to move to Michigan and marry Cecelia. The year was 1964. President Lyndon Johnson had just signed the Civil Rights Act which prohibited legal discrimination and segregation across the country. Led by their black pitching ace Bob Gibson, the St. Louis Cardinals defeated the Yankees in the World Series. A gallon of gasoline cost 30 cents. We would have two children in our 22 years of marriage. Cecelia was a fine woman. Cecelia had strength of character. She was honest and a great mother. We lost our first child, our daughter, after 30 days of life. Our son graduated from college and is now 45 years old. He's at work as a long-haul trucker as of this writing. Cecelia and I were divorced in 1986. She passed away in 1998.

In 1964, I went to work at Best Box Corrugated's plant located in Flint, Michigan. After only 30 days as an hourly employee, I was promoted to second shift group leader. Like I said, I knew my stuff. The people at Best Box may not have known a lot about the ins and outs of corrugated manufacturing, but they recognized that I did.

There was only one black male and two black females employed with the company when I arrived. All other employees were white. Sadly, this presented a problem right away.

Management wanted me to train people. The people I supervised as a group leader were all white. The plain truth is that they did not want to work for a black person. They clearly did not want to work for a black man who knew what he was doing. They wanted to be left alone to be lazy, do low-quality work, and collect a paycheck. They absolutely did not want me to teach them a better way to produce corrugated material. This went well up the rank and file. Even the general foreman did not understand the manufacturing process.

Management knew that my experience would help the general foreman. I worked as a group leader on second shift for three months. My experience in Chicago at Town Corrugated stood me well. However, they sadly underestimated the degree of prejudice within their company. It was a persistent, pervasive problem. In 1964, a black man supervising white employees was a novelty. Worse, it was problematic. Several male hourly employees left the company rather than take orders from a black man. I had to learn how to manage white people. White, hourly, prejudiced personnel.

Orders are not the best way to manage, anyway. Orders create resentment, whether the employee is white, black, Hispanic, or anything else. Suggestions are almost always the better method. If "suggestions" did not work, we'd have a "conversation."

"Look," I'd say. "I have an idea. Let's take what you're doing and adapt it this way. I think that'll solve the problem. You've helped me come up with a good solution. I really appreciate that." These days we call it "getting buy-in." Back then, I needed to get the employees to listen, learn, and cooperate without rancor.

I could tell them how I believed *our* new method would work. They'd get credit for a better idea and they'd become part of the decision-making process. Today, the business gurus would say I got the employees invested in the decision. In the 1960s, we just called it getting stuff done. This method worked 95% of time. I was a pro at applying this technique.

Part of this method came from my classes at Gambier College in my Chicago days. My professor at Gambier who taught collective bargaining also taught corporate management, how to manage union people of all races. After I was promoted to supervisor with authority and responsibility, a couple of white guys who operated equipment resigned from the company. They informed my boss, in the strongest terms, that they would not take orders from a "black guy." Except they didn't refer to me as a "black guy." We were not sorry to see them go. Folks like that, they turn into lousy employees and worse, co-workers. They spread that cancer throughout the plant at every turn.

Once those racist malcontents were gone, the rest of our employees began to accept me as their boss and leader. They could see I was fair and that I knew my stuff. Our second shift foreman was leaving the company for a different job, a step-up, and in his parting words to me were, "You'll win all these people over. You'll outsmart 'em."

My old firm was so advanced by comparison, Best Box had to promote me. It wasn't a matter of skin color. It was a matter of far more importance to the company: It was dollars and sense. I became a management supervisor.

I was no longer a union member and was completely salaried. Yes, at that time, it was a big move. I wore a white shirt and tie to work every day. I had real management responsibility. In time, I would take on the task of hiring and firing our firm's hourly employees.

Initially, my white colleagues viewed me with a great deal of skepticism. After a few months, they began to accept me as one of them. I would stay with Best Box Corrugated for fifteen years. I made a lot of friends in that time. When I started my own firm, both union and salaried folks came to work for me.

At the time, I did not even own a car. I had to ride the bus to work. Cars were not necessary in Chicago. Everyone took buses and trains all over the city. But in Flint, home of the modern automobile, public transportation around the city has always been an afterthought. No trains anywhere. Buses did not enter the suburbs where the plant was located. I had to walk two miles morning and night to get to the plant. That had to stop.

In 1965, after one year as a second shift supervisor, I was promoted to the first shift. With the promotion came a small raise. I decided to buy a car. As a second shift supervisor, I had to walk two miles at 11:30 at night to the bus stop. It has never been a good idea for black men to walk around that late after dark. Obviously, we're out there for some criminal activity.

The VP that hired me wanted to sell me his car. It was a small Chevrolet that didn't even have an AM radio. He arranged for our company to finance the purchase. I got a great rate and I didn't have to deal with a bank or financing company. President Johnson may have signed a law which banned discrimination in lending but as every black person knew, that didn't mean we got the same rates as white people. The lending officers just figured out slick ways to jerk us around.

With my promotion, I began to report to our general supervisor. He was not the brightest bulb in the chandelier. In 1966, he left the company. I was promoted once more. This promotion was huge. I became the manufacturing manager. I was responsible for the entire manufacturing operation. My old Chicago friend Ken Avery was the first black manager of a major corrugated plant in the U.S. Ken and I believed that I was the second.

1966. Only 11 years prior, Rosa Parks caused an uproar and

started a movement when she refused to move to the "colored section" of a Montgomery, Alabama bus. On March 7, 1965, "Bloody Sunday" took place. State troopers and police beat voting rights marchers to a bloody pulp as the marchers crossed the Pettus Bridge on their way from Selma to Montgomery.

On August 11, 1965, the Watts (a south-central Los Angeles ghetto) riots broke out in response to horrific LAPD brutality. The riots lasted five days, 34 were killed, 1,032 were injured on both sides, and 3,400 people were arrested. $40 million in property damages were accumulated. That's over $300 million in today's dollars.

So, yes, in 1966, putting a black man in charge of a major plant was a huge event. It was brave on the part of my employer. I felt the weight of both my race's credibility, as well as the normal stress of a man placed in charge of a major manufacturing facility. I was the first black man promoted to manage an entire plant in Flint.

Things change when you become management. You lose your rank and file buddies. You have to. If you're seen having beers after work with the guys, only bad things can happen. You automatically become accused of favoritism. Nothing ends a good working relationship with the rank and file quicker than the perception that you play favorites. Even if you don't play favorites, it looks that way. If it comes time to discipline one of your drinking buddies, does he expect special treatment?

It's not fair to the guys at the bar, either. Drinking with the boss makes you look like a brown-nose, a rat, a suck-up. I did not have rank and file buddies. Not black. Not white. You just can't.

I didn't have problems outside the company. When I spoke with management people at different companies, I was always treated with respect. Word gets around. Whenever a new man, always a man back then, would earn a major promotion, it was in the newspapers, the trade papers, office scuttlebutt, sales rep chat; it was no secret that a black man was now in charge at Best Box

Corrugated.

As I mentioned, a couple of white guys resigned from the company when I was first promoted to group leader. When I became the manufacturing manager, a handful of white employees left the company because felt they were passed over in favor of me.

Race had nothing to do with my promotion. Those men were passed over because I was better than they were. I knew more about the manufacturing processes. I was better at problem solving. I was more capable as a personnel manager. Yet, race had everything to do with those people quitting. It was not difficult to replace them. We had plenty of hungry, competent people to fill their shoes.

Were these difficult times? You bet they were. Alone by ourselves in managers' offices, we talked about race, about whites and blacks working side-by-side. I couldn't join the "right" clubs in Flint. It would be more than twenty years before that wall came down. There were neighborhoods where I could not buy a home. There were restaurants where I could not get a table, unless they knew that I was now "somebody."

But good things happened, too. A few years later, when I opened my own plant, a supplier who provided raw material to my company would take his best customers to Canada for a fishing trip. There were about twenty guys and I was the only black man in the group. I was always treated with respect and dignity. I gave and got the same crap to the white guys as they did to each other. Guys being guys, right? I never experienced a single problem with that group of white guys. I really loved being with them because we had a lot of fun. We would fish, drink booze and have a great time for five days.

Best Box Corrugated was a union shop. I did not have a problem working with their union because of my prior experience in Chicago. A key to negotiation, any negotiation, is to be able to see things clearly from the other guy's side. Only this time, I managed the entire plant operation. I was responsible for the well-being of

65 employees. Figuring in wives and kids, that about 300 people. Health care. Retirement. Income. Family issues. Good management is not just production management, it's human management, too.

I took that responsibility seriously. I couldn't totally leave my blue-collar days behind. Yet, if I couldn't convince the union of the fairness of my side, then maybe we can't make enough money to stay in business. I had to see the other side to be fair, but I had to see the big picture and be a careful steward of the company's money.

I made changes. I made sure that in our next round of hiring, we hired black people for hourly work. It wasn't that I shut out the white hires. It wasn't that if you were black, you got a job automatically. If you were competent, you got a job. I simply made sure that black people were represented. My own personal affirmative action program.

The white employees began to accept me as their boss. I could see them beginning to respect me without question. On a normal, day to day basis, I did not have a great number of problems. However, there were times when it was difficult to discipline a white employee. Fortunately, I had a good boss.

I reported directly to Jim White, the general manager. We had a good working relationship. Jim respected my skills and professionalism. I was always fair with my people. That made things easy for Jim. Ultimately, all major problems landed on Jim's desk and I worked my ass off to make sure those major problems didn't start on my time. My presence in the company was strengthened because everyone knew that Jim White was on my side.

Just the same, we did have an issue arise. Best Box's owner, John Simon, wanted a manufacturing manager between me and Jim. In other words, I would report to this new manager, and he would report to Jim. To me, this made no sense. Another layer of paperwork, another secretary on the payroll, another big executive salary.

At the time, I suspected this move was racial. Although the

company was very profitable with me as the manager in charge of all plant operations, I believe John Simon wanted someone white between me and GM Jim White. I believed that they saw me, a black man, as too close to the real power in the firm. They hired John Jones for the new position of manufacturing manager. To John Simon's credit, Jones did have corrugated plant experience.

My new title became general supervisor. I reported directly to John Jones. There is no way to sugarcoat it—John Jones was a terrible manager. It became obvious that this was a political hire. From the first weeks, I had nothing but problems with Jones. He did know the corrugated industry. It wasn't with manufacturing that I had issues with John Jones. It wasn't just that Jones was a horrible bigot. He was an incompetent manager. He stirred up trouble with personnel problems. He played favorites. He would tell one group one thing and turn right around and tell another group the opposite.

After that last go-around, I knew I could no longer report to this person. I was convinced that Jones would never accept a black man as a colleague. In 1968, I had a lengthy meeting with general manager Jim White. At that meeting, I simply told him that I could no longer work with Jones. One of us had to go. Here's why:

John Jones was a hateful, disgusting bigot. My second shift foreman was named Ron Pear. Ron was a good employee, a good co-worker, and a good man. He was also a black man. His position brought him into regular contact with Jones. Ron was dating a white woman. The woman's father was previously employed by Best Box Corrugated in the front office and had a friendly relationship with John Jones. The woman worked elsewhere.

The father had not been a part of his daughter's life for many years. In fact, they had not seen each other for most of her adult life. Just the same, he was upset when he discovered she was dating a black man. In his loathsome mind, the problem was even worse because she was dating a black man who was in a position of responsibility at his former employer.

Legally, Michigan has always been a forward-looking state. In 1883, Michigan's Supreme Court threw out all forms of legalized discrimination. The Court further allowed interracial marriage in the state. Yet it wasn't until 1967, around the time of this incident, that the U.S. Supreme Court held all anti-miscegenation to be unconstitutional. But court rulings don't overturn the mindset of the bigot.

The girl's father came to the plant on a Saturday looking for the owner, John Simon. The father stormed in loaded for bear, as if the private, legal dating relationships of our employees were our responsibility, or even any of our business. Simon was not in his office, but my new boss, John Jones, was parked behind his desk. With much shouting and slamming of fists on desks, the woman's father made a vigorous complaint against Ron.

Why? Because Ron was a black man dating this white bigot's adult daughter. Jones told him that he would handle the matter and there was no need for him to discuss the issue with the owner.

Monday afternoon, John Jones, my direct supervisor, remember, told me he needed to see my second shift foreman Ron Pear, ASAP. He did not tell me what he wanted to talk to him about. As Ron sat down for the meeting and the bile started to spew from Jones' mouth, it was shocking that Ron didn't explode across the desk and throttle him. After this incident shook out, Ron shared with me what had been said.

Jones said so many shameful and inappropriate things to Ron. He made him feel as if he was dirt. He insulted Ron as a man, as an employee, and as a black man. It was one of the vitriolic displays of racial hatred Ron said he'd ever heard. In short, Ron was less than human and had no business dating a white woman.

Jones did not know this woman. He did not know her father either. This fool-for-a manager based his entire revolting tirade on what the woman's father told him. Jones, that jackass, took everything the father said as gospel. He demoted a damn fine foreman. He took his keys to the plant. It was a kangaroo court. Fortunately, common sense and human decency prevailed.

Jim White, our general manager, was in the hospital at the time. I visited him in the hospital and informed him that if the current manufacturing manager remained with the company as my superior, I would leave. Immediately. Jim knew I was dead serious.

I absolutely could not continue to report to this person. I did not go into all the reasons why I felt so strongly against my immediate supervisor. Jim knew me, trusted me, believed in me. In me, Jim had a proven performer who was respected by all in the plant.

Jim White, a good man, felt that I was more important to the company than John Jones.

"As soon as I get back to the office," White assured me, "I will handle this situation. I promise you, Willie, the Jones issue will be the first thing on my agenda."

On Jim's first day back, Jones was axed. I was placed back in charge of all plant operations as manufacturing manager. My first move was to reinstate Ron Pear to his previous position with back pay. As for Jones, I never knew where he landed. Didn't care, either.

Six months later, the company decided to promote an office executive named Kyle Bert to manufacturing manager. I was told that I would report directly to Kyle. I knew Bert well and felt we could work together. Kyle felt the same way.

Although Bert did not have any corrugated plant or manufacturing experience, we made a good team. He did his job and I did mine. As a matter of fact, we became friends with a good working relationship that lasted many years.

I did not realize at the time that Kyle's promotion was John Simon's behind-the-scenes racism at work. Still scared that a black man had the direct ear of his chief, Simon did not want me working at a level where I would have daily access to Jim White. As a black man, I should report to a lower level executive, not the general manager. I never discussed this with Kyle Bert. As my boss, I did not know how he would accept any criticism of the company's owner from me.

Chapter 20
A Return to Chicago?

In 1975, I received a phone call at home from a man I did not know. The caller identified himself and told me that he was looking for an experienced, corrugated manufacturing person. It was critical that the man was a minority. He wanted to come to Flint and convince me to return to Chicago where I would run a plant. This person told me that this would be a big deal. He clearly stated that Sears Roebuck was interested in a minority man who would be part-owner of a corrugated operation in Chicago.

As soon as I hung up the phone, I called my good friend Ken Avery. Ken was still in Chicago. If anyone knew what this was about, it would be Ken. Ken had credentials every bit as strong as mine. I was not surprised when Ken told me that he'd had the same call from the same guy and that he declined their offer.

I was not interested in a move back to Chicago. I, too, declined.

A few months later, this same representative again approached Ken Avery. This time, the plan was different. The rep had two Fortune 500 companies ready to back a minority-owned corrugated plant in Chicago. This time, Ken accepted.

They did start a corrugated plant in Chicago. Ken Avery was installed as the president. Ken knew the business from the ground up. I sincerely felt Ken would make this new black-run company a winner from the get-go.

I visited Chicago and called Ken at the plant because I wanted to see him and wish him well. He did not return my call. This made no sense. Ken and I were old friends; we started as hourly employees together and climbed the ladder to upper management together. I knew the location of his plant and drove to see him unannounced. I entered the plant and asked for him. I was escorted to his office and he appeared to be quite surprised to see me.

He told me of all the problems the company was experiencing. The problems poured out of him. The poor man had been keeping this bottled up for several years. It was heartbreaking to sit and listen to all the lies he'd been told, all the heartbreaks he'd had to deal with, all the distress he'd taken onto himself. The company operated for two years and then failed. The company never made money. Not one dime.

Shortly after our meeting, Ken committed suicide. He left no note. I could not believe Ken Avery would take his own life. Ken and I were as close as brothers. I knew him as well as you can know a good friend. He was truly my best friend.

Ken loved motorcycles. Before he became involved with the corrugated ownership initiative, he decided to ride his motorcycle to Flint to visit me. If I think about it, I can still see Ken whipping across I-69 from Chicago to Flint on his trip. Our visit in his office was the last time I saw him alive. I think of him often and wonder what might have happened had I visited him sooner.

Chapter 21
The Beginning of the Dream:
My Own Business

While I was employed at the Best Box plant in 1975, I was approached by a black man who delivered used wooden pallets to the company. Clayton Thompson approached me about going into business him. The plan? We'd sell used wooden pallets on the open market.

Because he was known in Flint as a sharp businessman, I listened to Thompson's pitch. I liked his idea. We would purchase broken pallets from other companies, repair them, and then resell them as used wooden shipping pallets. It took several meetings, but I decided to go into business with him.

I owned 50 percent of the company and worked the second shift. Clayton Thompson wanted me to resign from the company where I was employed. He figured we'd both make more money if I devoted all my energy to our new venture. I declined. I didn't really trust Thompson. Something was off. Too quick to judgment. Too little planning. Too much "This is gonna be easy money." There's a lesson here: *If your gut says you don't trust someone, don't do a partnership with them.*

I should have listened to my gut. I discovered this guy Thompson was a disaster. He couldn't make a sound business decision if it was in a gift-wrapped package. With the first check we received, he decided to lease a Cadillac as a sign of success.

Thompson was also a liar. He told me that an entire load of pallets had been stolen.

"An entire load?" I asked him. "Someone stole a semi-trailer full of broken pallets? How did that happen?"

"The truck was hijacked. Right at gunpoint," he said.

I spoke with the state police. They had no knowledge of such a crime. Right then, I knew it was time to get out as fast as possible. I had no interest in remaining in business with this shyster.

Even the state police officer said, "You better have a word with your partner."

I gave my share of stock to Thompson and said goodbye. Gave it away. I took the loss as a "cheap at twice the price" lesson. He wanted to file a lawsuit against me because I left him. His attorney would not accept the case because he had no case against me. I just wanted to divorce myself from a fool.

From 1964 to 1977, I was a management employee with no intentions other than to earn a regular paycheck. I worked hard and was well paid. I was happy to stay at Best Box Corrugated. I had a little taste of entrepreneurship. I liked it but learned a valuable lesson: *Choose partners wisely.*

IndustryCorp, the world sales leader in their field, is headquartered in my adopted hometown of Flint. They were so dominant that it took a large staff of Washington lobbyists to avoid anti-trust action. It was said that when IndustryCorp sneezed, the ripple effect was so great that hundreds of smaller firms caught a cold.

I was not aware that they had started a program designed to help jumpstart minority-owned businesses. Their goal was to supply IndustryCorp with products and services from minority-owned businesses. The rules were straightforward. The business must be minority-owned and operated by a minority with no less than 51 percent ownership in the company. The program would be great for minorities who wanted to own their own business.

Of course, there were problems. Even in the 1970s, banks were not only reluctant to make loans to minorities, most banks refused to make loans to start-up companies. By 1970, the Great Northern Migration following the Civil War was at an end. There were 23 million African Americans in the U.S. at that time. They represented about 12 percent of the U.S. population. Yet, they owned and operated just a miniscule number of businesses. Someone in corporate White America decided it was time to help Black America change that figure.

Chapter 22
The Ups & Downs of Minority Sponsorship

Yet, leave it to other white-owned businesses to game that system. White-owned companies that provided products and services to IndustryCorp developed a method to take advantage of new business earmarked for minority-owned companies. It was called "sponsorship."

In other words, the owner of the non-minority-owned company would set up a new company. He would find a minority to front the company. The minority would own 51 percent of the stock and the non-minority owned 49 percent of the entity. Seems fair, right?

Here's where the game set in: The arrangement would set the minority-owned stock as five percent "voting" and 46 percent "non-voting." This would give the black owner a 51 percent stock ownership in the company.

The balance of the stock totaling 49 percent would be owned by the so-called sponsor, the white business owner. He would assign himself the other 95 percent of the voting shares in the company. While the sponsor could say, legally, that the business was majority-owned by the black man out front, with 95 percent of the voting stock, the white sponsor fully controlled all aspects of the company. Because minority-owned companies could receive preferential pricing, this arrangement was very profitable for the non-minority.

Legal? I suppose.

However, soon after the program was put into place, several minority men I knew broke away. They started their own companies without sponsors to provide seed money. These men knew their businesses. They knew their clients' needs. They put together great pricing programs for their clients.

Most importantly, they over-delivered. They were better than they promised. Higher grade products and on-time deliveries in an era when shoddy work and late delivery was the norm made them attractive as partners. Although the term "win-win situation" was not yet commonplace, that's exactly what this new group created. With the success of this firm, other minority businesses in this industry were formed.

Many firms that supplied IndustryCorp wanted to do business with minorities. They knew it was the right thing to do. But they couldn't do business solely on the skin color. The entire equation had to considered. When a minority-owned business provided the best products and service at a competitive price, the many "right-thinking" customers jumped at the chance.

It was this customer base that provided great opportunities to the minority-owned companies. Those early companies were the Jackie Robinsons of industry. Better, faster, more competitive. Customers responded. A firm that could produce a quality product with competitive prices grew fast.

In addition, IndustryCorp had a great program to assist minorities with their business plans. IndustryCorp had teams to help minority vendors plot a combined future with them. Many of those minority-owned companies are still highly profitable businesses today, 40 years after breaking away from their sponsors and heading out on their own.

In 1976, my employer, the owner of Best Box Corrugated, Mr. John Simon, approached me with a proposition. Simon owned three separate container companies. William Rush, the owner and the director of minority programs at a spring manufacturing company, attended college with John Simon. Rush and Simon discussed hiring and corporate ownership. Rush clued Simon in on how easy and profitable it was to set up a faux minority company.

In the late 1970s, minority-owned businesses were offered pricing and bid preferences in the container industry. Rush showed Simon how easy it would be for Best Box to set up a fronted minority-owned corporation if Simon would prop up a minority owner with no less than 51 percent ownership in the company.

John Simon discovered that Joe Brown, his Chief Financial Officer (CFO), could qualify as a minority. Mr. Simon wanted Brown and me to own 51 percent of a company he owned. No one knew Joe Brown was part Native American. Back then, a less "aware" time, we called them Indians.

Buyers would joke with him and say, "When did you become an Indian?"

"I am twenty-five percent Indian," Joe would reply.

"No shit? You don't look like an Indian," the buyers would answer. "You sure as hell don't act like an Indian. When did you decide you wanted to be an Indian?"

One manufacturing company, allied with IndustryCorp, stood their ground. They saw through these fronted companies and would not recognize Simon's new company as a minority-owned business. They did not accept my partner as an Indian. This company never granted minority certification to the fronted company. These arrangements with fronted minority companies lasted until 1979. Here's how it all went down:

Because the owner employed two men, one black and a self-proclaimed 25-percent Indian CFO, the fronted firm qualified as a minority-owned business. Simon decided to use both of us as minority owners. The ownership was created in the following manner. I would own 25.5 percent of stock. The "Indian" CFO would also own 25.5 percent of stock. Simon would own 49 percent of the outstanding stock. This arrangement would allow the company to be defined as a minority-owned company. This was the classic fronted minority-owned company of that time. You should know that Simon and Best Box were just one of many companies in that era to take advantage of the loophole.

The 51 percent of stock owned by the two minorities would be structured to make sure control of the company would remain with the 49 percent stockholder. The 51 percent of stock owned by the two minorities was structured as follows:

> **Minority Stockholders**: Brown and Artis to own in total 51% of stock at 25.5% each. This stock shall be "Class B" non-voting stock. They shall each hold 2.5% of "Class A" voting stock.

> **Majority Stockholder**: Simon shall own 49% of "Class B" non-voting stock. He shall own 95% of all "Class A" voting stock.

In this way, despite all appearances to the contrary, Simon held a lock on all corporate decisions. He held 95 percent of all voting power. Furthermore, Simon appointed two board members. Simon's chief corporate attorney, and Jim White, Best Box's general manager, would become a two-man board of directors. Therefore, Simon controlled the board and the company. This entire arrangement was designed and engineered by John Simon to further enhance his own personal financial gain. This scheme could be achieved because Simon employed both minorities.

John Simon, the guy who arranged to cook the ownership books, would never envision in his wildest dreams that very soon, these two employees would become his worst business nightmare.

The new "company" was recognized as a legitimate minority-owned organization. Because the company had legal classification as minority-owned, the sales increased from four hundred thousand dollars annually to over three million dollars in sales the first year. Astronomical growth. Unheard of.

I did not know if Joe Brown, in title the manager, received any additional salary. I do know that I did not. At this point, I was not aware of the amount of money paid to the front's manager. I had no idea of the salary structure. I never worked for the newly formed company one single day. Not one. I never set foot in the plant. I never saw any financials. I had no meetings. Nothing. I remained with Best Box Corrugated in my regular role as manager.

A meeting took place with a group of executives from one of our customers and the sham minority-owned company. John Simon was asked a telling question by a black woman on the customer's representative team.

"Where's the other minority owner? Why isn't he here?" she asked. "You'd think, we're a pretty big account for a new firm, wouldn't he want to be here? I'd like to meet the other guy."

I'm sure she asked the question because the minority sitting in the meeting did not look like an Indian. Remember, we had no proof that Brown was at all a minority. He certainly did not appear to have what we might be termed Native American features. He just claimed he was 25-percent American Indian.

Simon spoke up.

"He's at the other plant. You know, he used to manage that place. He still kind of thinks of it as his baby."

"That strikes me as odd," she said. "Seems like this should be his baby now, being an owner and all. He couldn't spare an hour to meet with us? I don't like that. If we're going to do this deal, I need to meet the guys who are in charge. This is a problem."

"Oh. Well, let me give him a call," said Simon. "I can have him come over so you can meet."

I received a phone call that instructed me to come over and meet some people. I was hard at work at my real job. The only thing I did was shake hands with the customer.

Simon did all the talking. Joe Brown, the Indian, said nothing. Willie Artis, the black man, said nothing.

I was present for about ten minutes and then, very politely, excused myself. I'm sure the visiting executives knew this company was yet another classic fronted minority owned company. Despite the realization that this was a front, they seemed willing to work with Best Box's front as if it were a legitimate minority owned company.

In 1978, the owner paid me $600 as a Christmas bonus. He paid the other minority $10,000. That is correct. The black man received a $50 per month bonus. Joe Brown received an $833 per month bonus. If you do the numbers correctly, you'll see he was paid 16.67% more than me. Yet, at that time, I had no idea of Simon's financial insult.

During the summer of 1978, Joe and I began to have conversations about our status with the newly formed company. We knew the corrugated business, Joe and me. From the ground up, we'd learned what it took to manufacture, price, and sell corrugated products. Were we experts? Pretty damn close.

We began these talks after a meeting with a buyer from a parts dealer who sold to IndustryCorp.

"You know, guys. You know business. You know this business," he said. "Maybe you've never been the boss before, but you should be. You know factories and you know numbers.

"Why are you working for Simon in this set-up? Take a look at yourselves—busting your asses for this guy, he's making the big money. Why don't you two: Joe, Willie, why don't you break away? Start your own container company?

"Look, here's the deal, fellas. I like you, I trust you, you're good guys. You two leave, start your own plant, come up with competitive prices, I promise you my first million in buys, minimum, will be with your new company. Think of it as seed money.

"We gotta buy our boxes somewhere. We want to buy them from you. That Simon, he's a sonuvabitch."

Brown and I looked at each other. I could see the lightbulb go on over Joe's head. I'm sure he could see mine.

My future partner, Joe Brown and I, met on a regular basis during the summer of 1978. Because we had different backgrounds, we felt that we could succeed with some help. Joe Brown was an accountant and a damn good one. The man knew numbers. Joe had no plant or operations experience. That was my strength. I was experienced with the physical plant, product manufacturing, and union issues. Between us, we were one helluva chief operating, chief executive, and chief financial officer. This could work, we decided.

A buyer Joe knew asked to meet with me. I didn't know him. We set up a luncheon. We talked for several hours. In the back of my head, I knew this meeting would go a long way towards determining the success or failure of our plans.

Fortunately, I impressed him. He felt strongly that we should move forward. The buyer felt that between us, Joe and I had the perfect combination of business expertise to be a success. This buyer was a big deal in the container business. We knew it was not just his opinion that carried weight, but his actions, too. When word got out he was doing business with us, other firms would follow his lead. He urged us to put a business plan together. He was confident that a firm owned by the two of us would take off.

We began to schedule meetings with a local attorney, Mason Stockbridge. We soon brought in an outside attorney as well. The three of us knew that this would become a nasty and semi-public business brawl. Stockbridge could not afford to be seen in this light.

Our outside attorney, Clark Taylor, practiced law in Bloomfield Hills, a wealthy Detroit suburb 45 miles to the south of Flint. He was known for his business law acumen. It was a bright move. This maneuver allowed Mason Stockbridge to work his connections behind the scenes. We were not in a position of power and needed to keep all our actions as quiet as possible.

In our first meeting with Taylor, we were asked how much bonus money was paid to us in 1977.

"Six hundred bucks," I said.

"How much?" Taylor asked.

Taylor looked baffled. He raised an eyebrow and asked me again, "How much?"

"Six hundred dollars," I said.

"What about you, Joe?" he asked.

"Um, Simon gave me ten grand," Brown answered.

If it's possible to be ashamed and proud at the same time, Brown was.

"Ten thousand dollars?" Taylor asked.

"Yes, sir. Ten thousand dollars," Brown said.

I almost fell out of my chair.

"That sonuvabitch," I said. "I got fifty bucks a month. You got ten grand? What the hell is going on?"

Joe didn't know. He wasn't privy to what I was getting any more than I was in on his cut.

It was quite apparent to me that Simon believed that I was not a threat. He felt that if he took care of Joe and paid him accordingly, he could keep me under his thumb. Pay off Joe, keep me squashed down, and the fronted minority business that was lining his pocket would keep right on lining it.

Although our stock purchase agreement with Simon allowed for us to purchase the fronted company, we knew that he would never sell the company to us. Because our bonus was scheduled to be paid before Christmas, we decided to wait until after the holidays to request a meeting. In January of 1979, after the bonuses were paid, I mailed a registered letter to Simon in Florida at his winter home. I requested a meeting to discuss the option per our agreement to purchase his interest in the company.

I had received my second $600 Christmas bonus. My partner received his second $10,000 bonus.

God bless us everyone, except that Scrooge. Simon, you're a real bastard, I thought at Christmas dinner.

Brown and I knew our meeting with Simon would be an exercise in futility. A meeting was scheduled by Simon to take place in the company office in April of 1979, several months after we notified Simon of our request.

A board meeting took place at six o'clock p.m. The board consisted of five people. Joe Brown and I were seated on the board, but it was under Simon's control, remember. Simon, his attorney, and Jim White were the other board members. They would always vote in his favor. In addition to his ownership of 95 percent of the voting shares, he also stacked the board in his favor.

His mouthpiece told us that his stock was not available until a certified appraiser was hired to determine stock value. Simon said he did not understand why we wanted to exercise our option to buy him out.

"Why do you want to do this? I got you up and running. You use my name to do business. Why do you want me out of the picture?"

Throughout this entire meeting, he never looked at me. He never looked at the black man in the room. Everything he said was directed entirely to Joe Brown.

To quote Ellison's *Invisible Man*, "I am invisible, understand, simply because people refuse to see me." I realized at this moment that in Simon's mind, it wasn't that I was sub-human, like my great-grandfather, an enslaved man. I did not even exist.

When Simon realized that we were not going away, he began to rant.

"You'll never succeed. I'll crush you, assholes. Look, I run this town in this business. I send out the word, nobody will meet with you, nobody.

"Look at you two! Everything you are in this town, it's thanks to me. Everything you learned, all the contacts you made, you are nothing without me! And you wanna squeeze me out? Bastards, you're nothing more than a bunch of selfish bastards. You're dead here, you know that? Dead!"

Saliva was flying across the room as he raved at us.

Joe and I sat quietly through his tirade. When he stopped, Joe spoke first.

"We feel we are being used as minorities. Everyone in town knows this business model is a scam. You didn't even see fit to pay us both accordingly."

Joe looked at me. The grotesque differences in our Christmas bonuses was on both our minds.

"Therefore, Mr. Simon," I said, "we would like to purchase your interest in the company as stipulated in our buy-sell agreement."

We always believed the agreement we had in place was worthless because it was written by his attorney. Clark Taylor confirmed our fears.

Simon asked us to leave the room for a few moments. When we were recalled to the conference, Simon terminated the employment of Joe Brown. Canned him, right there in front of me and our attorney. I was ordered to report back to the plant where I was the manager. Simon believed that the Joe Brown was the real problem. He saw Brown as the threat to Best Box, and a threat to him. It couldn't be the black guy, could it? Joe and I left the meeting and never returned to work for that company.

Simon made a huge mistake. He believed that his CFO was the problem. He felt that Brown would be a continuous thorn in his side. He believed that Brown was the sole reason his Best Box minority fronted company was being dismantled, piece by piece like a Lego toy, by these upstarts in the packaging business. It was clear that Simon had discounted me completely. In his mind, I was a marionette. That's why he axed Joe Brown yet sent me back to work as a manager of a highly profitable corrugated plant.

His real problem was not Joe Brown. It was me. As a racist, he just didn't know it. As a racist, he just couldn't grasp the idea of a competent black man at all. Invisible.

The owner failed to see the elephant in the room. He completely underestimated and ignored the black guy sitting in the office. He was completely blindsided because had he known what we were planning, he would have made every effort to block what we were trying to achieve.

I became his worst enemy. He never saw what was coming at him. I became the person who engineered major contract moves from his company to ours over a period of three years. It was not his former CFO. Joe Brown was a great accountant, but he could not sell. He would make us highly profitable.

I could sell. The phrase "Nothing happens until somebody sells something" has been attached to many great businessmen, and it is true. In those early days, I sold. And as a result, Joe Brown had numbers to crunch and plans to put forth.

Because of how my parents raised their children, their insistence that I work and learn, plus my personality, I mastered the sales arena. I developed millions of dollars in new business for Industrial Packing Company (IPC, for short), our new company. Although my background was manufacturing, I grew to love sales. There was a tremendous amount entertaining involved in sales. I love to entertain. Sales became my forte and I enjoyed every minute of it.

I spent a tremendous amount of time and energy with purchasing personnel who worked for IndustryCorp. Buyers knew I had been part of a fronted minority-owned business. I never complained about my involvement, about having to succumb to the wishes of an unethical business owner. If the subject came up during a conversation while developing new business, I would respond to any questions.

The British Prime Minister Benjamin Disraeli is credited with the phrase "Never complain. Never Explain." Henry Ford adopted it as his mantra. That was me. I never voluntarily started any dialogue regarding my involvement with a fronted company. Most people that engaged me in conversation were glad to see me out of that situation and moving forward with my own company. Over many years of business, my company created hundreds of jobs in our community and gained the support of our bank and customer base.

Joe and I had a 50/50 ownership stake as partners in the new firm. Neither of us had a controlling interest. We kept everything quiet as we brought our new firm into the marketplace. Only the attorneys and the stockholders were aware of how this new company had evolved from a sham minority owned company controlled by Simon and Best Box. In time, IPC would become the largest minority-owned firm in Flint, MI. At our peak, in 1999, we would employ 400 employees over three different sites.

As we moved forward, Joe and I did not forget that it was John Simon who, through his bigotry and miscalculation of the human equation, brought us together. A lifelong chain smoker, Simon suffered from emphysema and was required to carry an oxygen tank with him. We were sitting in a restaurant having lunch with a group of buyers one day and Simon came in with a tube attached to his nose. When he noticed us, he immediately turned around and left the restaurant. That was the last time we saw him alive.

I may have cursed John Simon on a regular basis, but I learned from him. He was a bastard, but he was a successful bastard. I've always been inquisitive, and I wondered how much salary he drew. One night, when I'd been working for him for a few years, and was just learning how much of a bastard he really was, I noticed that our CFO left a file cabinet unlocked.

I snooped.

I found the folder with executive salaries. Simon was far from the highest paid in salary. He made his money in other ways. He owned a leasing company that owned all his buildings and trucks. His packaging and trucking companies paid rent to his personal leasing firm. He owned the entire leasing firm on his own. It was brilliant. I realized I might need to stick around for a few more years and learn some things. He treated me poorly, but there was plenty there for me to learn. When IPC took shape, I set up my firm in exactly the same manner.

When John Simon passed away, Joe Brown and I paid our respects at the funeral home. Through his evil, Simon brought Joe and I together. In an eerie way, we owed Simon a bit of thanks.

Chapter 23
How to Get a Start in Packaging

The commercial packaging business, like every business in Fortune 500 America, is a fiercely competitive endeavor. The numbers are vast; tens of thousands of corrugated cartons crunched out at a time. Next time you drive past a plant of any kind, try and imagine the number of small parts that are manufactured off-site. Each part needs to be packaged perfectly before it can be shipped to the plant. It takes incredible design to use as little corrugated as possible yet provide maximum protection for each part. Think about Amazon and eBay, LG and Apple—hundreds of thousands of corrugated boxes are in use every moment of every day in the U.S. Someone makes those containers. We wanted our share of that business.

Packaging is part art, part science. Just down the road from my home in Flint, Michigan State University turns out 150 people with B.S. degrees in packaging every year. In fact, they have a dozen men and women with the Ph.D. degree teaching the sciences—Chemistry, Agriculture, Biology—all required courses to master packaging and design. Packaging today also requires high-level math, Calculus and Topology. In an ecologically-conscious era, the development of well-priced, "green" packaging is of the highest importance to every industry. Yet, even without degrees in packaging science, Joe and I managed to get things done.

Knowing that, you shouldn't be surprised that you can't just say, "I'm gonna start selling boxes to GE." It is a big-time undertaking that takes place partly in secret, and many pieces of the puzzle must fall in place simultaneously. You also need connections and guidance.

My wood pallet business was a semi-disaster—bad partner, lots of nights at work for little pay—but one connection I made was crucial to my success in the container business. Flint has several major Dow Jones corporations and I was given the chance to meet Mr. Lester Kimes, the minority coordinator for the biggest, IndustryCorp.

Kimes immediately struck me as a fair-minded person. I felt I could have an honest conversation with him. I wanted to discuss our new firm with him. By this time, I had a strong vision about IPC and I wanted him, an influential man in the Flint business community, to be aware of what I was trying to achieve.

At the outset of our conversation, Kimes got down to business.

"You still working with Clayton Thompson in that pallet business?" he asked.

"No way, I got away from that guy as fast as I could. I gave him my stock and sprinted for the door like Bullet Bob Hayes. Faster, maybe."

"Probably don't need to ask you if he's in on this deal?" Kimes asked.

"Nope. Not a chance in Hell," I said.

There was no reason to go into all the reasons I had for leaving the pallet business. Kimes had known Thompson long before I did. He didn't ask why I had bolted from the partnership. He knew that Thompson was not a solid businessman.

Never complain. Never explain.

I did volunteer that Thompson and I had different ideas—about how to structure the company, how to handle pricing, personnel. I stuck to business differences. I was careful not to badmouth him again. On the record for that meeting, our issues were strictly business.

We proceeded to discuss my new company. I explained what Joe Brown and I wanted to achieve as a company that was legitimate: A true minority-owned and operated company in Flint, Michigan. I explained to Mr. Kimes that we had broken away from Best Box because of our differences about minority-fronted businesses. No surprise, Kimes was familiar with the issues. Even in Fortune 500 corporate America, gossip flies fast. In fact, Best Box had been a supplier to Kimes' company for many years.

Kimes informed me that the information I provided to him about our intent with our new enterprise would harm a well-established company in Flint. That put him, he explained, in a difficult spot.

"Look, Willie, I am aware of the critical role you played while employed with Mr. Simon," he went on. "However, no matter how Simon treated you guys, and how he was skirting the law, he's still a respected businessman around here. Hell, he's built a pretty big business. He's been selling to us for years.

"I want you to know that I do understand what you are telling me. The problem is, I can't help you. Although I am the minority coordinator for this division, I do not have the power to promote what you are trying to achieve.

"I'll keep my mouth shut about this. You have my word on this. I promise. But you need to know the move you want to make could have an adverse effect on several people. Based on what I've heard around the grapevine, what you've told me about the company and your situation, I believe you are justified in what you want to accomplish in this matter. I wish you the best. I really do.

"But what you're looking for with your new company in this town? That's too much for me to handle. You've got a great idea, and I think you'll be a success, but you need backing at a higher level than me.

"With that said, I do know who can help you. You'll need to visit our company's supplier headquarters. I'll give you the name and phone number of the person you need to see. I'll call and let him know that you're going to call."

We stood and shook hands.

"Willie," he said, "good luck. I hope you succeed. I believe you will."

"Thank you, Mr. Kimes, for your help. We're gonna pull this off."

I discussed my meeting with my partner and we decided a meeting was necessary. I made the call to the supplier headquarters and set up a meeting with the person responsible for corporate minority business. I had no idea if the person was black or white. I arranged for Joe and me to meet with the executive in charge of minority business suppliers.

Joe Brown and I were amazed to discover we'd be meeting with a black man who reported straight to a director. Jack Curtis was a man with real power and responsibility in a Dow Jones firm. This may have been the 1970s, no longer rare, but it was still uncommon.

We were dumbfounded to find out that the director only one step over Curtis's head was an acquaintance of John Simon. They attended college together. John Simon, always looking to work the angles, had nurtured this relationship because he knew it would help him gain minority status for his fronted company. The minority programs kicked into gear in 1977, the same year Simon approached Joe Brown and me to own stock and front his "minority-owned" business.

Hard to believe, given that President Nixon was such a racist, but many of these programs were a direct result of his time in office. Legislation was brought from both sides of the aisle that boosted minority business. Desperate to regain a little foothold in the black community, Nixon signed on. When he left, both Presidents Ford and Carter continued to support black business initiatives.

During our meeting with Jack Curtis, he told us that what we wanted to achieve as a true minority business was a great thing. He said he would make every effort to assist us in making our new company a successful minority-owned and operated company. He further stated that IndustryCorp would be extremely pleased to see another minority-owned company succeed as a major supplier.

Chapter 24
It's All About the Money

We needed a bank that was willing to loan money to us for a new business. That might be a tough nut. One, we were new in the packaging industry. Two, we'd never owned a business before. Three, we would be going head to head with some of the biggest hitters in the business. Fourth, we were minorities. Any two should have been enough to sink us. It was not an easy process.

Straightaway, we tried to do business with a local bank. An attorney friend had a contact at this bank and thought they would listen closely to our proposal. The bank was willing to make a loan to us but only under a Small Business Association (SBA) loan agreement. This was a no-go.

SBA loans were distributed as lump-sums. This was fine if you need a chunk of cash. Imagine you are an existing business with cash flow problem. You discover you can get a great deal on a piece of land or building or major equipment if you paid in cash. That's a perfect scenario.

But for a business that needed to meet payroll twice a week, get a health plan up and running, pay suppliers, rent, and utilities—all the regular cash outlays a new business has but without much cash coming in—the SBA loan wouldn't cut it.

We tried to explain to them we needed to borrow money, but not in a lump sum as stipulated by the SBA, but as a revolving line of credit. The bank would not loan money to us without an SBA guarantee.

The bank decided they would loan us $250,000. Peanuts, really. We had asked for a loan of $500,000 to handle payroll and finance our inventory. We had provided the bank with a Pro Forma that clearly showed our need for one-half million dollars.

A Pro Forma is an accounting document that considers generally accepted business practices. Transactions, costs of doing business, sales projections—all of them are figured in as means to demonstrate a company's bona fides.

This bank was *the* well-established old money bank in the community. They were only willing to loan us enough money that would cause the company to fail. If we took the quarter million, Joe Brown showed me, we'd be out of business within the year.

It was heinous. With this loan, the bank could say that they supported minority business. They could also reinforce the racism of the banking industry: "Well, we loaned them the money. These minority businessmen, they don't know what they're doing." The loan officer was a black man who followed a tightly scripted process. The bank would loan only small amounts of money to minorities that would be guaranteed by the SBA.

Joe, our attorney, and I made a few phone calls to other minority-owned businesses in town. Most of these firms were turned down when requesting a loan from this bank. It was the exact same platform. Always loan far less than what was requested—just enough to get the doors open, and then fail.

We asked for another meeting to seek clarification on the loan process and to once more, ask for the additional money. The loan officer shrugged.

"Look, you guys are maxed out. We won't give you anything more. I can't help you. What's your next step? You want the 250 grand or not?"

"Our next step," I said as we stood up, "is to walk out that door and find a bank that can read financials without seeing a black guy and an Indian as the guys who put them together."

We turned and walked out. We didn't shake hands.

Richard Roddick, our CPA, suggested we take the loan and immediately try another bank. Having the money, even half of what we needed, Roddick convinced us, was better than no loan at all. He often worked with a different local bank and knew one of their senior loan officers. He arranged for a meeting to discuss our needs for capital.

When we arrived at the bank, the loan officer that Roddick had a relationship with was out of town. Instead, we met with a different loan officer. The initial meeting went extremely well. We discussed IndustryCorp's minority supplier program and how we were involved with a buyer that was willing to work with us. The loan officer was impressed and wanted to see our plant. It was obvious to us that the loan officer was interested in our proposal. We began to prepare for our next meeting with the same loan officer.

We updated our pro forma and business plan. Our sales forecast clearly indicated that we needed to borrow $500,000 as a revolving line of credit. Remember, we knew a lump-sum SBA loan would spell disaster for our startup. The loan officer understood exactly what we were saying regarding a revolving credit line and how it should be structured.

The officer wanted to meet our buyer and the person responsible for corporate minority business. The loan officer wanted to know how the minority program really worked. We arranged a luncheon that included all parties. We thoroughly discussed potential new business. We had the promised one million dollars in buys plus a small nuts and bolts container contract I had scared up in the interim.

The loan officer was impressed with our combined expertise. He felt strongly that with Joe Brown's accounting background and my skills in manufacturing and sales, we had a strong chance at success.

Our buyer lived up to his commitment. We were competitive with our first quotation and we were awarded a one-million-dollar contract. That's almost four million dollars in today's money. We now had a purchaser for a product produced by our fledgling container plant. The only possible snag? We needed to finance the product which required a revolving line of credit.

Once again, we all met: the buyer, the minority business coordinator, Joe Brown, me, Richard Roddick, and the loan officer met over lunch to discuss how we could make this contract the bridge we needed to get our new venture rolling.

The loan officer was impressed. He wanted to make the loan and work with us. He truly felt that we had a good plan and the new company had a good chance to be successful.

The loan officer already had our business plan and our pro forma. He added the signed bid contract to the paperwork. He told us he would get back to us after he completed his paperwork and met with the bank's loan committee. A few days after our luncheon, the loan officer call and informed us that the loan committee rejected our request. He was sorry this occurred, but the loan committee has the final word on loans.

We were heartbroken.

Chapter 25
What's in a Name? $650,000.

W e were aware that the loan officer believed in us and felt that we could succeed in this endeavor if the right financing was arranged. He decided to go back to the loan committee on our behalf. This time, he would use a different approach in his meeting with the loan committee. At this bank, we later learned, if a loan officer felt he had a lay-up on a loan, he would do an oral presentation. Our officer did not realize fully the implications of our minority status. He decided to make his presentation to the committee in writing.

When the committee members read the presentation, one of the them recognized the name A-R-T-I-S as a black family that he knew. This family had been in Flint for a long time. They were prime movers in the Flint area lumber business many years ago. One committee member, a local attorney, spoke up.

"I know this family, good people. We should do the loan."

That was pure, blind luck! There was a black family that lived in Flint named Artis. However, I did not know the family and we were not related. We just happened to have the same last name. There were not many black people around named Artis with one "t." Most of the Artis families that migrated North spelled their name A-R-T-T-I-S. If fact, many of black people in the Great Migration were a mixed bag. They had no idea where their names came from. As black people at the end of slavery, we were all given the last name of our owners. That's why so many black families share common last names, but no DNA.

Later in life, I had an opportunity to meet a couple members of the other "one-T" Artis family. We had a lot of fun with the name as we tried to figure out if we were related. We still don't know if we are relatives or not. The loan committee assumed that I was a part of that family and recommended the bank make the loan to us.

That is how our company, Industrial Packaging Company, was originally financed in 1979. The bank revisited our financials and wrote their own pro forma to determine the amount of money we needed. They told us that according to their numbers, $500,000 would be insufficient. We needed $650,000. The bank gladly provided us with a revolving line of credit for $650,000.

In 1979, Joe Brown and I signed a three-year lease on a 32,000-square foot building. This facility was used to start our company. The loan officer became a good friend. We worked together on a variety of business funding projects over the years. He became our go-to for all things financial. As my business grew, our relationship helped me become a successful man. In addition, as we paid our bills on time, our relationship helped the bank make money and helped our officer climb the corporate ranks. We remained in that building for the next three years. In 1984, we purchased a 117,000-square foot building for $800,000. When we needed a loan for our new building, where do you think Joe and I went? That's how important good relationships are.

Chapter 26
You Must Establish Sales Responsibilities

In 1979, shortly after our new company was formed, we knew we had to work our connections hard. We decided to establish our own sales territories. Joe already had a great relationship with a major IndustryCorp subdivision. Naturally, Joe would continue to be the point man with them.

Since my days back in Memphis as a butcher's helper, I'd always been a guy who had no problems making friends. I'm a guy who enjoys being out and about, so we decided that I'd be our new business guy. Because I had previously met with Lester Kimes, the minority coordinator at IndustryCorp, I made an appointment to see him first. I told him the company had been formed and I would like to begin discussions with other division buyers in IndustryCorp's hierarchy.

Kimes gave me the names of several buyers, including, the person responsible for contract packaging of bolts. Because we had a small nuts and bolts packaging contract, I decided to call on this buyer first. His name was Carl Diggs.

Carl Diggs was proud of his Hungarian heritage, and I'd never met a man from Hungary before. We swapped stories about our upbringing; Carl with his Hungarian grandmother, and me growing up in Memphis. We were more alike than either of us could have imagined. After several times in his office, we started to have lunch together. We went to lunch every Friday, and sometimes dinner in the evenings, as we built our relationship.

I was still driving that old Chevy with no AM radio. By now, it had part of the floor missing on the driver's side. I covered the hole with a piece of cardboard. I wasn't proud of it, but it ran. I figured that when IPC became a success, I'd have earned a new car. But when the water from the road started splashing up on my pants, I decided I had to do something. Joe Brown had a friend in the car business and he agreed to sell us two new cars with an inexpensive down payment on credit.

I bumped into Diggs in the lobby of his building and he noticed the new car. It was hard not to, after six months of seeing me drive around in a shade tree mechanic's special.

"You bought a new car?" Diggs said.

"Didn't have much choice, Charles. My old one was throwing so much water up through the floorboards, I was spending more on dry cleaning my suit pants than I was on gas and oil," I said.

The first nine months of our relationship, Carl Diggs did not award any business to me.

In January of 1980, Diggs called me into his office for a meeting. He had a legal-size envelope on his desk with a ribbon of white calculating paper stapled to it. It looked like a homemade ribbon you'd put on a gift package. What he had done was cut paper from a calculating machine into strips to look like a ribbon and stapled it to the envelope.

Inside the envelope?

My first contract with his company. Our first major contract for IPC.

"Congratulations, Willie. I tried to get this to you for Christmas, but I couldn't get all the required the paperwork done in time. This is just the first. We're going to do a lot of business together."

Today, 40 years later, that same envelope is in a glass frame on the wall of my office. The total dollar value of my first contract with this buyer was $65,000 annually. That wonderful Hungarian buyer was a great help to me over and above the first contract. My friend

Charles Diggs arranged for me to meet other buyers. He paved the way for me to grow my business at IPC. Thanks to the contacts and references that Diggs' provided, my business grew many millions of dollars over time.

We provided top notch products and service to Carl with competitive prices. Due to my company's business prowess, and our personal relationship, Carl told other buyers about me and my company. Although he has been retired for several years, occasionally, we meet for lunch just to say hello. A friendship established nearly forty years is still in existence today and will remain until one of us passes on.

Chapter 27
A New Proposal

In 1980, we were approached by a friend of Joe's, Roger Novak, who was also in the corrugated carton business. He repped a firm that manufactured a wide variety of corrugated products. Many companies, across a wide range of industries, used their products. Brown had known this man for many years, yet all Novak would say was that he had to meet with us both and he had a hot item on his hands. Neither my partner or I had any idea what was on his mind.

I discovered that Roger Novak wanted to unload a problem company. Along with four other businessmen, they had started a minority-owned corrugated company. They found a Native American willing to pose as the front. Yes, Novak wanted two guys who had fled a fronted minority owned company to take over a classic fronted minority-owned company.

Hilarious? Maybe. Funny, at any rate.

Their company was set up to sell corrugated packaging to other companies as a minority-owned company. We were not all that hot for the idea of rescuing them from their fronted operation. Joe and I were focused on growth within our industry. We had our hands full with IPC.

Yet, we were confident in our skills. In addition, with both of us minority men, we were interested in the idea of taking this fronted business, a phony business, into the realm of a true minority-owned business. It's not as if we were on a crusade, but we despised the fronted business model, and here was the chance to make a difference. Could we roll Novak's firm into ours? Could we run it as a standalone entity? It was worth careful consideration.

Roger Novak's plant was in a building on Flint's east side. For many years, this area of Flint had been heavily developed for commercial purposes. They had equipment in the plant and produced low volume short-run corrugated sold on the open market. In other words, relatively few containers were made here. Some were made to order for companies with a one-time need. Other containers were made in response to a perceived need by the owners and then sold to the best bidder.

The firm had cashflow issues. They did have a small but steady light assembly contract that paid some of the bills. There was another small contract that depended upon on of Novak's partners personal relationship with a vendor. If they lost either of those two deals, Novak's minority-owned firm would have crashed and burned within a month.

They had countless problems. Most of them came about because they got into the business with the lure of easy money due to the minority business program. They didn't know how to build corrugated products properly and they couldn't deliver on time. Quality and delivery—that covers about 80 percent of what any good company promises when they sign a contract—and they couldn't do either.

They started this company to take advantage of a minority business program but failed to hire experienced people. None of the five stockholders knew how to manage a corrugated sheet plant. The Native American minority owner had absolutely no responsibility with the operation. Zilch. He came to Flint every month to collect his paycheck and that was the end of his involvement.

When they discovered that my partner and I had started our own container business, and seemed to be on the path to success, they had this bright idea: "Let's sell the company to those guys."

I never did find out how they decided we were the guys. Were we dumb enough to buy it because we were minorities? We were so sharp that we could turn their failure into our success?

They desperately wanted to sell their fronted minority company to us. From their perspective, the sale should make sense to us. One, we were a legitimate minority-owned business. Two, they knew we came from a major corrugated company. Three, they knew that I could run a corrugated plant. Four, they knew that Joe Brown knew how to crunch the numbers.

I'll give them this: They were a persistent bunch. There is an old sales saying, "It's not a 'no' until you hear it three times." After two meetings, Joe and I just said "No." We agreed that we needed to spend our energies on our new company and we certainly didn't want to take on someone else's problem.

Yet, at the third meeting, we agreed to consider the proposal. I wanted to meet with Novak's one steady customer and get a feel for what they expected from a different owner. All the parties—Joe and I, Novak's people, and the customer's purchasing, personnel, and materials handling people—sat down.

The agenda was simple: *Is this a good deal for all three parties?* The meeting went well for all of us. The customer wanted us to become involved. They knew my experience, where I'd been, my position, my track record of success, and my extensive corrugated plant experience. The customer wanted to do business with a minority-owned firm. They were already looking forward to working with an experienced team.

Joe and I sat down with our people—our attorneys, our CPAs, a few trusted managers. We agreed; the deal made sense. There was no debt on any of the equipment. The location made sense. The existing contracts would serve as good seed money.

We scheduled meetings with Roger Novak and his four co-owners to discuss a purchase price. They were so poorly managed, we did not ask for an evaluation of assets. We knew that any evaluation would be useless. The company did have $80,000 in the bank. We settled the deal. They kept the eighty-grand, and we took ownership of the company.

"Deal?" we said.

"Deal."

The Native American stockholder lived in the northern part of Michigan. He drove south down I-75 to Flint and picked up his share of the eighty thousand. When Novak's team all signed their stock shares over, Joe Brown and I became sole owners of a corrugated sheet plant. We owned it. Not Joe and the bank and me. Just Joe and me.

I had problems with the company's name. To emphasize the Native American minority slant of the business, Novak and his people used a Native American name which translated into *Big Brown Box* in English. I felt we needed a name that was more business-like and easily understood. We brought that factory under the Industrial Packaging umbrella, bought new signage, and we own the name today. Today, some forty years later, that original customer is still a customer.

Chapter 28
We Play Some Hardball

For many years, Best Box had been the major supplier to IndustryCorp and its many divisions. They managed to corner the market on all the low volume, short-run corrugated business to one of the nation's largest manufacturers. This was excellent business and very profitable.

It is often assumed that the buyer holds all the power in a business relationship, but *it ain't necessarily so*. In the corrugated business, the seller/manufacturer holds certain cards. Many types of packaging are unique to each manufacturer. Think about the odd shapes so many things have: Lawn mowers and window screens and airplane engines all require a unique corrugated carton for shipping. It is often the case that the manufacturer and the packaging firm work very closely over a long time to produce packaging that is lightweight, durable, and cost-efficient for a product that is often a very odd shape. These kinds of reciprocal arrangements are highly valued in every industry. It's not like you can run down to the UPS Store and purchase 40,000 24-inch x 16-inch x 12-inch cartons and call it good.

Therefore, it was a huge shock to Best Box management when their best customer, a division of IndustryCorp, decided to quote the low-volume, short-run business with our new firm. We won the business. In fact, the customer's General Director made the decision to award that business to our company over a two-year period. Rare enough for an established company to get that sort of contract, and unheard of for a startup like ours.

Several colleagues at Best Box let me know that Mr. Simon was livid when the business was moved from his company to ours. If there is an adjective that goes beyond livid, I was told that would be an even better description.

"I thought the old man was gonna have a stroke!" was the semi-gleeful way it was described to me.

What tipped the new deal in our favor? It couldn't have been solely dollars and cents. Given economies of scale and profit margins, we could not have been markedly less expensive. I believe several factors were in play.

The customer was aware that Best Box set up a fronted minority-owned company which was in existence for two years. Strike one.

The customer was also aware that my partner and I were used as the fronted minorities for this company. Strike two.

We were a minority business, owned and operated by legitimate minorities. Strike three.

I was never told if these were the reasons this customer moved millions of dollars in business away from the Best Box fronted company to us. Logic would dictate that in total, these three reasons were enough.

Many suppliers in businesses allied with IndustryCorp did business with Best Box. To be fair, they made a good product. Later that same year, a different supplier in a different city quoted their Best Box packaging business with us.

This business was also awarded to us as well. In a year, we had taken millions of dollars away from our former employer—the firm that used and abused our minority status strictly to increase its own profits. It felt good.

Really good.

Chapter 29
We Can Pay Our Bills

In the early years, our company experienced ups and downs. Every startup goes through it. You hit a big contract; life is grand. You think you have a new contract; the buyer backs off, and in your mind, you have to un-spend the money. If you are tough, persistent, and concentrate on the process instead of the end-product, you'll get by. We were indeed tough and persistent. We managed to completely pay off the initial $650,000 line of credit with the bank.

We even got our revolving line of credit down to zero for a short period of time. In itself, this was a great achievement for Joe and me. That's a tribute to Joe's good number crunching and my frugality on the production end. When I look back, and I realize we financed our business using the same initial line of credit over the next few years, I'm a little astounded.

We worked hard. I was always selling. Joe was always forecasting and riding herd on our purchases. Our business model was solid and we had rapidly become a player. Fair prices, the highest quality possible, and excellent service were everything to our success. Word on the street was that we were a good packaging firm with whom to do business.

We approached our bank.

"Would you please increase our credit line?" we asked.

"Would we? We thought you'd never ask," they said.

The bank was very accommodating. We were profitable and

had built a solid relationship with this bank. After only several years in business, our credit was increased three-fold. From that original $650,000 we now had access to two million bucks. Now remember, this was the early 1980s, when the prime lending rate was at an all-time high of 21.5 percent, so we tried desperately not to use too much of our credit. Just the same, through careful spending, we continued to grow. Perhaps even more important was the psychological payoff.

"The banks trust us. We're doing something right."

We were extremely fortunate that we were involved with great people in the industry we served. They wanted us to be a good supplier to them. It may sound strange in a cutthroat business climate, yet our customers wanted IPC to be a success. Our customer base insisted on a quality product with on-time delivery. We made sure that we were a good supplier to them and their trust and business made us even more competitive. *Pricing, service, quality*...I'm a broken record, yet that will get you far in every field.

In the early years, before the arrival of computers, we had to quote new business with a calculator and a typewriter. It could take days to figure out what the customer wanted and what they were willing to pay. Then it would take days to figure out how we could make that happen. But whether we did it by hand or by spreadsheet, IPC has seen continued growth from its birth until today.

Chapter 30
I'm an Ivy Leaguer

In 1985, Mel Kaufen, the purchasing director at IndustryCorp, called to ask if I'd like to go to Dartmouth College for the summer. He explained that Dartmouth had designed a summer training program exclusively for minority business owners.

I wasn't exactly sure how to take the offer. On the one hand, I knew you can always use more education. Plus, I'd never been to New Hampshire and I'd heard it was a beautiful state. On the other hand, I wondered, *Is Mel trying to tell me I need to go to college? Does my lack of college show through?*

I graduated from high school, of course, but avoided any mention of it. Why? My high school diploma played no role in my business success. In fact, it played no role in my life in any way. I went to parochial school because my parents wanted me to do so. Schools attended by black children in the Deep South in the 1930s-1950s, especially those that were poor, did not receive an adequate education even if they graduated from high school. Teachers would pass poor kids on just to get rid of them. Jim Crow's reach was long. Jim Crow worked hard to keep black people from success right from the get-go. Separate but equal was an utter lie.

I was fortunate to have inspirations that exceeded what was expected of me after my school years in Memphis. As young kid, I always wanted to achieve more than what I had. I continued to think about what I observed in watching Mr. Joe handle money at the grocery store back in Memphis.

Kaufen's intent was nothing but positive. Dartmouth had put together an academic program that was conducted during the summer months to enhance business awareness for minority business owners. He saw my work ethic, my natural intelligence, and my hard-won business sense. The school had requested that major heavy industry companies sponsor minority suppliers. Dartmouth knew that heavy industry was the backbone of the American economy and they wanted to make sure that as many of the allied firms were as successful as possible. As I soon learned, Dartmouth's Tuck College of Business is one of the finest in the world. It was a huge honor.

Mel Kaufen asked me to attend the business program and provide him with a written report. I was the company's test balloon. His company was committed to other minority owned businesses, so he wanted to determine if the Dartmouth program had merit. If it did, Mel told me, they would sponsor many more minority business owners for the program.

He offered to split the cost with me. If IPC would pay for airfare, his firm would pick up the tuition, plus room and board. It sounded like a square deal to me. Mel and I shook hands. Lastly, he told me to provide my report to his boss, as he was the man who had to sign off on the tuition payments.

The Dartmouth program was outstanding. I was a graduate, as they say, of the school of hard knocks. My experiences, and my willingness to learn from them, had taken me far. Yet, when I came home from Dartmouth, I didn't feel just more capable, I was excited. I couldn't wait to implement many of the things I had learned at "summer school."

I couldn't wait to write my report, either. This program was so strong, I got right down to the report when I came home. Within the next couple of days, I would provide the report to Mel's supervisor at IndustryCorp. In my report, I said that the program would be extremely beneficial to every executive in the company's minority supplier base.

I have always believed that Dartmouth College played a massive role in my success in business and life. Over a five-year period of time, the minority business programs not only taught me how to own and manage my own multi-million dollar company, they also taught me a lot about life as well.

The next year, I heard that IndustryCorp was going to sponsor a former NBA all-star, Earl Scott, who had started a company that supplied raw product to IndustryCorp. Because of his basketball skills, his innate smarts, and his work ethic, he was already a college graduate. I gave him a call.

"Hey, Earl," I said. "Hear you're going to the minority business program at Dartmouth. You're gonna love it."

"Good to hear, thanks. You went last year, I heard?"

We talked for a while and I praised the program and the location and what it had meant to IPC.

"Earl, there's just one thing I need to warn you about."

"What's that?" he said.

I could hear a little caution in his voice.

"Yeah, don't stay in the university dorms. I'm 6'2". You gotta be what, 6'4", right? No way you're gonna get a good night's sleep in those student beds. Your feet are gonna hang off one end or your head's gonna bang into the headboard all night. Stay at the hotel next to the campus."

I laughed.

"Occupational hazard in the NBA, Willie. We all get used to it. I'll stay at the hotel. Thanks."

Since the Dartmouth program was continually updated, I returned for three more summer sessions. Every time, I came home with ideas I could put to immediate use. I have few regrets about my life, but one of the biggest is that I didn't have the opportunity to graduate from college in my younger days. I had to go to work.

Even with historically black colleges, it was tough for a poor black kid to gain admission in the late 1940s and early 1950s. I've done well, we want for nothing, and I sleep well at night knowing I've done right in my community, but there is one thing of which I am absolutely certain. Based on my experience at Dartmouth's Tuck School of Business, my net worth would be four times what it is now if I had graduated college in my twenties. At least four times. Probably more.

Chapter 31
No Longer Partners

In 1986, my friend and partner Joe Brown became too ill to stay on the job. Fortunately, we had a buy/sell agreement in place. He chose to exercise his option to sell his stock in the company to me. Joe and I both insisted upon such an agreement soon after we realized our new company was going to make it. We'd both seen too many firms crash and burn with the loss of a partner. We had purchased a disability insurance policy that paid a surviving stockholder in case of illness or injury. The policy allowed Brown to retire with a monthly income that would sustain him in a comfortable manner for the rest of his life.

Our holdings had increased as IPC became more successful. We owned a leasing company that was established in 1983. We formed the leasing company when we decided to purchase a 117,000 square-foot facility. How big was our new plant? Nearly three acres worth of footprint, three football fields including the end zones. That's a good-sized building.

Joe and I formed our leasing company separate from IPC. Tax law allowed us to use IPC corporate money to pay the lease on the new building to a company owned solely by me and Joe. Perfectly legal, and quite profitable.

After Brown retired from the company, the leasing company agreement stayed in place. We were paid according to the original agreement between the two entities. We continued to share in the profits of the leasing company for several years.

As often happens, it was a family issue that ended our relationship. Joe, on behalf of his daughter, co-signed an ownership agreement with a fast food chain. His daughter lacked Dad's business sense. She was a poor manager and financial problems occurred with this endeavor. The restaurant was losing money hand over fist.

Brown scheduled a meeting with me. He wanted to raise the rent being paid by IPC to our leasing company. Yes, he wanted to raise what was now my company's rent to offset the business losses incurred by his daughter's restaurant. As if I should help support his daughter's lack of business sense.

I refused.

"Joe," I said, "what you are asking me to do, this doesn't make sense to me. Not at all. You should realize you are no longer employed at the company. You're not a shareholder. You no longer have any say in IPC. You don't contribute. This isn't your company anymore.

"Explain to me, why should I pay more rent? Put yourself in my shoes. What if I came to you with this cockeyed proposal? No way, Joe, this is not gonna happen. Sorry about your daughter and all, but no way."

A few weeks later, Joe made another effort to get me to change my mind. I said "No" for the same reasons. He tried to convince me that putting a few more dollars in my personal pocket at the expense of my company was a good thing.

"No, Joe. This is not going to happen. Leave it alone."

He engaged an attorney and filed a lawsuit against me. He claimed that the rental rates were not competitive and should be increased to match current market prices. Of course, I was upset because my business partner, my co-founder and friend, was taking me to court. We'd been through a ton of corporate wars together. We'd been sucked into the system, we'd bucked the system, we built a damn fine business together.

It hurt. It hurt my feelings and it also insulted my business sense. Joe had to know that from every reasonable point of view, what he proposed was just stupid. I understood his dilemma. Money was leaking like a torpedoed ship from the fast food operation that he trusted his daughter to run. He wanted to recover his losses by raising the rental rates on our partnership.

Again, I said "No" to his proposal. It was, simply, a stupid idea. I was also a little insulted that Joe didn't think I'd see through it.

I spoke with my loan officer at the bank. After much discussion, he said, "Why don't you just pay him off? Dissolve the partnership, give him some cash to go away, and get rid of the guy? You don't need the headache. He's sittin' on his ass in Florida and you got a business to run."

It was an excellent idea. Under Michigan law, a partnership can be dissolved by either partner. I called my attorney and we put the plan in motion. Our corporate CPA evaluated the assets, developed the value of the LLC, and we split up the pie. My former partner was paid $400,000 in cash by the bank. I repaid the bank.

Done.

From that day in 1989, we never spoke again. I invited him to IPC's twentieth anniversary party. He did not respond. The next time I saw Joe Brown was at the funeral home during his wake.

Chapter 32
The Renaissance Zone Project

In 1986, IPC purchased a 40,000-square foot building for $250,000. This facility was used to repackage parts. We needed additional funds to help finance our growth. We borrowed $50,000 from the City of Flint. The City had obtained a special block grant to assist minority businesses within the city limits. We borrowed another $40,000 from an organization in Washington, D.C. that specialized in low interest loans to minority-owned companies. Those two loans were repaid in the agreed upon timeframe. Several other Flint firms were also part of the block grant program. The city official who managed the block grants informed us that at the time, we were the only company that repaid their loan to the City. As for the other firms, payments happened only after court intervention.

Because of our continued growth, I wanted to do something spectacular. Our company was doing well, and I wanted a project that would promise great things for IPC and our employees. I may have had some good ideas, yet without good people from the floor up, none of those ideas would've made us a dime without their hard work.

I made the rounds of our customer base. I let them know we were going big. Our new building was just a start. I knew our customers would not make commitments to increase our business based solely on my good talk and intentions. That is not the way they do business. When I asked for their support, they just sat and stared. Poker-faces, every one of them.

"Good luck, Willie, in the new endeavor. If you pull this off, it'll be great for the Flint community."

I couldn't tap dance around it—the business risk was huge.

I decided to move forward and approached the City of Flint. Flint had been awarded a Renaissance Zone. Businesses that moved into a Zone were granted tax-free status for up to fifteen years as a reward for opening in an area that was economically hard-hit.

I scheduled a meeting with James Sharp, a black man who was Flint's mayor. I told him I wanted to build a massive, modern container plant in Flint's Renaissance Zone. He was thrilled. On the scale I described, it would be a huge boost to the area's employment, and a feather in his cap as the leader of the City. He promised to assist in every way possible to advance the project. Along with my management team, we had decided to pitch the State of Michigan and use industrial revenue bonds to finance the project. Mayor Sharp promised to call in his favors to help make the bonds happen.

Our bank, the only bank I've ever used, agreed that industrial revenue bonds were an excellent idea. The City of Flint agreed to a long-term land lease. We negotiated a land lease of 100 years with an option for an additional 100 years. Because our plant was in a Renaissance Zone, our tax burden was much less. Remember, the first fifteen years of property taxes were waived.

Industrial bonds are complicated. Fortunately, it didn't fall on my people at IPC to sell them. That was up to the financial firms and their underwriters. Because of our excellent Standard & Poor's rating, our highly rated bonds were attractive to investors. On our end, the three percent financing allowed most of the monthly payment to pay down principal, rather than be swallowed up in debt service. You can imagine what it meant to our cash flow to be clear of property taxes for the fifteen years of Renaissance Zone tax abatement.

In the year 2000, construction began. Our new building would have a 2.5-acre, 110,000-square foot layout. With 24-foot-high ceilings, it cost 4.5 million dollars. With the help of the tax-free initiative, we stayed on schedule for a twenty-year payback.

Although IndustryCorp, our major customer, was silent when I approached them about my plan, once we moved our corrugated operation into the facility, we received instant validation for my daring and confidence with millions of dollars in new business.

Seventeen years later, this facility continues to be filled with corrugated materials waiting to be turned into boxes plus parts and components waiting to be placed in those containers and shipped all over the globe. IndustryCorp has factories in all corners of the world and we are proud to handle their shipping needs.

We now have four local facilities in Flint, Michigan which cover 267,000 square feet. That's nearly five football fields of factory footprint; a little over six acres of floorspace. Maintaining a great relationship with your customer base and your bank is essential to the growth of your company, regardless of the industry. *Keep people informed. No surprises.*

If we go back to birth of IPC, our initial credit line was $650,000. These days, our credit line is well into the millions. Because of our corporate growth, our ability to create innovative packaging solutions on time and budget, our credit line continues to be increased as we grow. It doesn't hurt that we pay all our bills on time, either.

We've maintained our relationship with this same bank since

Day One. We've never had to borrow from a different bank. After several years of business success, other banks tried to recruit our company as a customer. Obviously, we declined. Why would anyone leave a relationship that had such great benefits on both sides?

The original bank has been purchased a couple times. However, our banking relationship has not changed. Although I am retired, and the company has been sold, I continue to watch the company I established in 1979 grow because of the great relationships and people that worked with us over many years. While IPC is always on the hunt for new accounts, they continue to take the best care possible of every existing customer. As a result, IPC continues to make money, and when needed, that same bank is always able to lend money at a competitive rate.

Chapter 33
My Biggest Mistake

You should recall that in the late 1960s, Kyle Birt was hired over me at Best Box Corrugated. Despite John Simon's idea that Birt would be the boss of the black guy, Kyle didn't see it that way at all. On the depth chart, I may have been below Kyle but he respected my skills and I admired his. We were a good team. As I built my business at IPC, Kyle and I kept in touch.

I had considered bringing Kyle over to IPC. We did great stuff together at Best Box and I knew that under that right circumstances, we would do so again. Only this time, we'd be making the big money instead of John Simon. When the opportunity arose in 1984, I grabbed it. Kyle told me he was tired of the constant sparring, the in-fighting, that was required to stay on top at Best Box. Simon liked to set his people against each other, kind of a like a Roman dictator, and watch the hijinks. I offered Kyle the spot of manufacturing manager. He took it.

No surprise, Kyle did a fine job. In 1988, all of that caved in and it was all my fault. We did not have enough minority management. Sounds crazy, but it was so. I had no other black men or women in upper management. I brought in as many as I could for interviews, but I always managed to find something about them that brought me up short.

In 1988, I hired retired U.S. Army Colonel Jim Keller as the general manager of the company. He was a friend, he was a black man, and he had ten years of experience in the business. Kyle Bert was to report to him. I believed that we needed a general manager as part of the executive staff, what we would call C-Suite today, and I felt that Kyle would understand why I wanted a black man in that position. It may have been a good idea, but in execution, it was terrible. I envisioned a good relationship between these two men I considered friends. I knew both were good businesspeople.

The worst? I refused to believe my good idea was not working. It was very bad for Kyle. It also cut the legs out from under Jim Keller. Yet, I stuck to my guns. It *had* to be a great idea for the company. It put a black man at my right hand, and it gave Kyle continued broad authority throughout the plant. Sadly, my ego refused to factor the human element into the equation.

Kyle left me and IPC in 1988, shortly after I hired Keller. He went back to work for Simon at Best Box. He stayed there for just one year. He was a heavy smoker and unbeknownst to me, his emphysema forced him into an early retirement.

During the first few months of Kyle's retirement, I finally realized that Jim Keller was not up to snuff, and I terminated him. Yes, Keller was bright and well-educated. He was not a good fit, however. His hiring was a terrible decision and a bad choice. My desire to have a black executive overrode my sense about him as a good match for IPC.

As soon as I heard that Kyle was retired, I called him. I apologized for my terrible mistake. Before he could even accept or decline my apology, I offered him Keller's spot. Thank goodness, he took it.

Yes, his emphysema was bad. I was more than willing to work around that. When he didn't feel up to working from the office, he worked from home. When he needed to visit the doctors for treatment, we worked around it. Kyle was that smart and that valuable to us.

We worked together again from 1989 until 2004, when his

disease drove him into his final retirement. Over our forty years together, I worked for him, he worked for me, and we had a great friendship which lasted until he passed away at 85 in 2005.

His heavy smoking took its toll. Shortly before he died, I visited him at his home with just him, his wife and me. I was sad because I saw him using an oxygen tank to breathe. We had a chance to catch up. I had to do the talking.

Fate can be difficult to understand because one never knows where he or she will end up. I had a great deal of confidence in this man's ability to manage my company. It was repaid one-hundred-fold. Kyle was truly a good guy and was completely loyal to me. I always felt the same about him.

I visited Kyle during his last days in the hospital. His wife and children were with him. The hospital staff person wanted to move Kyle to a hospice facility. Kyle's wife did not want him moved. She knew that I had served on the board of directors for many years at the hospital and asked me if I could help keep him there. I told her that I knew the president and would have a conversation with her. I persuaded her to speak with the medical staff and please leave him at the hospital. The next day, Kyle passed away. I miss him.

My insistence on hiring Jim Keller taught me a lesson about people you want to hire. Being a minority might get you a foot in the door. However, you'd better have the skills to keep you there. In an odd twist, IPC had no minority executives for years. We employed every minority group imaginable at every capacity. Kyle and the rest of our team made certain of that. Yet, try as we did, it took years before we found a black man who would cure that minority executive problem.

Occasionally, customers would ask me, "How many minority executives are with you?" I could cite minority sales reps, and corporate trainers, and plant group leaders, yet still get the question, "Yeah, that's great, but how many execs?"

I'd have to shrug and say with some embarrassment, "Well,

me."

That changed when I hired Veronica Luster, the woman who would become Mrs. Veronica Artis, in 1989. If hiring Keller was my worst decision, hiring Veronica would turn out to be the best.

Chapter 34
I Meet Veronica Luster

I met Veronica Luster during the summer of 1985. It was during one of my summer sessions at Dartmouth College. Veronica was responsible for minority purchasing at Wisconsin Bell. We met on the last day of class. Fate, karma, luck; whatever you want to call it, it was all of those and more.

We were discussing business and how great the classes were and how beautiful New Hampshire was. She noticed my badge. On it were both my name and my company's name, Industrial Packaging Corporation. She told me that there were plenty of companies in Milwaukee that needed good container suppliers and she could help me make connections with them. We talked further about this, that, and the other. We exchanged business cards. As we parted, I told her that I would call her soon for an appointment. "Soon" meant the next week. Ms. Luster promised to help me set up meetings if I would visit her in Milwaukee.

I came to Milwaukee for two days. As promised, Veronica introduced me to the director of Wisconsin's Minority Supplier Development Council. I spent the entire day with him. We visited companies located in Milwaukee and Madison, the state capital 80 miles away.

I was well-received by these companies. I discovered they wanted to do business with a manufacturing company owned and operated by a minority. Fortunately for me, there were no minority-owned manufacturing plants in Milwaukee. In fact, there were none in the entire state of Wisconsin. It's not that Milwaukee had no minority-owned businesses. They had plenty, yet they were mainly service businesses; barber and beauty shops, small groceries, clothing stores, and the like. In the mid-1980s, minority-owned manufacturing companies did not exist in Milwaukee.

At the end of our travels, I sat down with Veronica and the minority director. I saw plenty of opportunity. A packaging plant, owned by a black man, would have access to a significant chunk of business. In addition, I would bring plenty of good-paying jobs to the area. I decided to return several weeks later for more serious discussions about IPC opening a corrugated plant in Milwaukee.

Veronica suggested that on this trip, I avoid the airport hotel. Rather, I should stay at a hotel in Brown Deer, a Milwaukee suburb. It also happened to be close to her home. This idea was not a bad one, I thought. Veronica was not just bright and capable. She was also seriously attractive.

I spent several days in Milwaukee as I visited companies. The minority coordinator accompanied me during these visits. I had the chance to assess the packaging and corrugated needs of many of these companies. I was already calculating their needs versus the square footage of plant IPC would need to produce corrugated at competitive prices.

I also had an opportunity to spend time with Veronica. We had dinner several times while I was in Milwaukee. While I was there to discuss the possibility of my business expanding into Milwaukee, a relationship with Veronica also developed.

The next time I visited Milwaukee, I scheduled meetings with bankers. I had learned with the Flint launch of IPC how an excellent relationship with a local bank was critical to business success. If my Milwaukee venture was going to take shape, I needed to meet with aggressive, forward-thinking bankers who understood my needs. I was pleased to discover they were seriously interested in becoming involved with a minority-owned and operated company based in

Milwaukee. The bank loan officers were filled with enthusiasm—they knew they were talking to a black entrepreneur who knew how to own and operate a manufacturing company.

Chapter 35
My Million-Dollar Business Mistake

Good news—the bank wanted to move forward with me. But first, they needed to visit my plants in Flint and Saginaw. Saginaw is a mid-sized town 40 miles north of Flint and home to parts manufacturers who do business with IndustryCorp. Makes sense; if you're going to loan a business owner a chunk of change, you want to make sure that your first impressions are based in the real world.

The loan officer and his boss came to Flint for a visit. We toured both of my plants in Flint and drove to Saginaw for a tour of that plant. They were extremely impressed. The fact that a black man had accomplished this level of business was well received by them.

How impressed? They asked one telling question:

"Mr. Artis, are you willing and able to make this work in Milwaukee?"

"That's not a question I can answer yet," I said. "There's a lot at stake here: Jobs, money, people's lives. Is there enough business in Milwaukee to support what I need to do on the other side?

"I'll need to do an extensive market study. It'll need to take in Milwaukee, Madison, a lot of Illinois. I'll need to talk to a lot of companies about this. What's their mindset? Are they willing to do business with a legitimate, minority-owned and operated business? It'll take a while. After the study is complete, then I'll schedule a meeting with the bank for further discussions.

"Look, here it is, late in '86. We should be able to decide by early '87. Regardless of which way the survey goes, we'll have a meeting. Based on what I hear, I'm optimistic, that's for sure, but I need the numbers."

I put our sales manager to work. He conducted an in-depth market study over several weeks. We talked to several dozen companies regarding the possibility of a new supplier to their company. Our pitch was straightforward:

"We produce the highest quality corrugated products at the most competitive price. We also have a dedicated contract packaging service. We've been doing this since 1979 in Flint, Michigan and since 1985 in Saginaw. Our smaller plant in Saginaw has a dollar of volume of $2 million per year and employs 70 people on a two-shift operation.

We are interested in bringing our expertise to the Milwaukee area. We believe that both our business and yours would benefit from our presence. Would you be open to bids on your container and packaging business from a company that is truly owned and operated by minorities?"

This new venture was a constant presence in my mind. New state. New tax laws. New banks. A new plant 400 driving miles away. Management team. Human resources. New buyers to court. Our business reputation. Was I putting my core business at risk here in Flint and Saginaw? Lots of tough decisions.

On the plus side of the ledger, I held group meetings with representatives from many of the companies affiliated with the Minority Business Program. These meetings were scheduled by its director, and they were all positive. Every participant appeared to be sincere in their desire to do business with a minority-owned and operated company.

We had positive market research in hand. The numbers were crunched. Add in the verbal intent I brought back from my group meetings, I met with the bank to play serious hardball about the financing I'd require. I provided them with the normal financial data required by any bank—projections, potential sales, audited financial statements—all from my company, IPC.

A new company in Milwaukee appealed to me. I liked the area. Land prices were reasonable. The market study indicated this would a great business venture. Time to flip the switch.

Chapter 36
Let's Get Started: The Usual Racists

While we had not yet officially signed papers with the bank, they gave me every indication that we were a go. With that knowledge in hand, I started to look for a building. The facility would have to accommodate a manufacturing factory. We needed major truck access and proximity to the freeways as well. I decided to name the company Wisconsin Corrugated.

We became aware of a building on the south side of Milwaukee. I called the owner, Mr. Brauer, and we had our first meeting. Not only was Brauer interested in selling the plant, he inquired about a partial ownership in the new company. The Brauer family were very wealthy people, well-respected and connected with the local business community, and they had tremendous resources. They had a great reputation, well-known throughout Milwaukee as straight shooters who knew how to make money. The Brauers owned a lot of downtown property, including the building which had my new bank as a tenant.

We were a good match. I decided that Mr. Brauer and I would go into business together. They purchased stock in my new company and leased the plant to us. The bank liked the idea because of Brauer's reputation. Brauer decided to finance a part of the venture based on my personal guarantee. The bank financed the major part of the business. That too, was based on my personal financial guarantee. I had a lot at risk with this Milwaukee project.

I truly believed this venture would not fail. We knew how to run a successful corrugated plant. We knew packaging. We had solid commitments from the business communities of Milwaukee, Madison, and northern Illinois. Furthermore, my entrepreneurial instinct continued to tell me this would be an excellent opportunity to diversify and enhance my Flint business. I would be able to meet and get to know many people in a different state not far from my home base. During the early stages of this new undertaking, I could see a successful venture.

At the same time, I was separating from my current wife. As I spent more time in Milwaukee, my relationship with Veronica Luster became more and more personal. We saw each other each time I visited Milwaukee. Veronica began to visit me in Flint. What started as a strictly business relationship had blossomed.

Mel Kaufen was the buying manager that originally asked me to attend Dartmouth College for minority business executive classes in 1985. Mel continued to remind me that he was the one responsible for me meeting Veronica. Kaufen was a great guy and was partly responsible my business growth in Flint. Up until Mel passed away, he wanted credit for Veronica coming into my life. He was absolutely correct and I was always happy to pass that credit his way. Mel? I thank you.

Our new Milwaukee bank financed all the equipment required to produce corrugated material. It takes time for the money and the purchase orders and the equipment manufacturer to get everything installed. We knew that success was predicated upon good product, good pricing, and good word of mouth. Once the machines were in place and we were ready to produce and sell corrugated to major customers, we scheduled an Open House. All the major companies were invited.

At the time, we felt the Open House was a success. We truly believed these people were ready to do business with us. The director of the Wisconsin Minority Supplier Development Council helped us schedule the Open House. He knew the players. He knew the newspaper people. He was our local fixer. It was with some pride he stood there with me as we showed off the new plant.

He believed, as our team did, that the attendees who represented the major corporations were there to help us get started with new business orders. To my absolute amazement, we discovered that the people attending the Open House were not decision makers or buyers. They were merely faces; lower level employees sent to represent their companies. It was a day of free drinks and snacks for them. These were people who attended minority council meetings as a front for their company.

We thought we were making our presentation to people who provided contracts to suppliers. They were not. Although we did not know this at the time, most of the companies had no intent of awarding business to a minority-owned company. It was all a show. A racist, bigoted show.

I discovered this nightmare when I scheduled a visit to see a buyer. The person who greeted me in the lobby was a guy that I had met at a minority function. He'd been at our Open House. He'd given me every impression that he was a buyer.

"Me, a buyer? Oh, no. Not me. No, sir. But I work for him. I'll put you guys on our next agenda. Gimme a couple of weeks. I'll get back with you."

Yeah, right.

The Wisconsin coordinator for minority business introduced me to most of these people during our functions. He should have known they were not buyers. He should have known they were clerks, not decision makers. Further, I should have discovered this farce myself sooner, but I didn't. The cost for opening this plant in Milwaukee was tremendous. However, I was not alone in believing this opportunity was real. The Brauer people also felt we could be successful in this venture. No one was better connected in Milwaukee than the Brauers.

So, what was up?

Racism, as usual.

I attended many functions in the Milwaukee area sponsored by a beer company. At these events, I had an opportunity to meet many people and introduce myself and our new minority company. On the surface, we were well-received. People gave me the glad hand, the pat on the back, the "Good for you, go get 'ems."

But underneath the surface, we were not welcome. These Milwaukee folks were as deeply prejudiced as anyone. It was just that the prejudice was hidden well. I did not realize just what I had gotten myself into. With a few exceptions, black people seemed to accept things the way they were in Milwaukee. There were no black-owned manufacturing companies in Milwaukee. Remember that, in fact, there were none in the state of Wisconsin, population 4.905 million. Not one.

We had everything in place. We were ready. We hired sales personnel, office personnel, a plant manager, and were in the process of hiring our hourly personnel. All of us—the bank, the new stockholders, and our team—believed all the right tools were in place to make this venture a success. The plant manager had over twenty years of experience in corrugated. The office manager came from a corrugated company and had sales and service experience working with customers.

We were awarded a small contract to produce corrugated cartons for a beer company. No surprise, right, that in Milwaukee, our first contract would be for beer? However, it was not the right product for a sheet plant. A sheet plant like ours produced flat sheets that are later turned into corrugated boxes and containers. In essence, a sheet plant creates the corrugated from which boxes are made in much the same way that a sheet metal plant produces sheets of metal that are later stamped into cars or refrigerators or metal doors.

We explained to them many times how much we appreciated the business but the product should be produced by a corrugated manufacturer. Although we did have the ability to produce some low-volume runs of finished cartons, we could not make money producing beer cartons. They did have a requirement for corrugated that could be produced by our company, but despite our competitive prices, we were not awarded any of the business.

We knew there was an IndustryCorp supplier located outside of Milwaukee. We also knew they needed corrugated material to ship the component parts that they manufactured. We already provided packaging services to one of their locations and our relationship with them was solid.

You should know that even within the confines of ultra-competitive bidding, where tenths of cents might sink or seal a deal, the personal touch matters. In fact, it probably matters more when competing price quotes are extremely close.

Whether we are buying lumber for our deck, meat for the grill, a car, or millions of dollars' worth of corrugated shipping containers, we all like to do business with people we like and trust. They knew we could meet their requirements.

We quoted the business. We were competitive. The supplier awarded their corrugated business to our company. We were extremely pleased with this new business. We were on our way. Once you break through with one company, it gets easier to get a foot in the door at another. Track records matter.

A second major corporation located just outside Milwaukee decided they wanted to move corrugated business to us. After we won the business, I had a meeting with the purchasing manager at the new account.

"Look here," he said. "We have a problem with our dock workers. One, these guys are on the take. We know the suppliers are sliding 'em stuff; cash, beer, tickets to ballgames, just to get their stuff taken care of, but we haven't been able to catch 'em. We're trying, but it's tough.

"I'm not telling you that to scare you off, but when they show up to unload trucks, they'll have their hands out. So now you'll know why.

"Here's the other thing. We have some real rednecks on our docks. Good workers, most of 'em, but still, not real fond of black folks. Or Mexicans, for that matter. But seeing as you're a black-owned company, and we've moved out some business from the good ole boy company we had been doing business with, well, I suspect we might hear a little noise from the dock men. Not up to them, of course, but just a little warning for your drivers to maybe lay low when they deliver."

That purchasing manager knew his people. They began to complain about our product, no matter what we did to satisfy their demands. It wasn't just the guys on the dock. The hourly workers, the ones who were hands-on with our product, beefed like there was no tomorrow. They would always find something wrong with the material. We continued to work with them to no avail. We were fortunate because the purchasing manager continued to award business to us as we were competitive on price and delivery.

Even back at the site of our original contract, the dock workers began to cause problems. Two separate companies, no way do these folks know each other. It seemed unlikely that the union was behind it. It was just racism, pure and simple. Black-owned business? Hate 'em. Give 'em trouble.

Our banker gave me a subtle nudge early on.

"We've found a suitable building for our new operation," I said.

"Well, that's good news. Where's it at?" he asked.

"South side of town."

"Hmm, well, that'll be a good lesson for those rednecks down there," he said.

With the dockworker troubles we were having, his throwaway comment took on a whole new, deeper meaning. I was not there to be the first guy on the block. I wasn't looking to "make a statement." I wanted to make money and offer good paying, steady work. I just wanted to take advantage of a business opportunity that had been presented to me.

After a few months of operations, our plant's hourly employees petitioned to form a union. Obviously, I did not want that to happen this quickly. Still, I was always a staunch union guy in my youth. As a business owner, I recognized the need for workers to have union protection. I knew we could handle the situation because of our experience with unions. It did not appear to be a major problem for us.

We decided to recognize the union as the official representative of all hourly employees. Labor law would have forced us to recognize the union anyway. However, by sending out a statement before the union leadership was seated, we felt it sent a signal that we would negotiate in good faith. In 1987, I sent Kyle, our Flint manufacturing manager, to Milwaukee to negotiate the union contract.

Kyle was well qualified to negotiate our initial contract. He handled negotiations with both Best Box and IPC for many years. Kyle had negotiated many contracts with our union in Michigan. He was known to be a stand-up guy, able to work out all union demands to the satisfaction of both sides.

Three days into negotiations, our man Kyle called me from Milwaukee.

"Listen up, Willie. This Robert Lindh guy I met with is a little nuts," Kyle said. "I don't think he wants to negotiate at all. Not for a second. Lindh has one position and that's it. There's no discussion going on here. He's got a scale for hourly and he just sits there. We make a counter-offer and he doesn't even look at it. Just sits there with his arms crossed and says, 'Nope.' We add in a fringe benefit, something he can take back to his people, and he just says, 'Nope.' I'm not sure what the hell he's thinking but something's up. Something's wrong."

"Kyle, what's his figure?" I asked.

Bert ran down the union's proposed pay scale for me.

Bert said, "This guy Lindh's a screwball. Nobody can meet that scale and still meet the factory nut. He's gotta know that. Everyone knows what it costs to run a plant like this."

"We say yes to that, we'll be outta business by the end of the year," I said.

Bert answered, "I told him that. I told him, 'Lindh, you go back to your guys and tell 'em if we meet that payroll, they'll all be looking for new jobs by the end of the year' and see what they say. And he just sat there and said, 'Them's our numbers. No numbers, no deal.'"

Lindh wanted the company to pay an hourly rate that would surely end the existence of the company. For some reason, he would not back off from his position. Everyone at the negotiation table understands how to do a deal. You have to have some give and take, and at the end, everyone should be a little bit satisfied and a little bit angry.

Kyle said, "There's something fishy here. There's an agenda behind this whole thing and I can't put my finger on it. I've met with dozens of union negotiators and every damn one of them wants to negotiate. Hell, it's like a game to them. They want a deal. Lindh, his deal? Seems to be *not* to do a deal for his union."

Although a strike was on the table as a threat, we continued to do business during negotiations. At the time, we did not understand this hardline method of negotiation for a union contract. Their means of negotiation was to not negotiate. We were sure that Lindh realized our company was a new venture and still in a start-up mode. Every startup is strapped for cashflow.

Startups are a kind of well-intentioned Ponzi scheme. You use the money that comes in during April to pay the bills you incurred in February and March. You don't meet April's numbers, then you dip into your company's line of credit to pay the bills. But then, you pay the bank a penalty with the interest they charge. You go to work, sell a bunch of stuff, and gradually, you can accumulate a cash cushion that lets you improve the plant and the employees' pay.

It is not a difficult process to understand. We continued to try and convince Lindh that we needed an opportunity to grow the business. To grow a business in a relatively closed market takes time. Most unions will negotiate a contract for a start-up company that allows the company to make money for the first three years and then they begin to share the proceeds with the rank and file.

Lindh even visited the local newspaper and minority agencies that were advocates for minority businesses in Milwaukee. He campaigned against me as an individual who was in Milwaukee to take advantage of black people.

This may have been the first time in history that a black man was accused of being a carpetbagger. Based on this man's campaign of misinformation, the local newspaper even printed a short article based on his lies. Lindh also paid calls upon several local black politicians to continue this campaign of falsehoods.

Upsetting? Absolutely. And further evidence that Lindh had an agenda, backed by a big someone behind the scenes.

That coward Lindh even visited Flint. He went to the Genesee County Court House to view my divorce papers. He then went back to the minority agencies in Milwaukee and told them I used the black people who were employed by my company in Milwaukee to pay for my divorce. He maintained I was doing some money laundering; stripping cash from the Milwaukee business to pay off my soon-to-be ex-wife. A total lie, but damaging back in Milwaukee where my reputation for clean business was not as well-known.

It became quite obvious that Lindh had an agenda. This bastard never had any intent of negotiating a union contract. He was not a negotiator. Lindh, the son-of-a-bitch, was bought and paid for by my competitors. He was hired to defame me and put the company out of business.

Unfortunately, my union employees had absolutely no idea what this asshole was trying to achieve at their expense. I talked to one of my competitors.

"What the hell is going on with this Lindh guy?" I asked. "He won't negotiate. He went to my hometown to try and dig up some dirt on me. He's talking shit to the newspapers. He's riding around the Northside talking to black councilmen. This is bullshit."

"You're right, Willie. It is bullshit and it makes me sick," he said. "I can't do anything about it. I told 'em it was bullshit and they told to stay the hell out. So I have. Until now.

"Here's the deal. A couple companies want you out. One, you're competition and they don't want that. Two, and here's the part that makes me sick, you're a black guy and they hate Blacks. So Lindh, he's gettin' paid by these guys to get rid of you, and he's riling up your black employees to try and get you to shut down. I'm sorry, Willie, but that's the plain truth."

I am not in business to fight racial prejudices or deal with Milwaukee's race problems. I was there to own and operate a company that would be successful and profitable. I decided to close the plant and move on. I wanted no part of a community that was divided by race. Quite frankly, I didn't give a damn about Milwaukee's race situation.

Sure, I fight for the rights of black people. I do it through economics. My company created employment for people who were unemployed. Before I arrived, most of my hourly people were on welfare and glad for a real job. We exploited no one. We did careful market research on pay scales before we opened. Our wage scales were right in line with comparable scales in our industry.

End of story—Lindh's agenda was not to help the hourly people, but to eliminate the company through false accusations against me.

I closed the plant and negotiated a financial settlement with the bank and stockholders. I lost over one million dollars in this venture. All creditors were paid in full over a period of time. The only good thing for me from this ordeal was Veronica Luster came into my life on a permanent basis.

Two months after I closed the plant, my attorney filed a defamation lawsuit against the union and their agent Robert Lindh in Milwaukee Circuit Court. We agreed to mediation at the suggestion of the court. I was paid tens of thousands of dollars, directly to me, as a financial settlement for defamation, slander, and character assassination.

All funds paid to me came directly from the union. In a fashion, this saddened me. The rank and file were not truly responsible for this. They were used as pawns by my competition, yet they were held financially at fault. Rest assured, the bastards behind this plot never repaid the union. The financial compensation did not match the grief I experienced.

The union's director who attended the mediation meeting was not happy over the money paid to me. He also realized that the union would never be repaid by the corporate owners behind this scheme. However, he did state that Lindh would never represent the union again. Small consolation to all concerned.

After the mediator decided in my favor and we agreed to terms, my attorney spoke to the union director.

"We still believe that our competitors paid you and Mr. Lindh to drive Mr. Artis's firm out of business."

The director was silent.

Chapter 37
A Long Distance New Beginning

Veronica Luster had been married before. She was the mother of two daughters. One daughter lived with her and was in the tenth grade. Her other daughter was already grown, a college graduate living and working in Washington, D.C. Veronica and I continued to see each for many more months. I would visit Milwaukee and she would visit Flint.

Long distance relationships are always tough. Veronica and I were fortunate enough that we could afford frequent travel. Still, it's unsettling. We all want permanence in our lives. Both of us were heavily invested in this relationship. We'd both been married before and were adult enough to know what we wanted. What we wanted was each other. The decision was simultaneous.

"Hey, Veronica…"

"Yes, Willie?"

"I was thinking. We should…"

"Get married."

We were married on November 25th, 1987. We held two celebrations, one in Flint and the other in Milwaukee.

For the first two years, we endured a long distance marriage. While we had the official recognition that each of us was in it for the long run, it wasn't any easier. I missed her. Born in Milwaukee, Veronica had lived all her life in Wisconsin, was a graduate of the University of Wisconsin, and had never lived in another state. When we were apart, I missed her terribly. When we were together, it pained to me to realize that in a day or two or three, I'd be headed back to Michigan.

Veronica had rapidly become the love of my life. The most beautiful woman in the world, she was also bright and witty and charming and willing to laugh at my weak jokes. As the owner of my company, I was, to a small degree, the master of my meeting schedule. Typically, I headed to Milwaukee nearly every weekend.

After two years of living in two different states, I grew tired of the travel and living alone for most of the week. I sensed that Veronica was also becoming restless and we felt that it was time for her to move. Veronica consulted with her "therapist," her beautician, Yvonne.

"You crazy, girl?" I always imagined the conversation went. "He's tall. He's got a little money. He is handsome. He loves your kids. He is crazy for you; poor man is here every weekend. Girl, please, go with this man Willie."

Yet at our stage of life, it wasn't so easy to come up with an exit strategy. Veronica had been with the phone company for twenty-five years. She had a lot of responsibility and took great pride in her role with Wisconsin Bell. In addition, she was well-compensated for her work. Jobs that pay as well as hers are not an everyday thing.

How could we bring her to Michigan? We needed to uproot her daughter and get her in a good school. Veronica needed a new job commensurate with what she'd been doing with Wisconsin Bell. We could handle the school situation; her daughter was okay with a move.

We kept coming back to the job.

We decided Veronica would become an executive at my company. I realized I would experience some level of difficulty from within and without the company. I have always believed that Veronica would end up working at my company. Aside from being my wife, her business and academic resume was outstanding. She could stand on her own merits. Even if we had not married, I would have done just about anything to hire her. I brought her in at a salary that I would have offered to anyone at her level. Yes, I gave my wife a raise.

As I look back over twenty-five years, I tell myself, "Wow, did you make a great decision!"

This woman who became my wife was now employed at my company. One man did leave the company out of fear of being replaced by Veronica. I reassured him that this was not my intent at all. I gave him my word that not only was his position not in jeopardy from Veronica, she wouldn't even be in his area.

"You'll have no problems there," I told him.

He decided to leave us anyway. I told him that I was sorry to see him leave and that I would be happy to provide the best possible recommendation for him as he moved on.

I was confident that Veronica's expertise and the way she carried herself around the plant would win over our employees. Respect is earned and I felt comfortable that, spouse or not, our people would recognize quickly that Ms. Luster was an asset to IPC. Within several months, my feelings were confirmed. Yes, she was "the boss's wife," but it was easy to tell that she belonged, regardless.

Veronica was no expert in corrugated, they all knew. She did not pretend to be. For every statement that she made on the floor and in meetings, she asked ten questions. She would get to be an expert by asking the experts.

What Veronica did know was business, and without making a big deal about it, that showed through with nearly every question she asked of our employees. Veronica's a humble woman; she mingled comfortably with all our people, salaried and hourly. She knew how to get along with other people.

I spoke with an assistant purchaser one day.

"You hired your wife? What are you thinking?"

"Yep, sure did. Woulda hired her no matter what. She's smart. She knows what's what. She knows corporate. Twenty-five years as an exec with Wisconsin Bell. She's gonna be a good one for us."

"Yeah, right. Who's gonna wanna talk to the boss's wife? Good luck with that, Willie."

I walked away. I never dealt with him anyway. I talked to his boss. Outside employees at some of our customers had this tendency to express their opinion regarding how you managed your company— including the hiring process.

As I made my calls around town and took in meetings, I always introduced her as our new executive. Not as my wife, but as a new executive employee of the company. You'd never catch us holding hands as we waited for a meeting. We were executives and business partners at work.

As the years passed, I had many moments of joy as I watched my wife become one of the most sought-after black businesswomen in the country. I knew Veronica was brilliant. I knew she had outstanding people skills. I knew she could get things done.

Around the world, the year 2008 was a tough time. Here in Flint, we wrestled with banking issues and the sub-prime lending crisis in addition to an economic depression that was the equal of the Great Depression. Yet, Veronica Luster-Artis was not one to sit back and cry.

Our company was faced with challenges. We had several multimillion-dollar contracts go south to Mexico. We knew that outsourcing had become a problem in the packaging industry, but we had always managed to remain relatively unscathed. We also had significant business issues with IndustryCorp insourcing.

For many years, economies of scale had dictated to IndustryCorp that packaging handled by outside firms made solid financial sense. But with the auto industry crash that accompanied the global financial crisis, many companies decided to bring their packaging back inside company walls.

It was Veronica who provided the leadership to secure grants to help rebuild our organization. She brought us together with the

Great Lakes Trade Adjustment Assistance Center. The GLTAAC is a federally funded, nonprofit organization that provides business assistance to manufacturers that have been directly hurt by imports. It is part of the Economic Growth Institute at the University of Michigan. Through grants provided by the agency, we upgraded to a more adaptable Systems, Applications and Products software (SAP) and it became more highly integrated within and outside our own walls. We developed professional educational videos and webinars that made a huge difference in the professionalism of our marketing people.

With Veronica's continued drive and focus, our company was successful in getting grants to implement lean and ISO principles throughout the organization. Her marketing skills pushed us to create mass market electronic mailings to over 1,000 targeted companies for diversification. More importantly, she led a drive to re-introduce our company to potential customers. She was also responsible for heading the program which brought us State of Michigan funds used to attract international sales.

Veronica Luster knew business.

In early 2012, Veronica was contacted by the chief of staff for the acting U.S. Department of Commerce Secretary. The Commerce Department wanted to set up a plant visit to launch and share information about President Obama's budget. Inside the President's budget was billions of dollars in help for manufacturers and small businesses.

Veronica hosted this event on behalf of our company. She commanded center stage with her presentation. She explained to those in attendance how this budget proposal would level the international playing field as it promoted funding for overseas trade. She explained how international trade could benefit a small business. The budget also provided tax credits to companies that move into places like Flint. She led a tour of our company which highlighted how small businesses can operate successfully in a Rust

Belt community. She held the business community, the press, and Commerce Department people in the palm of her hand with her flawless presentation.

Veronica's presentation must have reached the highest levels of government. In the summer of 2012, Veronica was contacted by the marketing firm hired by the Obama campaign for his second run for the Presidency. They asked Veronica to do a radio commercial that would be played across the country on prime stations to reach targeted audiences. The purpose of this nationwide commercial was to support President Obama's decision to save the automotive industry, a decision that saved millions of jobs and helped small businesses such as ours.

This commercial, which featured the voices of Veronica and the President, was personally approved by Obama campaign manager David Axelrod. It was heard by various audiences from New York, North Carolina, Washington, D.C., Las Vegas, Los Angeles and throughout Texas. The commercial ran for two months prior to the election and was widely heard. How do I know this? Our phone rang off the hook for months as friends and colleagues from around the country called to tell us how great it was to hear Veronica endorse Obama's policies on that radio spot.

Have we disagreed at the office? Of course. Being a business partner with your spouse can sometimes be a challenge. We're both highly confident businesspeople. Just like in any business relationship, we occasionally saw things differently. One of the secrets of my success has always been that I can switch perspectives from one side of the desk to the other. As a marketing wizard, that was also a strength of Veronica's. It made the resolution of differences so much easier. It also helped us leave work *at* work.

Perhaps Veronica's greatest strength is her ability to read people.

Veronica and I interviewed a potential executive employee. I was in favor of bringing him on board. Although I had several trepidations about him, I thought we should give this man a shot. Veronica strongly insisted that he sign a release so that we could have a professional background check performed. Although I didn't think it was necessary at the time, after much discussion about the merits of a background check, I came around to see Veronica's reasoning.

The results came back. They were not good. With this man's background, there was no way we could justify his hiring for an executive position. Although I was her boss and we didn't always agree, I learned to trust Veronica on a wide variety of business issues.

Over the years, it has not been difficult working with Veronica and being married to her at the same time. We are both serious businesspeople. We focused, right from the start, on leaving any differences of opinion over business at the office. I do not know if this arrangement would work for many people, but it did for us.

Veronica Artis has now been with the company for twenty-three years and counting. She began her career with the company as an executive. Today, she is Executive Vice-President with ownership in the organization. Our marriage and business relationship have worked tremendously well for over twenty-five years. It certainly appears that we will be married forever. Occasionally, we may have a day that things don't go well. But, at the end of the day, all is well.

As a matter of fact, not only has this been a pleasant and enjoyable experience for me, it has enriched my entire life overall. We both love to travel. As a result, we have literally seen the world: Five European countries, three Asian countries, and five countries in the Caribbean. I do love Paradise Island in the Bahamas. And in Barbados, servers at the resorts we visit are so numerous, they literally bump into each other in their haste to take care of you. Me, a dirt-poor Jim Crow-era kid from Memphis, and I have seen the world.

I have been involved with two step-grandchildren and watched them go through high school and now college. When I was a younger man, I never would have expected to so enjoy small children. Yet at Christmastime, the three-to-five-year-old kids would cover me in piles of Christmas decorations as if I were the tree. I can still hear those peals of little kid laughter. Precious times, indeed, thanks to my business partner, best friend, and wife Veronica.

Chapter 38
Welcome to the Club

“You playin’ much golf these days?” asked the voice on the phone. It was September 1990.

It was Woody Thicket. Woody was a local attorney, well-known around the courthouse and the clubhouse. He was sharp. While not my regular attorney, we’d done work together in the past and enjoyed each other’s company.

“Yeah, a bit. Not as much as I’d like, you know. My wife and I are finally living in the same state. Plus, still cleaning up the mess from that Milwaukee project. I’d play more, but dang, you gotta figure out where you’re gonna play, find some guys, everyone get the time out of the office, throw the clubs in the car, drive somewhere…

“It’s tough, right? Turns into a whole damn production, even if you just wanna grab a quick nine. And since you always end up playing eighteen, there’s drinks and lunch or dinner.

“Yeah, I’d like to play more, but turns out, it’s more work than work is.”

“Willie,” I heard Woody say, “I am so glad to hear you complain like that. How would you like to join the nicest country club in town?”

"Never really entered my mind, Woody. Like the game, sure, but let's be real here, none of the clubs around Flint want black members," I said.

"That has changed, my friend Willie. That has changed," said Woody. "Warwick Hills wants a black member, and we want it to be you."

I burst out laughing.

"You gotta be kidding me, Woody. Warwick's never wanted black members. Every black man in this town with money in his pocket knows that. You guys having a Shoal Creek problem?"

In the 1990s, *GOLF Magazine* published the results of a study conducted by the *Charlotte (N.C.) Observer* that showed that 17 clubs which staged highly prestigious and lucrative golf tournaments for the PGA Tour were held at clubs that barred black people from membership. In 1990, Shoal Creek Country Club, one of the clubs with discriminatory membership practices, was set to stage for the PGA Championships.

Jaime Diaz, in a report for the *New York Times*, explained:

Reeling from criticism that it holds many of its most prestigious tournaments at private clubs with all-white memberships, golf has been caught in a moral issue so powerful that the social and political vacuum in which the game has long existed has probably been altered forever.

The statement last month by Hall W. Thompson, founder of the Shoal Creek Country Club near Birmingham, Ala., the site of the 1990 Professional Golfers' Association Championship, that "we don't discriminate in any other area except the blacks," was so bluntly phrased that the repercussions have caused the sport to come under intense attack over a situation that for years has been relatively ignored.

In response to Thompson's statement, Rev. Joseph Lowery, head of the Southern Christian Leadership Council said, "To cooperate with evil is to affirm it. This honest man, Mr. Thompson, has exposed the sophisticated layer of deceit and hypocrisy that veils the racism that still exists in our society today."

The PGA Tour moved quickly to distance itself from the controversy and stated that "In no way does the Tour condone racism and we will not return to clubs that have a written or *de facto* policy which bars blacks from memberships."

How did Shoal Creek act to appease the PGA and keep the tourney which would generate millions of dollars in revenue for the club? They found a black doctor, a non-golfer, who was willing to figuratively stand by the door and wave as patrons walked by.

So yes, I laughed when my friend Woody asked if I wanted to join Warwick Hills.

"Willie," said Woody, "I know this is a pretty big deal. First black guy and all that. So we'd like to set up a meeting. I know you'd be curious about 'Why me? Why now?' so how about we do this meeting?

"We do have a Shoal Creek problem. You know Warwick hosts the Buick Open, right?"

It's impossible to live around Flint and not know about the Buick Open. It is the biggest sporting event held in town. From 1978 to 2009, the greatest names in golf descended upon Grand Blanc, Michigan (just south of Flint) for the tourney. Along with winners like Fred Couples, Tiger Woods, Vijay Singh, and Jim Furyk, all of the *CBS* golf team showed up, too. Jim Nantz sightings at Ziggy's, the local ice cream parlor, were breathlessly reported on the evening news. So, yeah, I knew about the "Buick." It's a huge deal, especially for those of us in industries allied with the Buick brand. Let me tell you, in Flint, everyone—doctors, lawyers, dentists, shopkeepers and industrialists—we are all allied with Buick.

"Here's the deal, Willie. Everyone on the Board knows you, likes what you're about, knows you're a good guy. So the club prez asked me to raise this with you." Woody said.

"Well, that's pretty interesting. Really interesting. Who's the club president these days, anyways?" I asked.

"Oh, that'd be Carl Slice these days."

"What the hell?" I said. "Damn, Carl's my neighbor. Hell, I talk with him all the time. See him every week when we take out the garbage. Why'd he have you call? He could've called me himself."

"Yeah, well, Carl was kinda nervous about asking you himself. He knew we were friendly, and lemme be honest, he thought it'd be uncomfortable for both of you, being neighbors and all, if you said no, so he asked me to open the door for him.

"So whaddaya say? Can I tell him you'll talk to him?"

I agreed to meet with Carl. He came to my home. It was not much of a walk, just had to cross the street. We lived directly across from each other.

Carl had an envelope in his hand as he entered my home. I poured some iced tea and we sat in the den. Carl and I had always been friendly, right from the moment I moved into the Warwick Hills neighborhood.

Carl began to talk to Veronica and me about the club's problem. With no minority members, they could lose their tournament. The PGA had decided to cease doing business with clubs that discriminated on the basis of color. Discriminatory clubs either found black members quickly or they lost their slot on the Tour.

Aside from the three major championships staged in the U.S., there are approximately 40 PGA Tour events. They are a source of great pride for every club involved. They are also extremely profitable. As the typical host club membership is filled with wealthy business leaders, the men who stand for the boards of the clubs understand the value of a PGA tourney.

Carl said, "Look, we know who you are. You've done well in this town. To a man, we think you'd be a great addition to the club. We'd love to have you as a member."

"Carl," I said. "I am not in the business of breaking down

barriers. I have better things to do. Just so you know. But I am interested.

"Let me tell you right up front. The club's all-white, right? Right. Okay, so if Veronica and I decide to join, and we bump into one thing, one damned thing that's because we're black, we have any difficulty because of our color, I walk away.

"Right away. Not later, after I send a letter or make a call, but right then. No bullshit on this. Oh, and one other thing—I pay full ticket. No first-year discounts, none of that crap. I'm going full boat or this isn't happening."

I had to be frank with Carl and let him know that my family and I would not accept any form of prejudice or bigotry; any unsavory or unscrupulous act or attitude towards me and the family was completely unacceptable.

"Willie, I make you this promise right here, right now. If you experience any problem whatsoever, I'll quit with you. And I've been a member for more than 20 years. What's more, we've already had this conversation on the Board, and they back me 100%. They'll quit, too. We're in this together, Willie."

Strong talk. I believed him.

Veronica and I excused ourselves to the kitchen for a quick discussion.

"What do you think, dear?" I asked Veronica.

"You like to play golf. I like to play golf. They have a great pool. The food's good, and the club is right up the road. It'll be a good place to relax, a good place to entertain clients. You're already friends with plenty of the members. We can afford it. We're gonna have grandkids someday, they have kid programs.

"You trust Carl's word, right? And he knows you well enough to know you mean business, right? I've never heard you be more clear.

"I say it's a go. Let's join."

I am pleased to say that joining Warwick was one of the best decisions I ever made. Two current members sponsored me. Other members wanted to sign on as sponsors as well, but the rules were two sponsors only. I have to admit, it was gratifying, as a black couple and local businesspeople, to see the esteem with which we were held by the community.

We were treated like royalty by the staff, servers and other members. Of course, this was the norm for all the members. Warwick's staff took great pride in the level of service they provided. The golf course was impeccable. The clubhouse and locker rooms were always immaculate. The tennis courts were well maintained. The professional teaching staff were all stellar instructors. The pool was always pristine and the youth swimming program was the finest within a 60-mile radius.

I'd been friends with Detroit's Dr. Marvin Cutter for years. We'd been brought together because of our work with several charitable organizations in the state. We'd played golf together and drank a few together. We could let our hair down and not worry about what the other guy might think. Cutter was a prominent surgeon, often featured in the "Best of" features in Detroit-area magazines.

Naturally, I invited Cutter up to Warwick to play golf. He liked the course, enjoyed the grille, and wanted to join. He asked if I would sponsor him.

I said, "Absolutely, nothing would make me happier, but I need to find one more sponsor."

I asked Greg Hacker, a local attorney, if he'd like to be Cutter's second sponsor.

"Sponsor a friend of yours? I'd be honored. Thanks for asking me," Hacker said. "Let's schedule a lunch so I can get to know him. But of course, I am happy to sign on."

With that lunch, and Greg Hacker's co-sponsorship, my old friend Dr. Marvin Cutter became Warwick's second black member.

At this writing, Warwick Hills has approximately 300 members. Over my years as a member, the club has had as many as six black members. I have never heard of any black member experiencing any problem at the club because of skin color. As the "senior" black member, if something was amiss, I suspect I might have been the first one to receive a phone call from a disrespected member, but that call has never come. My family and my guests have always been well treated. Every year, my wife would invite three black women to play in the ladies' golf tournament and they always had a great time.

I was asked to serve on the Board of Directors. After joining the board, I became aware of how the club was managed and I wanted to make several changes. I became chairman of the personnel committee and was a member of the finance committee. I wanted to see the club run like a business. The board agreed with my suggestions.

Many changes were made. Our club manager, with us for eighteen years, was replaced. He had no idea where the club was headed. In his position of authority, I felt, as a Board we all felt, that we needed someone with vision and ideas on how to grow the club. We needed a true general manager, not just someone to handle the grill room.

We went to a general manager concept and hired someone with a degree in club management who had shown promise at a smaller club. We paid him well, listened to his ideas, and were rewarded for our confidence. During the slower months, we regularly stage outside events, fundraisers, business meetings for Chambers of Commerce and such, school sports banquets; they raise awareness of the club and generate significant off-season cashflow for the club.

A new outside accountant, again with club management experience, was hired. We could no longer afford to let members manage the accounts. True, some of those members were CPAs, but they merely assigned the accounts to interns. The dollars were too big, and for true fiscal due diligence, the finances needed to be audited outside of the club's walls.

All club renovations were quoted to get a better price. No longer could members in the construction business be allowed to treat the club's work as a slam-dunk for their firms. When work needed to be done, if a member wanted to quote the business, we were willing to look at their blind bid, just as with any other vendor. But the days of the club being a cash cow were over.

We also struck a deal with the club golf pro. Traditionally, a teaching pro manages the golf club pro shop, and s/he profits from it. However, in today's highly competitive golf equipment business, that exposes the pro to a significant amount of risk. Golf gear is pricey, and if it doesn't sell, the pro is left holding the bag (pun intended).

This is especially true in a market like Michigan where a course is playable for perhaps five or six months a year. We did a deal so that the club would share in the costs, share in the profits, and share the risk. In addition, the profit-sharing encouraged club members to shop at Warwick's pro shop rather than a sporting goods store or online.

I remained on the board for three years. I was asked if I wanted to become president of the club. I declined because I was busy enough running my own company.

I joined Warwick Hills Golf & Country Club on October 1, 1990. Twenty-seven years later, I'm still a member and have enjoyed every minute of it.

Chapter 39
Take Me Back to Memphis:
Jim Crow No More

In 2006, I had a great idea regarding my two brothers, Boots and Howard. During our school years, Boots worked after school at Memphis' most famous downtown hotel, The Peabody. Of course, this was during the Jim Crow years in Memphis. At the time, segregation was at its angriest and most repellent high point. Bob was not allowed to enter or walk through the lobby of the Peabody. Black people could work at the hotel as kitchen help, carry laundry, mop and scrub rest rooms; low-skilled and low-paid domestic work. Black employees had to enter and leave through the rear door of the hotel. They could not go anywhere close to the lobby or the front door. Black people were not to be seen by the white guests as anything but the most menial of laborers. We might offend their "sensibilities."

I called Boots and Howard. Howard lived in Milwaukee. Boots lived in Chicago. I asked them if they would like to visit our old hometown of Memphis. Both were extremely excited. I told them I would treat them to a great trip. I would pay the airfare and hotel expenses. The whole nine yards. I've made awfully good money in my life. I couldn't think of a better way to spend it. We would stay at the finest hotel in the state. We might even see some of the people that we grew up with.

Boots was thrilled. It had been nearly seventy years since he'd had worked at the Peabody Hotel. Our trip would give him the opportunity to see the front entrance of the hotel where he worked.

In the many years since the repeal of Jim Crow, Boots had not seen the hotel.

We met at the airport where I had a chauffeur-driven limousine waiting for us. When we arrived at the hotel, our driver pulled up to the front. A black doorman opened the lobby door for us.

A black man was working at the front of the hotel. In full view of all the white and black patrons, the first hotel employee one would see would be a black man. Shocking in 1945. Normal in 2006.

The doorman called for a bellboy—a white bellboy—to handle our luggage. Even more shocking, a black man was giving directions to a white man in the lobby of what once was Memphis' most segregated business.

We went inside to check in. Robert stood in the lobby for a few minutes. It a good, long while for Boots to take in all in. Black people worked at the check-in counter. We saw black people greeting patrons in the restaurant. A black man carrying the tools of an electrician walked by to an elevator bank.

Boots was amazed at what he was seeing in the lobby. He continued to stare at the people. He looked truly bewildered at the surroundings. He saw white people cleaning the lobby and wiping furniture. He saw white people waiting on black people in the restaurant. In his mind, things had been reversed in a manner that he thought he would never see. Boots looked stunned as a black person checked us in.

The people were young. It was quite obvious they had never experienced the kind of segregation to which we were subjected. Black and white people were having coffee together. Black and white employees spoke in small groups, as would any co-workers, as they walked across the lobby. Boots continued to walk around in a daze. His old high school days returned as he was exposed to areas that he was never allowed by law to see, although he had been employed at that hotel.

A white bellboy brought our luggage in from the limo. A black man checked us in. A different white bellboy took our luggage to our rooms. In turn, he settled our goods in our rooms, opened the shades, showed us the TV hidden inside the room's armoire, pointed out the remote control, and showed us our room's temperature controls.

I tipped him for the three of us. Boots' jaw dropped. As the young man left our rooms, he said, "Now that's something I'd never thought I'd see in the Peabody. I figured that white and blacks would be working together. I figured the old Jim Crow stuff would be gone. I knew there'd be black folks out front. I mean, I was a little surprised to actually see it, you know? But still, not shocked, right?

"But to see money change hands, from my brother's black hand into a white man's hand like you just did, man, that's just something I never would've imagined seeing in Memphis. And never, no way, in the Peabody.

"Man, thank you for that, Willie. Thank you."

By now, Boots, Howard, and I were all welling up, remembering what it was like to be poor black kids in Memphis in the 1930s through 1950s.

We had an opportunity to see an event the three of us had heard about, but of course, as black people, we had never seen. The Peabody is famous for their *ducks*. These small ducklings were trained to walk across the lobby, walk up a small ladder, and then, dive into a pond of water. They performed this act every day and had done so for many years. The ducks even had their own *duck-master*. He wore a white formal jacket and his full-time job was to train and manage these ducks. The ducks and the duck-master had their own quarters in the hotel penthouse.

The ducks started back in the 1930s. The hotel's general manager, Frank Schutt, and his buddy, Chip Barwick, had been on a duck hunting trip to Arkansas. In those times, it was legal to use live ducks—tethered to a float or weighted in the pond—as decoys. As the story goes, the men had a little too much Tennessee sippin' whiskey and thought it would be a hoot to let three of their live decoys loose in the hotel's lobby fountain. They were certain it would be funny. The guests thought it was just the bees' knees. It became such a well-known event that people would line up in the lobby to watch the duck march. It became a trademark and was great for business.

In 1940, the hotel hired a bellboy named Ed Pembroke who had been a circus animal trainer. He volunteered to bring the ducks to the fountain each day. He taught the ducklings to march down a red carpet, climb the ladder, and dive into a pond. Today, the tradition continues.

The three of us drove all over Memphis. We made sure to drive past many of the town's theaters. Memphis has always had dozens of movie theaters. In our day, six were "Colored Only." Three downtown theaters allowed black moviegoers to buy tickets, but of course, those tickets came with humiliations.

In our youth, we had to enter by a side entrance. We had to purchase our popcorn and soft drinks at a "Colored Only" concessions stand. And so as not to sully the whiteness of the audience, we were required to sit in the "Colored Only" balcony. The prime seats, on the floor, were "Whites Only." The tickets, however, cost the same. As we passed by the theaters of our youth—now open to all—you could hear our sighs of recognition and regret.

We had a great time reminiscing about our childhood. We saw a few people we knew growing up in Memphis. Most of the people we knew had passed away. We were all much older than when we last saw each other, yet, we were able still to recognize each other, and we still enjoyed the company. It's rare when, as men in our seventies, you have the chance to recapture your youth.

Several months after our trip, our last old Memphis neighborhood friend passed away.

My dear brother Robert passed at the age of 79 in May of 2008. Our kind brother Howard passed at the age of 83 in December of

2012. Only two of our parents' children are still alive. My sister Jessie is 88. Me, I'm 85. Jessie lives with her oldest daughter in Chattanooga, Tennessee. My sister is a God-fearing, churchgoing woman. Deeply religious, the church is the center of her life. Jessie and I talk to each other regularly. At our age, I always wonder when we hang up if that will be the last time I hear a sibling's voice. My oldest sister passed away many years ago at the age of 68.

Chapter 40
Thinking Back on a Memphis Boyhood

A s a boy, I loved to visit the Memphis Zoo. It's in Midtown, a distinctly white neighborhood during my youth. During the year, black people could visit the zoo on Thursdays. That's right. One day a week for a public zoo located in Overton Park, a public park. Just like everything in Memphis, public facilities, paid for by the tax money of all citizens, were ruled by Jim Crow.

The zoo is across the street from Rhodes College. Originally a Masonic-based college, then a Presbyterian school, Rhodes wasn't even integrated until 1964 when Lorenzo Childress and Coby Smith stepped on the Rhodes College campus as the first black students. While Rhodes holds a celebration of that moment every fall, I promise you that in 1964, no one was any too happy to see young black men on campus doing anything but pushing brooms or emptying trash.

As children, we really enjoyed the experience. All kids love the zoo. Animals we'd never seen, zoo snacks, all the people pointing at cages; "Ooh, look at that one! My Lord, who knew elephants were so big. That's bigger than your truck, Pops!"

July 4, 1946 was a Thursday. *Our* day. The one day each week when black kids and their parents could visit the zoo. Hundreds, maybe thousands of black families excited to visit the Memphis Zoo on our nation's birthday.

The city of Memphis changed "Black Day" to Tuesday. That's the way to celebrate our nation's independence—remind its black citizens that they were still second-rate.

Memphis had an amusement park, Fairgrounds Amusement Park, with many great rides for children and adults. Fairgrounds had the Pippin Roller Coaster. Made from wood, it was said to be Elvis Presley's favorite ride. It had the Grand Carousel, too. For a little kid, floating up and down on a hobby horse whirling in a giant circle with a grand view of the Fairgrounds was a big deal. Summer, of course, meant not just rides but ice cream and hot dogs and soft pretzels. Being a southern town, the amusement park was open most of the year. White people could visit the park whenever they felt like it. Black people were allowed to visit for three days in October. So popular was the Park that black schools would reduce their class schedules so kids could go and ride the rides. October.

Three days. Disgraceful.

Chapter 41
The Theater: Movies, Blues, Vegas and Ray

A s a teenager in the late 1940s, I was enthralled by the movies. We all were. Right after the war, everyone old enough to understand the threat from the Axis Powers could finally take deep breaths for the first time in six years. Memphis was a major movie town. Post-war, the city had over 120 movie theaters for a population of just under 400,000 people. I heard it said that Memphis had one movie seat for every ten people in town. Unless you were black, that is.

Our theater was the W.C. Handy Theater. Located at 2363 Park Avenue, in the Orange Mound section of Memphis, it sat 1,100 black people eager for moving picture entertainment. Orange Mound was a special place. It was the first "nice" neighborhood designed for black folks in Memphis. Named after the great black composer and musician, W.C. Handy, the theater opened in 1947. In an odd coincidence, one of the owners was Kemmons Wilson, who would later found the Holiday Inn chain in 1952.

Handy, who lived from 1878 to 1958, was known as the "Father of the Blues." While he certainly did not invent the blues, his dance band style pushed it into the forefront of music. Vernon and Irene Castle, the famous dance team, performed their new step, the foxtrot, to Handy's "St. Louis Blues."

In addition to movies and newsreels, the theater was famous for stage shows by black entertainers. Blues and jazz musicians would frequently play at the Handy Theater. In 1953 alone, Little

Esther, Lionel Hampton, Duke Ellington, Lloyd Price, and Ivory Joe Hunter all played the Handy.

I remember as a teenager a public announcement was made: The great Nat "King" Cole would appear at the Handy. *For one night only!*

After the announcement was made and handbills were posted around Memphis in black neighborhoods, it was discovered that white people also wanted to see the great singer and entertainer. One problem. The Handy and the show were issued their permits under Jim Crow law. The Handy was "Blacks Only."

A large group of white people decided that they wanted to see Nat Cole play the piano and sing in his sweet, smooth baritone, too. They petitioned the city of Memphis for permission to see the Nat King Cole show at a "Blacks Only" theater. The city decided that just this once, white people could also attend the show. It'd be okay, City Council said, for just this one time, if black and white people watched a great talent together.

However, Jim Crow still ruled. The theater had to be segregated. White and black people could be in the same theater, but they could not sit together. The Handy did not have a balcony. Theater management roped off the left side of the theater for "Whites Only" seating. The center and right side of the theater was seating for black people. Police were in attendance to make sure the color line was not breached. The inimitable Nat King Cole performed a magnificent show before a strangely segregated audience in Memphis, Tennessee. Me? I had seats front and center.

In 1950, I went to the Handy to see a well-known blues singer and guitar player, Lowell Fulson. Along with T-Bone Walker, Fulson was one of the first great electric guitar bluesmen. Lowell had Ray Charles in his band before Ray was Ray. He had Stanley Turrentine on saxophone in one of his bands. Fulson's first big hit was "Three O'Clock Blues" in 1948. B.B. King released his version of it in 1952. "Three O'Clock Blues" was the song that sent everyone over the moon for B.B.

The normal routine was that you would see a movie and then a stage show. When the stage show was over, you would see the same movie again and then another stage show. When I arrived for Fulson's show, I sat down while the movie was playing. There was a person sitting in front of me in the aisle seat with his head down. It was drooping so far down, I thought he was asleep. Possibly, I thought, he might've been passed-out drunk.

I did not pay any attention to this person. When the movie was almost over, someone came by, nudged the guy, and said, "Come on, Ray, it's time to go. Let's go. Come on, now."

He then held this person by the arm and they walked down the aisle toward the stage and then through the curtains on the side. I could tell the fellow was blind by the way he was being led down the aisle. I didn't give it a second thought. Until the movie was over and the band started playing, that is.

Yep, I saw the same guy at the piano. If you've ever been to a big blues revue, you know the routine: Get the crowd more and more wound up, bring it way down low towards the end, introduce the players in the band, and then blow the roof off the place with the last number. That fellow passed out in his seat in front of me was introduced as Ray Charles.

In those days, he was just a blind piano player playing in a blues band. Ray was no saint, you know. Twelve children, nine different women. Years later, in an interview I read, Ray said he'd been a junkie since he was 16. That explained why he was passed out in front of me.

During the early 1960s, I lived in Chicago, and Ray Charles was now world famous. I had the opportunity to see him at the McCormick Theater inside McCormick Place on Lake Shore Drive. There was a cast on Ray's left hand. They announced that Mr. Charles had fallen in his bathtub, hurt his hand, and he'd play organ instead of piano. By this time, Ray was an incredible performer. He was a star, not just a piano-playing sideman. It was one of those shows that 50 years later, I can still picture in my head and hear in my ears. I wasn't the only one in awe. The entire audience was thrilled. We could not stop talking as we filed out about what a great entertainer this man was tonight.

In 2012, I read a book written by Isabel Wilkerson. *The Warmth of Other Suns: The Epic Story of America's Great Migration*, won the National Book Critics' Circle Award for Nonfiction in 2012. The story is about black citizens leaving the south for a better life; in essence, they became immigrants in their own country. It took Ms. Wilkerson 15 years and over 3,000 interviews to put her book together.

As I flipped through the first few pages, I saw that a chapter was dedicated to Dr. Robert Joseph Pershing Foster. As a fan of Ray Charles, something clicked. Dr. Foster, I recalled, after much hard work and prejudice, had become a Hollywood doctor to the black stars. Ray had suffered a serious hand injury and it was not from a "fall in the bathtub." The physician who saved Ray's hand? Dr. Foster.

Ray did not fall in the bathtub; Ray had a temper. Ray also had a serious love affair with alcohol. You mix the two in a highball glass and you get a drunken, angry man smashing his hand through a glass coffee table. In those days, long before social media, medical and personal issues had to be handled very carefully, lest the public get offended. Hence, the quiet call for Dr. Foster to piece Ray back together.

Dr. Foster was present in the audience to monitor Ray's health that evening in 1962. Ray Charles, in fact, commissioned and recorded a song about Dr. Foster, "Hide nor Hair." In the lyrics, Ray's character is a man burning in bed from fever, caused by—we assume—his need for a fix, and his girl runs out on him with Dr. Foster. Foster had a reputation as a considerable ladies' man, every bit as predatory as Ray. But the song was intended as a tip of the

Chapter 42
Ah, Sweet, Sweet Beale Street

During my early years, the 1930s through 1950s, Beale Street was the one street where black people congregated, just having fun and a good time. Ella may have sung about Basin Street in New Orleans as the place where:

The band's there to meet us,
Old friends to greet us
Where the elite always meet
Heaven on earth, they call it Basin Street

but Louie Armstrong spoke the truth when he sang:
I've seen the lights of gay Broadway
Old Market Street down by the Frisco Bay,
I've strolled the Prado, I've gambled on the Bourse;
The Seven Wonders of the World I've seen,
And many are the places I have been
Take my advice, folks, and see Beale Street first!

During the middle of the 20th century, there really was nothing like Beale Street. Clubs, restaurants, joints, theaters, performers on the street; music was everywhere, and when people went down to Beale Street, you put on your best. Women in high heels and gowns, men in such fine suits, even on weeknights. You headed to Beale, you came ready to look fine. Who played the clubs on Beale Street?

cap, not a notice of anger.

I had the good fortune to see the great Ray Charles in concert at a Las Vegas casino shortly before he passed away in 2004 at the age of 74.

Vegas: It was no haven for black people. In 1947, four Jewish-owned, black-patronized casinos opened on Jackson Street in the new "Black District." Black performers often played the undercards at the "Whites Only" casinos—Lena Horne at the Flamingo in 1947, Pearl Bailey at the El Rancho in 1948, Nat King Cole at the El Rancho in 1951. Yet, they could not stay in the hotels where they entertained the high rollers.

It would be 1953 when the Will Maston Trio, starring Sammy Davis, Jr. would be the first black group or artist to headline a show on the Strip for $5,000 per week. That's nearly $50,000 today. Still, Sammy and his people couldn't stay in the hotel.

It took Frank Sinatra to fully integrate the clubs of Las Vegas. The Chairman invited Sammy to open his show at the Sands. Due to Frank's nod, Sammy's trio was offered $7,500 a week to headline at the Frontier on the Strip in November of 1954.

The Will Maston Trio, featuring Sammy Davis, Jr., became the first Black Americans given complimentary room, board, drinks, and casino access to a hotel on the Las Vegas Strip.

You could write a book 400 pages long about all the blues and jazz greats that played Beale Street during those years.

Like a lot of urban centers, urban renewal and the general degradation of cities took their toll in the 1960s and 1970s. However, with the inception of the Memphis in May Festival and BBQ Competition, and the Beale Street Music Festival in 1977, the area has staged a dramatic comeback.

In 2006, when my two brothers and I made our big return to Memphis, we walked Beale Street. It was early Saturday evening. The Beale Street area was already a beehive, crammed with people. As we got closer to the corner of Beale and Main, we saw police placing barricades across the road. The streets were blocked off. Nervous that something bad had happened, we asked one of the officers, "What's up with the barriers?"

"Oh, we do this every weekend," one said. "It gets so crowded down here, we don't want cars driving down Beale Street. Weekend nights, we always turn this into a giant pedestrian mall. Have a great time, fellows!"

We were astonished. People were walking around with drinks. Cans. Bottles. Back in our day, you wanted a nip, you hid it in a brown paper bag or a pocket flask. Today on Beale Street, not only were people leaving bars and clubs and bistros with drinks, drinks were sold from those same establishments right out of "walk-up windows."

That's right. You could walk into a bar and leave with a drink. You could walk up to that same bar's windows and get a drink in a "to-go" cup with a lid. In the 1940s and 1950s, there was no quicker way for black folks on Beale Street to get arrested than to be seen having a sip on the street. Public drinking would get a black man or woman tossed into the pokey for at least the rest of the weekend; maybe more, depending on the mood of the judge. It'd earn you a hefty fine, too. Can't pay the fine? Back in stir.

Yet, that wasn't the biggest deal. The biggest deal was all the people wandering around Beale Street. They were white people. Young white people. Loads of them, as crowded as we ever remembered Beale Street in the glory days of our youth.

They were drinking beer and walking on the sidewalk and walking in the middle of the street. There were thousands of young white people having a great time. At first, we saw no black people other than the three of us. As the evening wore on, we saw more and more black folks. It was an integrated, happy and partying crowd on Beale Street that night.

Our minds went back to the time when Memphis hired its first two black police officers. They could not carry guns. They were authorized to arrest black people, however. It violated Jim Crow law for a black man to arrest a white person. Further, their beat was confined to one street: Beale Street. You read that correctly: Not only was their authority limited to only black people, the arrest had to take place on Beale Street.

If they saw a white person committing a crime, they could not arrest that person. They could hold the person and you can predict how well that went. Once they had the person "held," they could call a white police officer to make the arrest. Those rules were strictly enforced. Even when it came down to protecting the public from criminals, Gentleman Jim Crow was a relentless bastard.

As the three of us walked Beale Street, we were quite surprised to see the major change of scenery from our time in Memphis. The street was clean and orderly. They were nice shops for shopping. Many of the restaurants offered indoor and outdoor dining. The same three segregated, "Blacks Only" movie theaters we visited as kids were still there and looked the same. Neat, clean, and with remodeled facades, they were far from rundown buildings. We had a few drinks and a bite to eat before returning to the hotel. It was a wonderful reminder of our younger days.

Later that evening, several of our relatives, all younger, visited us at the hotel. Seeing so many black people working in the front of the hotel had zero meaning to them. They were accustomed to integration of the races. They'd never been subjected to the barbarous Jim Crow laws. They went to school with white people, lived in mixed neighborhoods, and had absolutely no understanding of the atrocities and abominations of Jim Crow law. Later, my brothers and I realized they could not relate to our lives in the pre-Vietnam War era because they were born after Memphis had been integrated.

I've always felt that Memphis was less difficult to integrate than most southern cities. For some strange reason, white people decided that black people were not all that bad to live around. The exception was the public swimming pools. Rather than allow black people and white people to swim together in the same public pools, the city chose to close all public swimming pools.

It was not all wonderful, of course. It would be many years before black people and white people lived in the same neighborhoods, shopped in the same stores, had their children attend the same schools. It took a long time for institutional segregation to subside. In many ways, it still has not.

Yet, after the Jim Crow laws were struck down, black and white people were able to co-exist: they attended the same movie theaters, rode in the same taxi cabs, and ate in the same restaurants. Black and white kids began to attend the same schools. Never again would black kids be forced to sit in the back of the bus, lest some white folks near the front take offense at seeing, hearing or touching them if they had to share a seat.

I thank both Martin Luther King, Jr. and Rosa Parks for this. There are times when I wish that I was born in a later time. I could have had a much better life without the Jim Crow laws that caused all black people so much harm. Jim Crow didn't just keep black people down and destroy their opportunities for financial advancement, it destroyed lives. How many great artists, businesspeople, scientists, doctors and lawyers did we lose because of this despicable policy?

Chapter 43
Riding with the King: B.B. King

One November evening in 2013, I could not fall asleep. I got out of bed, crept down the hall, and turned on the TV. Channel surfing, I stumbled onto a documentary, *The African-Americans: Many Rivers to Cross*. Professor Henry Gates was conducting interviews with black people in Memphis.

By now, I'm sure most people are familiar with Dr. Gates. He's a professor at Harvard. He's a historian; he discovered the first two books written in America by black authors, both women. He's a filmmaker with a series on PBS. He's an advocate for the inclusion of black writers' work into the Western canon of literature. He was the first black man to win a Mellon Foundation fellowship. He earned his Ph.D. at Cambridge in English literature. When Gates has something to say, we should probably listen.

Dr. Gates was at Memphis radio WDIA speaking with a disc jockey. Growing up, WDIA was my favorite station. WDIA played an important part in media history. Here's the story:

When it went live in 1947, WDIA-1070 AM played Country-Western and some of the day's popular tunes. It did not do well. Nat Williams, a black Memphis high school teacher, convinced John Pepper and Bert Ferguson, the station's white owners, to air his new show, *Tan Town Jubilee*, in October of 1948. *Tan Town* was the first radio program in the U.S. that targeted black listeners. It was an immediate hit and pushed WDIA to Number 2 in the Memphis radio ratings. Seeing the writing on the wall, and counting the dollars, Pepper and Ferguson made the switch to all-black targeted programming and rapidly became the Number One station in Memphis.

WDIA launched dozens of careers. Martha Jean the Queen got her start there. Hot Rod Hulbert got famous there. Rufus "Walkin' the Dog" Thomas had a show on WDIA where he frequently played and sang live, in addition to spinning the platters that matter. Elvis credited WDIA with inspiring his love of black music. B.B. King had a show on WDIA which he credited with building his audience, a critical movement in his later success as a bluesman.

While WDIA brought back memories, I wracked my brain but could not place the DJ. He was an elderly black male.

"Sir, you have been at that desk for over six decades, haven't you?" asked Dr. Gates.

"Yes, sir. Yes, I have, Dr. Gates. Just over 60 years, mmhmm," the gentleman said.

"And I also know, Ford Nelson, that you were a part of the B.B. King Blues Band," said Dr. Gates.

I heard the name Ford Nelson and I sat straight up. It was 2:00 a.m. and in fact, I jumped out of my chair because I could not believe my eyes.

Ford Nelson.

"That's right, sir. I was B.B.'s piano player. Oh, way back in the early 50s, when he was startin' out on his own. I tell you, we had some players back then. Hank Crawford on sax, he could blow. And that Solomon Hardy could play, right? We had Floyd Newman on sax, too. He was big with that whole Stax records crew, started the Mar-Keys and the Memphis Horns. Heck, if I couldn't make the date, sometimes Ike Turner would sit in for me. And Teddy Curry on drums, he never got enough credit. Yes, sir, that was quite an outfit."

My wife Veronica was asleep so I could not tell her what I had just seen. It would not affect her anyway, because she did not live in Memphis. That morning, I told her what I had seen. I knew Ford when I was a kid growing up in Memphis.

Ford Nelson was a schoolteacher and he played piano. He played for years in the B.B. King Blues Band. When Ford could not make a playing date with BB, my older brother Howard would replace him. With the Nelsons living two blocks away, Ford's younger brother, Lindburg (also a fine player) and I attended the same Catholic school.

Howard was a decent player, not nearly in Ford's class, but he could play well enough to sit in for gigs with B.B. in Ford's absence. Ford was a terrific player, truly an outstanding pianist. Unlike a lot of blues and jazz players from the era, Ford could read music. That marked Ford as a pro's pro.

As I mentioned, B.B. had a radio show on WDIA which was instrumental in B.B.'s career getting off the ground. Ford, a teacher, worked endlessly with B.B. on his on-air persona. He coached him hard with his spoken English. B.B., as did many of us, spoke in a drawl peppered with slang. Ford insisted that B.B. speak in "correct" English on the radio. It was on his show that Riley earned the nickname that would earn him fame and millions. His full name was Riley B. King. He was tagged as *The Beale Street Blues Boy* on the air. Later, that would be shortened to *Blues Boy*. As he got famous, that was shortened even further to B.B.

As a friend of the family, B.B. allowed me to ride in the car with him to gigs.

There were times when Howard and B.B. had too much to drink and could not drive home. We had to sit in the car until one of them became sober enough to drive. If Ford was with them when B.B. was drinking, they had to park the car and wait for B.B. to sober up. You see, Ford was not only a teetotaler, he did not know how to drive.

Eric Clapton didn't record *Riding with the King* until 2000, but it in 1949, I knew that riding with B.B. was a big deal. While

B.B. was not a huge national star yet, he was certainly a big deal in Memphis. I was nine years younger than B.B., so for a 15-year-old boy to be hanging out with a 24-year-old musician—a good-looking guy who knew his way around women—that was a real big deal. I saw some things.

B.B. would play in the local veterans' hospital for free. He loved to entertain the vets. We'd head over the Mississippi to play joints in West Memphis, Arkansas. Those were real joints, let me tell you, and every chance I got, I rode with the fellows. The buildings were no more than barns with dirt floors and tables filled with black people drinking corn liquor from fruit jars. This was the chitlin' circuit.

It could get real interesting for a kid. You went to the bathroom, you heard some squeals from a stall, and maybe you'd see four feet, two feet in oxfords and two feet in heels...well, you didn't ask if everything was all right in there. Yet still, these people were like me; they loved the blues and nobody, absolutely nobody, could really play and sing the blues like B.B. and his band on those nights.

My father entered the picture and stopped me from going to gigs with B.B. and the boys because I was falling asleep in school. Some nights, we'd get home as the sun was coming up, just in time for school. I'd go to school on no sleep, too wound up from the night's show to catch even an hour or two in the car.

Sister Ann Joseph was my teacher in elementary school and she was keeping tabs on me. She called home and told my mother that I was falling asleep, out cold, right at my desk. My mother put her foot down and told my father to put a stop to the B.B. King activity.

"Son, you are falling asleep in school because you like guitar music and the blues. Those days are done. No more riding in B.B.'s car during school days. Weekends, we'll see. Summers? I guess. But your late nights out at roadhouses during school nights are over."

"Yes, sir," I answered.

This was not a discussion. I couldn't argue. I was exhausted.

Still, I enjoyed those days as a young teenager. I was going places where other kids my age were not. I would brag to other kids about my experience traveling with B.B. and the things I saw. Most of the kids did not believe me. That was, until they saw B.B.'s 1947 Chevrolet parked in front of my house and heard the loud music coming from my parents' living room. Even if they thought I was lying to them, they believed me then.

BB, Howard, and a few of our neighbors who were off work would come to our home to listen to B.B. play. Those folks would drink all day. All day. The drinking would start when B.B. walked into the house, even before the guitars made it into the house. Those guys, they loved their liquor.

They would always pool their money and buy half-pints of Jim Beam, one at a time. They would never buy a quart, just those little eight-ounce bottles you could hide up a sleeve or down a sock. They'd make ten trips to the liquor store, about once every half hour, and come back with those puny little bottles. Heck, Jim Beam was made just four hours away in Clermont, Kentucky. All the time they wasted, they could've driven up to Clermont for a half-gallon. They were always careful to end the party and clear out before Dad got home from work.

B.B. was a regular visitor to our home in the summer for other reasons. My sister Jessie was an attractive woman. Married, yes, but attractive. B.B. was not much of a respecter of marriage vows, his own or anyone else's. Ole B.B., you see, had his eye on Jessie. He kept that fact to himself. After a fashion.

"Damn, Howard," he said to my brother, "Damn, how come every time I come out to see you guys, I look for Jessie, and I'm tellin' you, that girl is always pregnant?

"Well, B.B.," Howard said, "she is a married woman. Why shouldn't she be pregnant?"

"Don' never see her husband around here, do you?" B.B. asked.

"B.B., he's on the road for business a lot," Howard said.

"Well, there you go," said B.B. "He's away. And I am right here."

B.B., oh my, he really loved the ladies and let me tell you, the ladies really loved the King. We all remember B.B. in his last years as that big, heavyset fellow playing a few notes from a chair, but that was not the young B.B. I knew. The young B.B. had a charming line for every pretty girl, a winning smile, and of course, he could play and sing like no one else.

He truly was, in the words of a 1956 Chuck Berry song, a *brown-eyed handsome man*. Brown-eyed, of course, being code for brown-skinned. After one of his shows in Arkansas, he stopped at a house in Memphis and a woman came out. B.B. called me "Elgie," from Eldrage, my middle name.

"Hey, Elgie!" said B.B. "Get your little ass up front with Howard and don't look back. You look back, I'll kick that little ass."

And with that, I was exposed to lovemaking at a very young age.

No surprise, as I got older, I remained a fan, although I never got backstage at any of B.B.'s shows as a grown man. I did see B.B. many times throughout his career. Several times, I saw B.B. with the great blues singer Bobby Blue Bland. B.B. and Bobby Blue Bland both came out of the same Beale Street music scene in Memphis. In fact, when Bobby was inducted into the Rock & Roll Hall of Fame, they said "Bobby Blue Bland is second in stature only to B.B. King as the finest to come out of the Beale Street scene." Maybe because Bobby didn't play guitar there was no rivalry, just admiration and friendship between the two.

I saw them in the mid-1970s at Flint's IMA Auditorium. Bobby, as usual, opened the show. The man could just flat-out sing. Yet after an hour, the crowd got restless and began to scream for B.B.

"Hey, ya'll, c'mon now, I'm working haaaard up here. B.B.'s on his way. We all want to see the King," said Bobby.

With that, B.B. poked his head out the curtains and smiled. The crowd went berserk. Bobby knew what was happening. B.B. pulled his head back. Bobby turned in mock surprise. Bobby turned to the audience; B.B. walked out and gave Bobby a huge hug. The crowd got even louder. With that, B.B. said what he always said, "Aw, man, I'm sorry I'm late. The dang bus broke down."

B.B. had the bad habit of being late to his performances.

I saw B.B. and Bobby on what would be their last tour together in 2006 at the Fox Theater in Detroit. By now, B.B. was obese and diabetic and Bobby was not much better. As usual, Bobby opened with a few numbers. B.B. came out with his band and played a few songs as well. B.B. was, by now, only able to play from a chair. After a few songs, Bobby came out and they sat together on stage. They sang a few songs together, traded stories, and swapped a few lies. It was like sitting on the front porch, listening to a couple of the local guys talk about "back in the day."

Eric Clapton seemed to solve King's habitual lateness. I saw Clapton and B.B. several times. Clapton was a huge fan of B.B. King's, prominent in spreading B.B.'s music among the young, white population. Clapton's play was highly influenced by B.B.'s style and Eric had no qualms about letting people know. As Eric spread the gospel of B.B. King, the B.B. King audiences became much more integrated and King began to start his shows on time.

Was there a cause and effect there? I cannot say. What was marvelous was seeing a white man and a black man playing the blues side by side with such obvious friendship and admiration between them. It made me think back to watching B.B. playing those West Memphis juke joints and the only white faces were on the cops who sometimes rousted the bars.

Clapton covered much of B.B.'s health care costs as well. Black musicians from the 1940s and 1950s were generally screwed over in royal fashion by the white men who ran the business and B.B. was no exception. Not only did Clapton take care of health care for B.B., he did everything he could to help B.B. gain financial rights to his back catalog of songs and his royalties. Clapton may have made some racist remarks as a younger man, but as he matured, he did everything in his power to atone for them. That's all we can ask, right, that people turn away from sin? A good man, Eric Clapton.

Chapter 44
Strikes Strike Out

We continued to build our business. Over the years, my company, Industrial Packaging, became the largest minority-owned and operated company in Flint, MI. We employed over 400 people at the peak of IndustryCorp's profitability. Our gross sales approached $20,000,000 in sales annually. We had the best of relationships with our customer base and the bank. We owned three large manufacturing facilities located in both Flint proper and Genesee County. Once established, we were profitable for many years.

The late 1990s were excellent years in the auto business. Well-recovered from the dire economics of the early 1980s, sales had recovered and that was excellent news for all the allied industries, including ours in packaging. However, the union decided to call an unexpected strike against the auto manufacturers during the summer of 1998.

The strike lasted 54 days. The effects of the strike created tremendous problems for many companies. On June 5, 3,400 workers at the Flint Metal Fabricating Center walked off the job. Several days later, another 5,800 Flint Assembly workers joined them. That was 9,200 men and women in critical areas such as parts and bodies.

The strike shut down 30 IndustryCorp main assembly plants and 100 IndustryCorp parts plants across the country. Around 195,000 workers were laid off during the production halts. If you figure in the strikers, that was around 200,000 workers suddenly jobless. While they were jobless, the union paid them each $150 per week in strike pay and continued to pay their life and health insurance premiums from their seven hundred million-dollar strike fund.

Proving the adage that "As goes IndustryCorp, so goes the nation," President Clinton called for an agreement after two weeks of strike.

"I encourage the parties to work it out. They have, apparently, very legitimate and substantial differences, but we have a collective bargaining system in this nation, which I support, and I believe they can work it out. And I hope they do so in a timely fashion."

The strike was settled on July 29, 1998, even before the scheduled meetings with a mediator. IndustryCorp agreed to invest equipment in several plants, to not close several plants scheduled to be shuttered, and workers agreed to a fifteen percent increase in required parts output in many plants.

The strike pushed production schedules back by months. It delayed the introductions of the new model year. This caused the old models to be sold as new yet at deep discounts. In total, the strike cost IndustryCorp over two billion in profits.

Further, the entire Genesee County community was adversely affected by the union strike. The supplier base, the companies that produce allied goods such as seats and windshields for IndustryCorp, was damaged to the point where several suppliers went out of business.

In 1998, IndustryCorp employed over 30,000 workers in the Greater Flint/Genesee County area. In the earlier, glory years of the post-war era, IndustryCorp employed 80,000 people. Thousands more were employed in industries closely tied to the success of IndustryCorp. By 2015, IndustryCorp employed just over 7,000 men and women in the Genesee County area.

Stupidity? Yes.

Retribution? Perhaps.

The strike was not very smart on the part of the union; a very short-sighted move. IndustryCorp had just recovered from their nadir of the 1970s. It was clear to all of us in the local business community that IndustryCorp was just a nudge away from collapse again. The 1998 strike was that nudge. Not only did they do severe damage to the community and the supplier base, their show of force was suicide for them, as well. Just in the Flint area alone, the permanent job loss from 1998 to the present was nearly 25,000 jobs. That's a lot of people paying dues. The union has never recovered. It is my belief it never will.

When IndustryCorp was thriving, they begrudgingly shared the wealth with the workers. Workers were, by many standards, overpaid. IndustryCorp viewed their workforce as chattel. Yet, the bar had been set. Greed on both sides compromised any chances of a healthy business relationship.

The rancor and animosity that hung over the worker-factory relationship in Flint spilled over into allied industries. Several large allied firms decided to cut their losses. They began a process of operational reductions in the area. They moved production. They shuttered factories. Over the next several years, many plants were closed, and the buildings were torn down.

Today, there are hundreds of acres of vacant land throughout Genesee County. There is no possibility of rebuilding in this part of Michigan. The memory of that 1998 strike is still strong. Major corporations are not willing to locate in this area and deal with a union with a reputation of calling a strike against any employer at the drop of a hat. The union has had a severe decline in membership. Their confrontational attitude towards management is a major reason that manufacturers locate their new plants in other states.

Several companies have built plants in southern states. On many occasions, the union has made efforts to organize employees without success. Obviously, a southern work force believes they can coexist with management without the representation of a union.

Major corporations are unwilling to manufacture their products in our area because of organized labor which creates a ripple effect on small suppliers. Opportunities to provide services and products to other companies by local suppliers do not exist. We have an excellent work force in Genesee County. Our people have great experience and an admirable work ethic. We have people capable of producing quality products every day. However, we do not have manufacturers in our area to employ them.

All unions do not conduct their business in this manner. You may recall that I was once a union man. I was a proud member, and I was proud to have served my union brothers and sisters well and honestly as a union representative.

As an employer, I have been associated with other unions that negotiated fairly and worked diligently on behalf of their membership. Contracts were negotiated fairly and equitable. Strikes were the last resort. The job, the contract negotiations, could get done without a strike. Strikes harm the company. Strikes harm the employees.

Unfortunately, the union in the Flint area does not always understand how to negotiate with management. Neither are they willing to do so without confrontations, strikes, and the desire to destroy management and weaken the company. I believe this goes back to the Sit-Down Strike of 1937.

During the Great Depression, workers' conditions were horrific. The pay was terrible. The benefits were few. Worker safety was a non-issue. If a man was injured on the job, there'd be dozens more waiting to take his place. IndustryCorp maintained a network of spies throughout their factories to report back to management any workers who spoke out against the company in any way. IndustryCorp controlled the City of Flint. No political, business, or economic moves were made without the okay of the higher-ups at IndustryCorp.

Spies were everywhere within the city, as well. The first time a union organizer came to Flint in 1936, he hadn't been in his hotel for more than a few minutes when he received a phone call with a muffled voice saying, "You better get back where you came from if you don't want to leave town in a wooden box."

It was tough for IndustryCorp workers in the beginning, and the antagonism never faded away.

When Joe Brown and I founded our company in 1979, I truly believed we would be organized by a union. We were a Flint business and Flint has been a union town since the Sit-Down Strike was settled. Also, I felt we would be a better company if we were organized by a fair-minded union that would allow the company and the employees to become successful. I knew that my team and I would be fair. I understood the values, both psychological and financial, of a solid union. I looked forward to a positive partner.

A union can help a favorite company. In 2005, a manufacturer from England located a competing packaging plant in Flint. The new factory was organized by the same union that represented our workers. The union demanded a ridiculous wage scale for the new factory workers. They issued an ultimatum—sign the contract or we strike. The company closed the plant and returned to England.

When we first opened the doors of IPC in 1979, we knew our first contract would have to give the business a chance to be successful. It was important that the union rank and file understood that a new company in an intensely competitive market might not make it past year three if wages and benefits for years one and two were too generous.

On the other hand, they needed assurances that if the contract was tipped slightly in the company's favor for the first several years, those good feelings would be recognized in subsequent contracts. You can't exactly put that into the contracts. There must be strong personal relationships between the people on both sides of the negotiating table.

Knowing that, I hired a person I knew well, Nora Price. She had worked for me before and we understood each other motives. She knew I would keep my word and I trusted her implicitly. She was an hourly employee with a union background who understood the economics of a start-up business.

I felt that Nora would be the one to organize my employees and she would be their lead negotiator for our first long-term union contract. Further, I knew Ms. Price would encourage employees to sign union membership cards in an orderly manner.

You've heard stories about unions and their sometimes "heavy" hands. They're true. Unions have often threatened, coerced, and committed crimes against the working man and woman to gain an unscrupulous foothold in a plant. I knew that wouldn't happen with Nora in charge.

Nora had no problem accumulating enough authentic employee signatures on signed cards. Her team presented the signed cards to the company and we decided to recognize the union just thirty days after we finished hiring. A fair union, a fair employer; solid footing for success.

In later years, Nora Price, union organizer, became a strong member of our management team and worked for IPC until she retired. With her knowledge of the shop floor and her natural business intelligence, we wanted her more in the boardroom that we needed her in the box-room.

Over the years, IPC has experienced two union strikes. One strike was a major work stoppage. An outside union encouraged our employees to strike for greater benefits and wages far beyond the company's ability to pay. This occurred at one of our plants in a different city. This not uncommon. Outside union leaders will attempt to influence the workforce with "pie-in-the-sky" promises to wedge themselves into a new business. If they succeed, they use that as way to drive the old union out.

Why? There is a tremendous amount of money in the union

business. The dues are not outrageous, but there are so many workers. In 1979, the United Auto Workers had 1,500,000 dues paying members. As of 2014, that number dropped dramatically, all the way down to 391,000 workers. However, from dues alone—no stocks, bonds, mutual fund investments—the UAW still brought in $115 million per year in dues income. As you can see, the incentive to take over a plant is strong.

As we heard of the outside union movements in our plants, we became wary. Their attempted takeover was so blatantly in violation of National Labor Relation Board (NLRB) rules that the local arm of the NLRB became involved, sat the other union down, and advised them in strong terms that they were in violation of the law. The strike lasted two weeks and it cut decidedly into our profitability for that quarter. Far more importantly, our union employees returned to work, more strongly educated, under the original union contract.

The second strike was minor and lasted only three days. A small number of employees decided to strike during negotiations. There was no real reason to strike. We were close on a variety of small issues. The strike was not authorized by the union. We quickly came to an agreement. The contract was brought to the rank and file, approved, and all was fine.

Except for a husband and wife who both worked for me. The wife went on strike. The husband did not. The husband would drop his wife at the picket line and then walk right into the plant.

"I'm not walking your picket line," he said. "You're on your own. You wanna do this, you go right ahead. Jes' don't expect me to follow you. I'm not walkin' any picket line."

Obviously, they had a good married life.

For 34 years, my company and the union have sat down and negotiated many contracts. It has been a "live and let live" environment that has been good for both sides. We learned to live with each other with a high level of respect. We always had a policy of hiring the very best people we could, from custodial to set-up to floor workers. I was always proud of the overall intelligence of our rank and file. This made negotiations go more smoothly.

Our contracted union employees could find themselves in a difficult financial situation. Strikes were not a good solution for them, either. They chose to negotiate rather than walk in a picket line. This approach made more sense to them. The financial drain on the union was also a major factor. Should a union take its employees out on strike, the employees begin to draw on union reserves. As part of their dues, workers are entitled to a small stipend of strike pay. The union will pay their health, life, and disability insurance premiums. There are no dues coming in. For a union to take its membership out of work, they put themselves in quite a financial bind.

In writing this story, one would think that I was opposed to unions. Quite simply, I am not. At one time in America, unions were absolutely necessary. Employees organized into a union to make life better for them. I am also absolutely certain that is not the case today.

The environment today between unions and management has improved tremendously. No one, no way, wants a work stoppage to take place. In the 40 years I have owned my own company, I have worked closely with all manner of union employees. The last 40 years, I have seen major changes in union and management relationships. Not just major changes. Dramatic changes.

Declining union membership has played a role. This forced the union to acquire a better understanding of management difficulties. Situations occur almost daily that must be resolved. Whether it involves hourly vs. salary, production and work rules, interpersonal issues between hourly employees – somebody in management must become involved. It's not easy. I believe unions concluded that a work stoppage causes major difficulty on both sides. Strikes? No one really wins.

Additionally, overseas manufacture has had a massive impact

on the U.S. worker's place. While 12 million Americans still work in manufacturing, since 2000, 5 million manufacturing jobs have vanished. 2.4 million of those jobs have been shipped overseas.

The reason for this change is simple: lower wages and benefit costs increase corporate profitability. This process also allowed for an increase in corporate overall profitability. Say what you will about companies being green, or good corporate citizens, or on a list of *100 Best Places to Work Right Now!,* it is all about the bottom line. You don't turn a profit, you cannot stay in business. Should you decide to become a public entity, you now have shareholders and analysts that demand performance and answers.

Many American jobs were eliminated with this change in business philosophy. A maneuver of this magnitude most certainly causes a severe loss of employment. The public is willing to pay a certain amount of money for a quality product, but you don't dare go over that price by more than a few cents or dollars. Employee costs often set the bar for wholesale costs from manufacturer to dealer.

The 2015 *Forbes* corrected wage in India, (i.e., corrected for differences in the prices of basic goods between the U.S. and India), was around $1.88 per hour. Healthcare in India is mandated for all workers by the State in their constitution. Here in the U.S., according to the Kaiser Foundation, a worker's family health coverage costs the company around $12,000 per year. Already, the deck is stacked against U.S. manufactured goods in the pricing department.

When a company is faced with high wages that have a negative effect on profits, management will make decisions that upset a union. Even though the union realizes these issues will ultimately cause financial losses, the rank and file often demand action. Yet, the company must react in a manner that will allow the company to return to profitability. If not, all is lost.

The decisions made by management to implement major changes are critical to the future and well-being of every company.

Companies must balance the "long game" against the quarterly financial statement. Too often, unions respond in a kneejerk fashion. Their members can't always look five years, or even two years down the road. They have bills to pay right now. But so does the company. There's the rub: unions don't often realize that management must always balance the *now* vs. the *long now*.

At IPC, we've always balanced the two. On October 22, 1999, my company received a letter from the White House signed by President Bill Clinton. The President congratulated us on our 20th anniversary as a minority owned business. For any manufacturing business to last 20 years is noteworthy. Yet for a minority-owned business, that is extraordinary. In business, twenty years is several lifetimes. Half of all businesses don't make it to five years. About 1/3 of businesses make it to ten. When you look at minority-owned business, 9 out of 10 black-owned businesses fail within five years. Furthermore, although statistics may not exist, for cities with ingrained corporate racism such as Flint, I can say with some pride that my firm, Industrial Packaging Company, may be one of a kind.

Over the years, IPC has been the recipient of many certificates and awards from the city, state, and federal governments. I'm sure these honors are a direct result of the longevity of a company owned by a black man. Yet, this black man had the wisdom to bring the best people on board. He was no fool.

The data is clear: Minority-owned companies are not known for their long existence. Minority manufacturing companies are even more short lived. The financial requirements are difficult to obtain. Union officials, knowing the data, look at black-owned firms differently. Even in the latter part of the 20th century and into today, white workers are often unhappy being directed by black management.

Banks are unwilling to provide the necessary credit lines to startups owned by minorities. They hold black-owned businesses to a different standard of accountability. However, when a minority does become involved with a bank and the company is managed by skilled personnel and the company generates significant annual profits, the company is most likely to continue to work with that bank. My experience—and that of many other minority-owned businesses—is that we recognize and reward such loyalty.

This might be the most important piece of business advice in this book: *Build a relationship with your bank and loan officer.* When you find a bank that will work with you, keep them in the loop. Teach your bank about your industry. Keep them apprised of any changes within your customer base. Use the most diligent CPA firm you can afford and shoot those reports straight from your desk to the bank. Attach your own executive summary to the top of the quarter's financials.

When times are good, this might seem like overkill, but times will also be bad, I guarantee it, and that's when you will be desperate for the bank's help. If the loan department doesn't understand your business nearly as well as you, you will be out of luck, and that'll be the last time you lock your business's front door.

Chapter 45
The Ugly Side of Business

Owning your own company is an enjoyable experience. Mel Brooks, as King Louis XVI in his movie *History of the World, Pt. I,* may have said it best: "It's good to be the king." Of course, you will have ups and downs. It's not always about the money. It's the personalities, the human side of business, that will be the real gut-wrenching moment. There are times when you must decide how to handle delicate and fragile situations. You may find yourself in a compromising position that you did not create. A deep conversation for which you were not prepared may occur with an individual. You might have to wrestle with some discomfort because of a request made from out in left field by an employee or colleague or business associate. Whatever ownership throws in your way, your first step is always the same: *Deep breath. Take a step back. Do not engage on someone else's terms.* Much to my chagrin, I have experienced situations that forced me to learn that lesson. Let me share a few of those experiences with you.

A buyer for a key account asked me for something unexpected.

"Willie, listen, I need to ask you a favor," he said.

"I'm listening. Business or personal?" I said.

"A little of both, Willie. My brother needs a job. But here's the deal. He has a little medical condition, there's this situation, see. It's a chemical imbalance. He's taking care of it, he sees the doc, it doesn't get in the way of his working..."

"A medical condition. Hmm, I gotta ask. Why me? You've got

contacts everywhere. You see where I'm going, right?"

My first thought was, *I don't hire this guy's brother and it's bye-bye business.*

"Oh, sure," he said, reading my mind. "No, it's not like that. You got the business. See, you're a good guy, you got decent folks out on your floor, I think he'll do good for you, and if there's issues along the way, well, you're a fair man, Willie, I know that. So, yeah, it's maybe more personal. No strings. Whaddaya say? Can we do this? Give it a shot?"

I hired his brother.

After three weeks, one of my managers came to my office.

"Willie," he said, "we can't keep this guy."

"Why not? What's up?"

"Well, it's like this. Okay, this is weird. He wanders out to the parking lot a coupla times a day..."

"So he leaves his job without permission. We've dealt with that. Write him up. Let the shop steward know. What's the problem?"

"Um, yeah, well, lemme finish. He wanders out to the parking lot, Willie, and he stares up to the sun, and starts talking to himself. I mean, like real conversations. He does both sides. He, like, talks to the sun and then the sun answers.

"Willie, people are talking. Every time I go out there to bring him back in, people are asking me 'What is wrong with that guy?' 'Hey, how much longer we gonna keep that guy around? I'm gettin' tired of coverin' for 'im.' One guy even said, 'Boss, thinking I should start putting a knife in my boot?' He was laughing when he said it, but still.

"This has gotta stop, Boss."

"Got it. I'll handle it. Give me a couple of days."

I called the buyer. Believe me, it was easier to ask for a signature on a seven-figure contract than to bring up this issue. I had to get my point across without any damage to our business relationship.

"Listen, this is tough," I said. "It's about your brother. We gotta talk. Here's what's happening over here."

I relayed the conversation with my manager. I explained the conversations my manager had held with the other workers. Fortunately, the buyer understood.

"Willie, I appreciate that you took a chance on my brother. He's been fighting this his whole life and it's always like this. Things get straightened away, and then they go to Hell again. Thanks for trying, Willie. I owe you one."

Believe me, all situations do not turn out this way.

I was making an out-of-town sales call. My buyer, Donny Kramer was a 45-year-old man. He was gay. Today, we are much more aware and accepting. In today's business world, LGBTQ status is nothing. It's like color or religion.

"Oh, you're gay. Okay, now about this contract..."

But this was 1984 and sexual preference was much more hush-hush. From my perspective, I never cared much about how a person chose to live his life. But gay or straight, I don't want to hear about anyone's sex life. Not even my own.

Donny and I would go out to lunch. He made it difficult to talk business with him. I was there to build a relationship that would help both our companies prosper. But Donny wanted to talk about his 18- year-old boyfriend, Sammy.

I suppose there are plenty of straight guys who are 45 years old with 18-year-old girlfriends who want to brag about their girls. I don't want to hear about that, either. With Donny, it was Sammy, even in his absence, who dominated the conversation. "Sammy did this. Oh, let me tell you about this cute thing Sammy did."

It was just wrong. That's not appropriate talk for any sort of business situation. Donny had been married. He had two adult children. You want to share something about your kids, I'm happy to listen. But I'm here to sell you cartons and packaging goods for your employer. I am not here to listen to you brag about your teenaged lover.

Donny had a knack for making me uncomfortable. At one meeting, I asked, "Where's the men's room?"

Donny said, "Oh, I'll go with you."

I said, "Well, I'll hit it on my way out, then. Thanks, Donny."

Maybe it meant something, maybe it meant nothing, but most men don't go to the restroom in groups. It was several years before I was able to shake hands with him without him scratching the palm of my hand with his index finger. Was this a come-on? A sign of some kind? I didn't know, but it made me very uncomfortable.

I worked with Donny for two years and was able to increase my business with him. These were the most difficult sales calls I had to make in 35 years of sales. His un-businesslike demeanor threw me off. As much as possible, I would distract him from talking about Sammy. I simply did not want to hear that shit.

I mastered the art of deflecting the conversation from Sammy to business. It was never easy, but I managed. Every time he'd turn the conversation to Sammy, I'd nod and say, "That's great, now, what's the feedback from the guys on the floor about that new packaging system we put together?"

It wasn't easy. Sammy was always present in our conversations.

"Sammy came home late last night, and guess what he brought me?"

"Oh, I couldn't begin to guess. Hey, let me show you this new prototype corrugated we're thinking of bringing in. I'd like your opinion on it."

It was hard work. It made me uncomfortable. Donny was persistent—he wanted to talk about Sammy. I was persistent—I wanted to sell corrugated. I did not want to hear about his love-life. I won. After two years, Donny figured that I was not going to be his therapist or his shoulder to cry on or someone to whom he could brag about snagging a teenaged lover. It took two years of me treating him fairly, but firmly, and we finally developed an appropriate business relationship. I'm not homophobic, and I showed him that.

I just wanted a business relationship. The remainder of our years together, they purchased a lot of products and services from us. When I passed the account on to a new sales rep, we shared a warm goodbye.

For most businesspeople, making a deal is relatively simple. *My company will provide these goods and services for $X. Here's what you get. Here's what I get. We both prosper.* It may take a while to settle on terms, but that's just negotiations. Every businessman or woman thrives on negotiation. It's fair and honest; above-board. That's how business should be done.

But for some, making a deal involves a certain amount of quid pro quo. Payola, tickets, trips, favors, girls. For those, no deal is going to get done unless a pocket gets lined with a little something. *I'll get this contract approved for you if you can do this for me. Quietly. And on the side. Cash.*

I'd worked with Ryan Follett for years. We weren't friends, but we'd always had a good working relationship. One morning, my phone rang, and it was Ryan. Odd, because Ryan and I usually talked about twice a year. Once before our contract was due to come up and several months later to make sure all was well. Over the years, Follett's contracts had made me a lot of money.

"Hey, Willie, Ryan here. Need a little favor. You mind having breakfast with a buddy of mine?"

"Sure, why not? Do I know this guy?" I asked.

"You do. It's Bill Henry. You remember Bill, right? Worked for me for about five years until he switched to pharmaceutical sales."

"Well, okay, but what's up? His pharmacy company wants me to handle his packaging?"

"Nope. Bill wants back into the business and he'd really like to work for you. Bill's a good friend. Can you meet with him?" said Follett.

"Ryan, I gotta tell you, I'll have breakfast with him, but we don't have anything for him. I'm just trying to be polite and honest here.

I can only see Bill in a couple of spots for us, and those spots, well, we've got great people there already."

"Sure, sure. I understand. But Bill really wants out of drug sales and he's a good guy. He wants to work for you and I really think you need him."

We had breakfast. I explained to him what I said to Ryan; that we did not have a suitable position open for him at that time.

"Maybe in the future," I said, "I'm always willing to talk with you, but for right now, I'm afraid it's a no-go. I tried to explain that to Follett but maybe he didn't pass that on to you."

Two days later, I received a letter from Ryan Follett. It was an ultimatum hidden inside a "friendly piece of advice." Follett's letter said you should hire Bill Henry because you need the experience he has to offer. That was the friendly advice.

But in the very next paragraph came the ultimatum: "If you don't hire Bill Henry, a letter will go to upper management that says you lack the personnel to be our supplier any longer. We'll void those contracts and you can try and sue us if you want."

It reminded me of the Mafia shaking down a store owner for protection: "Nice store you got here, buddy. Be a shame if anything, you know, like a fire or sumpin' happened to it." From Follett's tone, it was clear that if I failed to hire Bill Henry, I'd have a serious situation on my hands. Those contracts were worth millions of dollars.

I caved. I hired Bill Henry and he worked for my company for six months. It was a complete waste of time and money. Bill was absolutely useless as an employee. He was a cancer in the office.

This was one of the very few times when I compromised my own integrity and business sense because those contracts dictated that I should do so. I had an asshole on my payroll and could not do anything about it.

I knew Ryan's boss, Rick Brooks. Not well, but when I decided to have a conversation with him, Brooks took my call to set up the meeting. I walked into Brooks' office and we traded the usual pleasantries. Without a word, I handed him the letter that Follett had sent me.

As Brooks read it, his eyes got big. His face turned red. He looked at me.

"Follett sent you this?"

"Yes, sir. He did."

"On company stationery?"

"That's the letter he sent me, Rick. About eight months ago."

He read it again. I could see he was steaming.

"You know that's not how we do things around here, Willie. Why didn't you bring this to me sooner?"

"Well, I believe in chain of command and this could get ugly so..."

"Oh, it's going to get ugly, Willie. I promise you. Really ugly," said Brooks.

"Thanks, Rick, but just do me one favor...Can you keep my name out of it? I still gotta deal with Follett, and I gotta do something about Henry," I said.

"No problem," said Brooks. "This'll just be some office scuttlebutt. Heard it around the watercooler."

I discovered that Brooks called Follett into the office the next day and kicked his ass for an hour. In addition to getting dressed-down, a letter was put into Follett's file and he was barred from visiting our premises again. How did I know this? I knew some people on the inside, too.

Bill Henry was an ass. He did nothing at work, literally nothing. He'd wander the floor and the halls with a cup of coffee, badmouthing me and IPC and IndustryCorp suppliers in general. I had made no secret of why I'd been forced to hire Henry and my people had my back. Henry was friendless. People would turn on their heels and walk away when he approached. The week after I met with Brooks, I found Henry literally standing next to the coffee machine.

"Well, Mr. Henry. How much longer will you stay with us?"

The look on my face was the same one that you'd have on your face if you found a flaming bag of dog excrement on your porch.

Several days later, Henry did not come into the office. He never returned.

One of our top IPC salesmen, Carl Diggs, came to see me the week after Henry left our employ. You might remember Carl as the Hungarian buyer who "gifted" me with my first big contract when I first started IPC. Carl was so good, when he became available, I had to hire him.

"Can you have lunch with Ryan Follett and me?" Carl asked.

"I guess. Not exactly sure why, but yeah, okay," I said.

"Well, I don't know what's up," said Carl. "Ryan asked me to put together a lunch so I said I'd ask."

I had an inkling. I knew that Ryan was ticked that his boss, Rick Brooks, had torn him a new one, and I'd bet that he had put two and two together. My suspicions were that Ryan thought I had told his boss about how he'd leaned on me to hire his useless buddy Bill Henry.

We met for lunch. I wasn't hungry. I pretended to be unaware that his boss had any knowledge of how Bill Henry came to work for me. It was, of course, a bald-faced lie.

"What are you talking about, Follett? I hardly know Brooks. Going over your head like that would cause me more trouble with IndustryCorp than I have with Henry wandering around my place. I never had a conversation with your boss. It was probably someone in your office. Hell, Henry's an asshole. Probably he just pissed off the wrong guy in your office and that's who ratted you out."

I would like to have been a fly on wall during that Brooks-Follett meeting. I know that it got loud and ugly. Deservedly so. The overwhelming number of people I did business with were on the up and up. That's why the jackasses like Ryan Follett stand out so clearly. I never saw Ryan Follett after that lunch. He was replaced as our buyer. I don't know what happened to him and I don't give a damn where he ended up.

In 1988, we decided to put forth a concentrated effort to diversify our business portfolio. In our core business, we provided packaging services to the automotive industry. However, the early 1980s were terrible years for motor vehicle sales. While the auto business was in a recovery mode, we had been hit hard by the downturn. We felt that if we could diversify our base, we'd be better positioned to withstand future downturns.

However, we had to make sure we did not disrupt any of our current relationships with contractors. These were cherished and profitable relationships. We had to make certain that our current clients did not get the impression that as we expanded, they'd no longer be our main focus.

We began the diversification simply. We visited firms that used packaging services. We pitched companies where we felt we could make inroads, building upon our success in the auto business. At the same time, we increased the TLC we lavished upon our current accounts.

We began to make inroads. New contracts were being signed. Relationships were being built. However, we started to encounter a certain type of dialogue that caused all of us, from frontline sales to my CEO's office, a notable level of discomfort. It was a new conversation and we all heard it.

Buyers from our new clients were asking for bribes. I was not accustomed to individuals requesting favors as a condition for business. I realized that this was a penalty I would have to pay for going outside my core constituency. In my main industry, payola and bribery were extremely rare. But I found that in other industries, not only were bribes accepted, they were expected.

I discovered the downside to certain elements of business that can uproot a portion of your integrity. I hated it. But I did it. I wanted to do business in that industry and that was the price I had to pay to feed new sales to my company. Not surprisingly, these were people that I didn't particularly care to be around.

Unfortunately, there were times you take those people to lunch and try to increase your business with their companies. While entertaining clients was almost always a joy, these meetings were not. While my core business was with people that I loved to be associated with, people with whom I've maintained relationships long after our retirements, these folks with their hands out were the exact opposite. As the old saying goes, don't wrestle in the mud with pigs. You'll get up filthy and the pigs enjoy it.

It is inevitable: *During the course of your business life, some ugliness will flare up.* You learn to deal with individuals that conduct themselves outside the upright and transparent manner in which business is generally consummated. Fortunately, the time you spend with them is short.

I have lived in the business world for 40 years and have enjoyed most of it. There have been times when I did not enjoy certain situations. Some of those occurrences were caused by my own actions which I had to correct. When I made a business mistake, when I pushed the wrong button, I learned to analyze the problem and take the necessary steps to repair the damage. One key lesson: *It doesn't matter where the mistake was made or who caused the problem, you cannot allow an adverse situation to jeopardize the company; its goals, image, or portfolio.* When there's a problem; identify it, solve it, and take steps so that it never happens again. *Blame solves nothing.*

That is my own philosophy in life and business.

Chapter 46
My Brother Makes Me a Believer

It was early in 2008 when I spoke on the phone with my brother Boots in Chicago. The topic? A man who had just announced that he was running for president of the United States. A black man.

My take? This guy is completely out his mind. Why would you attempt something so impossible? Boots and I repeated this conversation several times over the next few weeks.

"Look, Boots. The only guy I know who had tried to do something this impossible was Jesse Jackson. And we all knew Jesse couldn't win, wouldn't win. That was all about making a statement. You know that. But this guy's serious. He's really running for President."

Jesse Jackson made a strong statement back in 1988. He won nearly 7 million votes during the campaign. He flat-out won seven Democratic primaries: Alabama, the District of Columbia, Georgia, Louisiana, Mississippi, Puerto Rico, and Virginia. He picked up four caucus wins, too: Delaware, Michigan, South Carolina, and Vermont. But you'll notice only one big ticket state, Michigan, among his wins. Michael Dukakis ended up with the Democratic nomination but was trounced by Bush/Quayle, winning only ten states. Who's to say that Jesse couldn't have done better?

But I never for an instant thought that Jesse back in 1988, or this new black guy in 2008 could win. I was a broken record in conversation with my brother.

"Boots, there is no way, no living way, a black man gets elected president in this country. No woman, neither. Only a white man is electable in this racist society. Don't care how rich you are, how smart you are, how many degrees you got, you a black man, you will not be President."

I can remember one conversation like it was yesterday, not ten years.

"Hey, Boots. This guy. Who is he, anyway? Where's he from? He started out as a campaign manager, right, and now he's in the Senate? But c'mon, Boots, that's thousands of miles away from the White House.

"Seriously, there's a couple black guys on the South Side that'll vote for him, maybe some white folks because he headed up *Harvard Law Review*, but we're joking here. You gotta tell me the truth: Is this guy in his right mind?"

Boots set me straight. "Lemme tell you about this Obama. Not only is he in his right mind, he is an absolutely brilliant individual. Flat out, he's a great man. He's so great that he can get elected no matter what color he is. All of us will vote for him, and you are going to be shocked at how many white folks recognize him as brilliant. He's that sharp. Man, it just shines off him. He's gonna be president. Not just 'cause I wish it, but because people will see it, they'll know it."

It had been a long time since I'd heard my brother get so wound up, so emotional, so dead-set about anything besides family.

"Okay, brother, have it your way," I said, "but I think you've been drinking if you think this guy Obama can win a national election and occupy the White House. Robert (I never called my brother by his Christian name), we won't live long enough to see a black man elected in the USA. Our *grandchildren* won't see it, either. No livin' way."

I could hear Boots sigh on the other end of the line.

"You wait and see. You just wait and see. I will be able to say, 'Willie, I told you so.'"

Come November 4, 2008, there were no dry eyes in the Artis home. Barack Obama's election thrilled me beyond all belief. I had only one regret. My dear brother, my lifelong best friend Boots, passed away at age 79 on May 16, 2008. My brother did not live to see his prediction come true. In the six months of campaign between my brother's death and the election, I found myself reaching for the phone to call Boots, only to realize he was no longer available to answer the phone.

If I was thrilled, Boots would've been ecstatic. He was so damn proud that a black man was running, his pride would've been immeasurable at a black man in the Oval Office. Boots was 100% certain that Barack Obama would win. His faith never wavered.

It saddens me terribly when I think of the missed conversations with Boots during Obama's eight years in office. He would have said to me, over and over, "Willie, you gosh darned idiot, I told you so. From now on, you will listen to me when I talk to you."

He was always my older brother. I would agree with him.

Chapter 47
My Dinners with Barack:
Five Invitations to the White House

O h, how I have longed to be able to sit down with Boots and tell him about the five times Veronica and I have been invited to the White House. I would love to tell him that Veronica and I have had the opportunity to meet, converse, shake hands, and be photographed with President Obama and First Lady Michelle Obama. Boots would've been dumbfounded; his little brother had the chance to look our first black president in the eye, shake hands, and say "Thank you, Mr. President." As I was greeted by the President, I heard Mrs. Obama say to my wife, "It's lovely to meet you, Mrs. Artis."

Veronica and I have had quite a run at the White House. We were present when the President announced he would seek a second term. We celebrated with the Obamas, and several hundred others, at three Christmas parties.

We were also present when the Obamas honored Berry Gordy, Jr., the founder of Motown, on February 24, 2011. Not only was Berry Gordy responsible for "The Sound of Young America"—his Detroit-based company was the top grossing black-owned business in the United States. Perhaps you saw it on **PBS** as part of the *In Performance at the White House* series. If you get the chance, look for Veronica and me in the row behind the Obamas, just a few seats off to the side of them. I'm the tall guy with the huge smile plastered on his face.

The President made the opening remarks. He called Motown "The soundtrack of the Civil Rights era." He told the Motown origin story; how Gordy borrowed $800 to set up shop in the basement of a rental house on Detroit's W. Grand Boulevard. In closing, he paid tribute to Motown for creating a music where black and white people—in the midst of incredible turmoil—could come together in happiness.

Jamie Foxx served as emcee for an incredible lineup of talent. Foxx, John Legend, Seal, and Nick Jonas opened the show with a Temptations medley. Sheryl Crow (who later told me she started her career as a backup singer for Michael Jackson) did a couple of Jackson Five songs. John Legend did an amazing "Heard It Through the Grapevine." Natasha Bedingfield, Jordin Sparks, and Ledisi sang a Supremes medley, right down to the dance moves. We all had the privilege of watching Smokey Robinson clap and sing along from the audience as Bedingfield sang Smokey's hit "Tracks of My Tears."

After several more songs, Stevie Wonder came onstage to sing "You Are the Sunshine of My Life." He spoke to Gordy from the stage:

"Berry, thank you for this incredible Motown ride. And to all of you in the crowd, I need you to get up, get up and celebrate by 'dancing in the streets.'"

That was the cue for all the performers, plus Martha and the Vandellas, to come on stage and close the show out with one of Motown's greatest hits. Martha brought the band down low as the President, Ms. Obama, and Sasha came on stage to join the crew for a high-energy end to the show.

Before and after the show, we worked the room, worked it hard. Every one of those stars, many of them favorites of ours, were right there. Many of them looked as starstruck as we were. Among our two photo albums from that evening, we have shots with Vice-President Biden and his wife, with Sheryl Crow, and with Seal. Veronica was hugged and kissed by Smokey when he confused her with a friend from his Motown days. We stood and had drinks with Stevie Wonder. I do realize I live a bit of a blessed life.

To spend time at the White House, the home to all our presidents since John Adams in 1800, is an extraordinary experience. We walked the same halls as Lincoln. We have visited both the East and West Wing. The East Wing is the formal guest entrance, home to the formal lobby with its portrait gallery. It also serves as the headquarters for the First Lady. The West Wing, as we all know from the television show, is home to the executive offices. We also have seen the working offices, including the Oval Office. The oval office is the most magnificent, awe-inspiring place I have ever seen.

The Oval Office is very bright with a beautiful, rich color scheme. There were two busts sitting in the office. A bust of Abraham Lincoln and a bust of Martin Luther King, Jr. were on display when I visited during President Obama's time in office. It was clear the president wanted to pay homage to these great men who made tremendous contributions to this country. I wonder today, in 2019, if the King bust is still on display.

The first time we saw the future president was in Chicago. It was the spring of 2007, shortly after he announced in mid-February his formal entry into the race. We shook hands, but in the busy crowd, we did not speak.

However, he came to Kalamazoo, Michigan, 130 miles west of my Flint home, in 2010 and we did spend some time together. Not only did we shake hands, we shared an amiable conversation. There were twenty of us present in a meeting room in a downtown hotel. I shared how thrilled my brother was with his candidacy, especially given our youth in the Jim Crow south. I felt that he was sincerely impressed with what I had accomplished as a businessman with roots in the South.

The president was not in Kalamazoo solely to meet a small group of supporters. He was there to visit Kalamazoo Central High School and grant them an award for writing the best essay on education in a nationwide competition that was part of his Race to the Top education initiative. He would later return to the high school to deliver their commencement address. Michigan Democratic officials invited us to attend a small gathering of his supporters before his high school appearance.

Veronica and I had never been exposed to the security and traffic control that surrounds a presidential candidate. Fortunately, we decided to drive to Kalamazoo early in the morning. The drive from Flint to Kalamazoo is not lengthy, an easy and uncrowded two hours long.

After we arrived at the hotel, we had time for breakfast and waited for the President to arrive. I looked out of the window from the hotel and there was not one single vehicle in the street. There was absolutely no moving traffic in sight. No cars in any direction. We could hear the helicopters overhead. We were moved into the meeting room, simultaneous to a horde of security and media people bursting through the hotel's entrances. It was both heartwarming and disturbing to experience the cool efficiency that surrounds the President outside of the secure confines of the White House.

We met up with President Obama again in Columbus, Ohio in March of 2012. Upon arrival in Columbus, we were brought to an outbuilding attached to the massive Ohio State University Horseshoe stadium complex. At this meeting, thirty people were present. We patiently bided our time for a few minutes with the President. The President visited each group. He shook hands, thanked us for our support, and asked what he could do for us in Washington.

"What are your concerns? How are we doing? Do you see the

country headed in the right direction?"

The President is a methodical man. He made 100% certain to greet everyone in the room. A White House staff photographer trailed him. He took photos of each group with the President and they were mailed to our homes. Whenever the President was to be in our area for fundraisers, our contact at the White House always made certain we were invited.

As strong supporters of the President, we were also invited to the homes of powerful donors and celebrities when Obama would be present. We were invited to a dinner at Denise Illitch's home. Ms. Illitch is the daughter of the late Mike Illitch, the founder of Little Caesar's Pizza. He also owned Major League baseball's Detroit Tigers and the NHL's Detroit Red Wings. Mike was known as one of the wisest, kindest, and most generous of team owners.

More importantly, he was a brilliant and hard-working businessman. He opened his first pizza restaurant in the Detroit suburb of Garden City in 1959. Mr. Illitch passed on February 10, 2017. Active to the end, "Mr. I" and Little Caesar's had 2016 gross sales of $4 billion dollars, spread across all continents with 4,500 stores. Pizza!Pizza! indeed.

Fifty people were invited to have dinner with the President. Veronica and I were asked, along with four other people, to greet the President in the Illitch library. A bust cast in silver plate of President Obama was sitting on a pedestal. Photographs of the Illitch family standing in the Oval Office were also on display. Obviously, Illitch money played a significant role in President Obama's re-election.

When the President arrived, he was invited into the library. The six of us stood waiting. Veronica and I were beyond proud to be included in that elite half-dozen. He came directly to Veronica and me. We shook hands and he began to speak with us.

"Whaddaya hear? How's business? Everyone in good health? Are things better than before 2008?"

The President is a smooth politician. When he speaks to you,

you get the sense that he cares most sincerely about you. When you speak to him, it's as if you are the only person in the room. With that sort of focus, I would have hated to be a witness under his cross-examination.

His intelligence shines through. You do not become the president of the *Harvard Law Review* without exceptional intelligence. More importantly, Barack Obama was elected in 1990 as the first black president of the *Harvard Law Review* in its 104 years. As we all know by now, to be the first minority to lead any august and previously white organization, you can't be merely first among equals. You must stand head and shoulders about the rest.

He then moved to the other two couples and spoke with them. I watched him closely. As he spoke, his face was alive. As he listened, you could see his brain store the data. Focused, just as he was with us. He spent ten minutes or so with each couple. At the conclusion, as always, the photographs. On the basketball court in D.C., he might be one of the boys. Yet for the rest of his public life, he was Mr. President. Chances to hang out with a President come rarely and we all want to save the memory. He is charming, interesting, and the most powerful man in the world.

The six of us, the President, and his team were ushered into the foyer where the President spoke to the fifty people present. He thanked us all for our support, briefly outlined his administration's latest accomplishments, and gave us a peek into the next few months. With that, Ms. Illitch host jokingly announced, "We will not be serving pizza for dinner."

The lamb chops were fabulous.

Ms. Illitch has a lovely and large home in the Bingham Farms area of the Detroit suburbs. Built in 2000, her 14,000 square foot home with 5.5 baths sits on 1.5 acres of wooded, lush property. We dined in the foyer; it was large enough for ten tables, each table seating ten. I know because I asked. It was a night to remember.

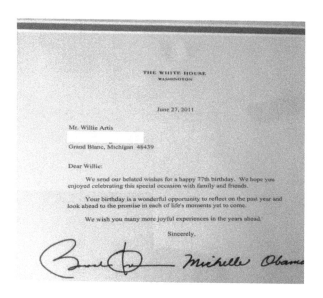

Chapter 48
Letters from the White House:
My Birthday Present

Once a family hits a certain level of income, presents present a problem. When you can afford expensive things, it truly is the thought that counts. For my 77th birthday, Veronica engineered a spectacular gift. With a thousand guesses, I never would have expected to receive such a gift in my lifetime.

Veronica—I need to say upfront with the utmost love and respect—can be a pitbull. That is what made her such a business success. She is a kind, loving woman, but she knows how to reach her objectives. When she talks with someone about an important issue, when it is something she really wants, there is no misunderstanding. Veronica Luster Artis gets her point across.

She called her contact at the White House.

"My husband Willie has been a staunch and generous supporter of the President since he announced his candidacy. It would be a very nice gesture, one that would mean a lot to both Willie and myself, if President Obama could recognize Willie on his 77th birthday. Willie turned 77 on May 30, 2011. Who do I need to speak with to make this happen?"

"I can make that happen, Mrs. Artis," her contact said. "I'll get with the President and First Lady's social secretary. This will be taken care of. The President and Mrs. Obama will be happy to send out birthday greetings to your husband."

On June 30, 2011, I received a letter from the White House. Not to brag, but as contributors to the campaign, we did occasionally receive mail on White House stationary. When I opened the letter, it was not the usual solicitation and invitation.

To my absolute amazement, it was a letter from President and Mrs. Obama. Of course, at the time, I had no idea that Veronica had put this whole thing together with her contact at the White House as my 77th birthday present.

I raced through the house.

"Veronica! Veronica!! You're never going to believe this! C'mere, lemme show you what's in the mail. Veronica, it's a birthday letter from the President!"

She looked up at me, bored.

"Oh, really? Hmm."

At that point, her bored face broke in a huge grin.

"Happy Birthday, sweetheart. Happy 77th birthday."

I was so excited I decided to have the letter framed. The letter is not computer generated and robo-signed. It is actual correspondence signed by the President and First Lady.

The letter is currently displayed in my living room. Often, our guests will walk over to the etagere to read the framed letter; to view the contents and the signatures. If I'm honest, for the first few years I had that letter, if you were in my home and didn't notice the letter, I might well walk you over to it and tell the story of how Veronica put the whole thing together.

I am not a celebrity. I am occasionally recognized around town as a successful businessman. No one outside of our business community would be likely to recognize me. For a regular guy like me, to receive a letter from the President of the United States that congratulates you on your birthday with all best wishes is an extraordinary experience. Although I made contributions to his campaign and have met with him on multiple occasions, to be acknowledged by President Obama is one of my life's most remarkable events.

It's at times like this that I really miss my brother, Boots. As I think back, Boots might've appreciated this letter even more than me. It makes me sad to think that Boots was so close to seeing a black man take the oath of office. It saddens me even more when I think how much Boots would've loved to know that his own baby brother had the chance to hobnob with the President and First Lady. Whenever I stand in front of that letter, I think how much Boots would've enjoyed reading a letter written to his brother and signed by the President and First Lady.

My Letter

The White House
Washington, D.C.
June 27, 2011

Willie E. Artis

Grand Blanc, Michigan 48439

Dear Willie,

We send our belated wishes for a happy 77th birthday. We hope you enjoyed celebrating this special occasion with family and friends.

Your birthday is a wonderful opportunity to reflect on the past year and look ahead to the promise in each life's moments yet to come.

We wish you many more joyful experiences in the years ahead.

Sincerely,
Barack Obama

Michelle Obama

Chapter 49
How to Party with a President

I have been blessed to be able to give money to a black man campaigning for the president of our country. I will admit, I was doubtful. As much as I admired his courage in running, I didn't honestly expect that he could win. Yes, I cheered loudly as I watched the returns be finalized but there was still a tiny part of me that doubted the reality of the whole outcome. Not that it was a dream, it all seemed so unlikely, so otherworldly. A black man was President in my lifetime.

I have always donated money to local people who campaigned for local office. Local politics are important. They have an immediate impact on our lives and our business success. However, those donations were dwarfed in comparison to the amount of money I gave to the Obama campaign. Let's not kid ourselves, it was those checks that gained me access to the President and politics at the highest level.

As a result, we were often invited to attend White House events. Veronica and I had to go through background checks prior to every one of our White House visits for Christmas parties and concerts. No surprise, the background checks are extensive. Phone calls are made. Documents are checked and rechecked. The phone calls are made again, just to see if people will answer the same way each time. Perhaps even visits are made. I wouldn't know. They're called the Secret Service for a reason. Obviously, if you're going to be in contact with the world's most important man, everything possible must be done to identify every possible risk.

Seeing the President and the First Lady at these affairs and being able to talk directly to them is an exciting experience. I will remember those nights for the balance of my life. Should you have that chance, you will never forget the moment when you are introduced and walk into the White House.

I have created an album of memorabilia that contains our photographs from the Obama's events that we attended. We have a wide range of shots: Photos of Veronica, me, the President and Mrs. Obama; Mrs. Obama and my wife; me shaking hands with President Obama. When I open those albums, I am reminded of my great luck in life. Imagine, from a little kid who started out as a butcher's helper in the ghetto of Jim Crow Memphis to a millionaire businessman who stands with the President of the United States.

You attend enough of these events, you will meet many people at these affairs that are famous. Actors, entertainers, and high-level business celebrities were all invited to celebrate the Christmas season with the Obamas. Some you will recognize by name and you summon up some courage to walk over to a Morgan Freeman or a Tom Hanks or Meryl Streep, stick out your hand, introduce yourself, and tell them you love their work. We've spoken with Stevie Wonder, Jamie Fox, Jordin Sparks, Mellody Hobson, the wife of George Lucas, to name-drop a few of our favorite stars.

Others will look familiar and you cannot quite place them. You'll also notice that many of the elite will look every bit as awed as you to be having dinner at the White House. One thing every guest shares is that everyone is having a huge amount of fun.

At one Christmas party I saw a familiar-looking man in the buffet line loading up his plate. I continued to stare at him. I thought I knew him yet could not quite place him. I realized I'd often seen him on television and in the movies. I approached him and introduced myself. It was Wendell Pierce, star of HBO shows like *Treme* and *The Wire*. I've since added *Parker*, a Jason Statham thriller that co-stars Pierce, to my DVD collection. Whenever I watch it, I think back to our pleasant conversation that evening.

Nearly everyone in the crowd made significant contributions to the President's campaign. Many of the celebrities gave not just large sums of cash, but also offered up endorsements and campaigned on Obama's behalf. These parties were not enormous. Perhaps one hundred people were in attendance. It pleased me to see so many people of various colors and faiths in attendance. President Obama had truly brought his party together with his campaign.

At the last Christmas party we attended, the President addressed all the people in attendance.  He discussed his many accomplishments in his first term in office. I could sense that the crowd was getting anxious. He had not yet said anything about "moving forward, in the years to come"—nothing about a second term. He let us hang for a few minutes longer, and with a large grin he said, "I would like to announce that I will run for a second term as your president." The applause from the crowd in the green room was overwhelming.

Again, as I was caught up in the joy of the moment, I flashed back to Boots, the man who convinced me that Obama was going to be not just our next president, but our first black president. Unable to share my experience with my brother, I gave several photographs to his widow, our dearest Ann Artis, a woman we love deeply. Ann resides in a nursing home. She has never recovered from the death of her husband, my brother Boots.

Chapter 50
It's Time to Think About Retirement

Many decisions had to be made before I reached age 75. I had owned and managed my company for over 30 years. You've probably heard business owners talk about their companies as their "babies" and I was no different. Every entrepreneur has an idea, s/he figures out how to make that idea a reality, and then brings the idea to market. For the rest of that company's life, you live and breathe business. You sing with joy in good times, and you brood and sulk in bad. You land a big contract, close a great deal, and you're like a grandparent showing off photos of a grandbaby. It's pride. It's immensely satisfying. It's addictive.

In earlier years, I had tried to sell my firm on the open market. My P & L numbers were good. My contracts were solid. My staff, from the ground floor on up, were the finest anywhere. We had low turnover. We took great pride in hiring the best people and paying them a fair wage. My firm's relationship with our union and our suppliers was outstanding. We were a great buy.

I was surprised to learn that buyers of companies were not interested. It wasn't that IPC wasn't of interest. Prospective buyers liked the company, the connections, the P&L. What they didn't like was Flint, Michigan. Some buyers didn't see a future for the packaging industry. They felt that two trends would sink the independent packaging firm. One trend was towards in-sourcing. The feeling was that the auto industry would start packaging and shipping their own products, rather than use an outside supplier.

The other fear was that an Amazon/Fedex-type of packaging company would swoop in—a mega-packaging company—and drive the independents out of business. Other potential buyers turned up their noses at the idea of local banking.

But mostly, it was location. There was no denial on my part. Flint was struggling. From 1960 to 2010, the population of Flint was nearly half. In 1978, IndustryCorp employed 80,000 people in Flint. By the time I began to think of selling in 2010, they were down to 8,000 employees. This plunged the region into a recession all its own. You can't forget the massive recession of 2008, either. Oh, and there was that matter of the $17 billion bailout of GM and Chrysler in December of 2008. This was initiated by President Bush and finalized by President Obama. You should also remember that Flint's city government was so poorly managed that two separate GOP Governors of Michigan, Engler and Snyder, placed the city under emergency financial management to enforce some degree of fiscal responsibility.

In that same period, Flint repeatedly made the news as one of the deadliest cities in America. Granted, most of the crime was within two very small areas of the city, but you could not fight the public perception that Flint in the first part of the 21st century was a war zone.

In retrospect, I should not have been surprised. I had conversations with agencies located in New York, Chicago, and Philadelphia. They all expressed a fear of unions. They also had the typical big-city attitude. They felt that there was no way that Flint could provide highly qualified people capable of corporate management; they were convinced that it would be impossible to attract bright people to the Flint area. This information was provided to me, quietly, by brokers within those big-city agencies.

All of this made me both sad and a little befuddled. I decided to change tacks.

It was not in my best interest, nor my company's, to continue on the same path. I needed someone inside the local industry, perhaps even someone within my own company, to take over the reins. No surprise, this was a difficult task. I needed someone who was willing to work the long hours, someone who knew the business from the ground-up, and someone who would be acceptable to the banks as my successor.

I stayed at the helm and kept my eyes and ears open. Over the next couple of years, I realized that while I was getting older, the problem was not going to solve itself. I was waiting for the right person to appear. I could not afford to wait much longer. I was determined—I refused to be seen as a doddering 80 year old man too old to run the show.

As I approached the age of 75, I had to dig deeper into my own mind. After much soul-searching, conversations with my wife Veronica, and several other trusted colleagues, I recognized the company must be sold. It is hard to express how difficult a decision this was. If you've raised children to adulthood, you understand what I mean. We birth our children, rear them, educate them, get them off to college, and send them into the real world as our emissaries into the future. It tears at your heart and fills you with pride as you see your children turn into fine adults with their own lives.

This move was not all that different. I created this company, learned with it, steered it through storms, and turned it into a business that created a significant lifestyle for my family. As a man who grew up poorer than poor, that I could also help thousands of people support their families with my company was a point of pride in my life. My company was 40 years old, still growing, still moving forward. It was extremely difficult, but I convinced myself that the time was right for another man or woman to take the helm of IPC.

Selling your own company to another person is a poignant experience. It's not your baby anymore. That's not your office in the corner. Those are no longer your plants cranking out cartons by the thousands. Those are not your machines filling the cartons with parts for clients that you've nurtured for 40 years.

No matter. When you hit a point in life and you see clearly that your skills are diminished, your age makes you ineffective, your legacy will be tarnished, that if you continue you jeopardize the well-being of many dear people—that's when you say, "I need to go."

Willie reviewing plant operations in Flint

Chapter 51
Time to Put the "Success" into a Succession Plan

Throughout this memoir, I have tried to drop in bits of some hard-won business wisdom. Here's my last one: *If you own a small business, start planning for your exit from the firm long before you anticipate leaving.* Talk with your business attorneys. Talk to your CPAs. If you want to walk out the door when you turn 70 as a comfortably well-off man or woman, start thinking about it when you are 45 or 50. If you wait much longer, the plan can easily become a desperation ploy. And desperation is never good. Yes, succession plans are that important and that complex.

I tried to convince one of our upper level managers to take an ownership position in the company. I was not successful with this person. I am eternally grateful that this effort failed. What happened? This.

I had made a tremendous effort to encourage one of our high-level managers to become more deeply involved in IPC. I knew I needed a successor and I felt this fellow might be interested in taking an ownership stake in the company. Over many months, I worked hard to convince one of my favorite people, Kyle Pinto, to take a real interest in ownership. I worked this deal darned near as hard as any deal I did with any vendor. If you think about it, this deal was far more important than any deal I'd done since my company became successful. The future of IPC as it moved into the 21st century rested on this deal getting done. Thank God it didn't.

I had always thought highly of Kyle Pinto. He was a hard-working man. He had earned many corporate responsibilities. Pinto had academic credentials. Kyle had twenty years' experience in our field. We brought him in, he quickly moved to a high level, and he'd been outstanding in his several years of employment with us.

"This is the guy," I said to myself. I said it to Veronica. I really believed Kyle was the guy who would lead the company for many more years. We had meetings. I took him to meetings with me. I introduced him around. Yet, when I'd raise the topic of ownership, I could feel him backing away.

I'm a guy who listens to his gut. On the one hand, everything seemed perfect for us. Kyle was competent. He was well-regarded in our building and with the banks, our vendors, and our accounts. He could do this. And why wouldn't he want to? More money, prestige, more satisfaction as he grew the company in his image.

Yet, I was getting nowhere with him. I dropped the matter for several weeks and then it hit me: I was getting no place with my efforts to involve him in ownership because Kyle was scared.

Scared? He was terrified. He had no idea about risk. He was apprehensive about nearly every issue. I reviewed his time with us. Unless it was a sure thing, he had always been an "Oh, no, what if XYZ goes wrong?" guy. I needed a "Great idea! How can we make this happen?" person as my successor.

Kyle Pinto did not trust himself. He did not believe in himself. He needed someone to report to. He needed a boss. He needed a go-to person. I believe that he concluded that as an owner of the company, all of that would be absent, and he would have to make final decisions by himself.

All businesses are cyclical. Whether you build homes or refrigerators, some years will be good, some will be so-so, and some will be terrible. Continue to build good products and take care of your customers and business will return. You must trust your core competency. Sadly, Mr. Pinto didn't.

In 2007, the entire business world was hammered. When that $8 trillion-dollar housing bubble burst, everyone took the hit. Two of our major clients were no exception. They had to cut back drastically. As a result, IPC took a big hit, too. Our numbers were bad, but then, so were everyone else's. Depending on how you read your economic history, it may have been a worse depression that the Crash of 1929.

When Kyle looked at the numbers, he became even more scared. Our numbers were bad. Our best customers' numbers were bad. Everyone's numbers were bad. This made him even more apprehensive about ownership.

Obviously, we had to take certain financial measures to remain stable because the company had been affected. We cut back everywhere we could. And a few places where we really couldn't. Throughout this time, despite the downturn, I continued to speak with him.

"Look, Kyle, we provide a crucial product to IndustryCorp. They're the world leader. They've weathered storms like this before. They came out of the Crash of '29 strong. They came out of the '73-'75 Recession just fine. They know how to handle this. They'll be okay. And then we'll be okay."

"But what if they don't?" Pinto said. "What if this is the time they crater for good? Then where will I be? You'll have all your funds from the buyout, and me? Well, I'll be stuck with nearly bankrupt company, no cash of my own. I'll be ruined."

"Come on, now. They'll make adjustments," I said. "They'll get back to profitability. They've got the best people in the world, they've got factories and sales all over the world. They're not going anywhere. We stick with them, they'll stick with us. It'll be okay. This can't be the first time you've been through a downturn."

"Well, no, it's not, but I've never been in the hot seat at a time like this before and I don't think I like it."

I could read the fear in Kyle's face.

"I think I'm headed elsewhere, Willie. Probably in another state. I can't just sit here."

I don't think he understood the severity of our customers' situation. Kyle Pinto was highly valuable to me. I didn't like the idea that he'd bail on us when things got tough. Scared? Sure, he was scared, but he was still good at his job.

He told me about his plans for a startup in a southern state and it left me scratching my head.

"You do your market research, Kyle? Window treatments? Drapes and such? Really? Is your heart in this? Seems like there aren't too many customers for that in the South. Most of the folks down there are retired. I can't imagine it going well. This isn't you. This is you."

I waved my arm around his office. I pointed towards the window at our plant.

"This is you. You know this business. You're damn good at this business. Stick around. I'll keep you where you are, stop bugging you about buying me out. You're a good man, Pinto. I need your help until this whole thing gets straightened out."

"Sorry, Willie, but I can't stay. This is making me crazy. I know this'll fly. Thanks, but I'm done."

Kyle Pinto left us for the South and started his own firm. In less than a year, his company was belly-up; he lost all his savings, defaulted on a loan, and had to look for work. He became an employee instead of an employer. I'm sure he was a good employee. But I'm even more glad he never took over my chair.

I chose more wisely in 2009. I began preliminary discussions with another executive employee. This person had been with us for many years. As a matter of fact, Betty Aims started with us at the age of eighteen. Ms. Aims had grown with the company and had many years of experience. She had excelled at lower level management, so much so that we had to find room for her upstairs within several years. Once moved to upper level management, she continued to be an innovator and problem solver for IPC. Everything Betty did turned to gold.

Why? She studied. She researched. Betty was able to look at nearly every side of a problem, and do it quickly, before she came to a well-reasoned answer. Betty never graduated college. As far as I know, she took just a few classes at the community college. That fueled her drive. Everything about Betty revolved around success in the workplace. Her immense native intelligence, her ability to problem-solve, her curiosity—all created the perfect second CEO for my company.

It is always difficult to be the "next guy" after someone has been successful. I was successful, there is no doubt. Look at sports. A college coach like Bo Schembechler; his successor Gary Moeller struggled and failed to fill those cleats. Moeller, successful on the field, succumbed to the pressure and resigned in disgrace following a string of alcoholic incidents. Casey Stengel won eight World Series titles with the New York Yankees between 1949 and 1960. Who remembers anyone that came after? It was a cast of failures until Billy Martin took over in 1975.

Are you surprised that I should have chosen a woman as my successor? You shouldn't be. Yes, I was a 73-year-old man. I understand that many men of my age would not have been inclined to choose a female successor. Yet, I was also a 73-year-old man who grew up in the Jim Crow South. All my life, I fought to be judged on the quality of my work, not the color of my skin. All my life, I had sought out the best people for my company, regardless of color or religion or gender. This was no different. This woman simply stood head and shoulders over anyone else in my employ.

Our initial conversation went extremely well. I had always felt that Betty loved her work. I had always known that Betty had an excellent feel for personnel decisions. I knew she knew the business; that's why we so quickly moved her into management. Most importantly, Betty Aims knew what she didn't know. I've never been afraid to ask an expert in a particular field to decode some difficult problem for me. As a CEO, you can't let your ego ruin your decision-making. Your job is to manage the big picture. No one can know everything. If you can't bring yourself to ask an expert for help, then you're a fool.

I decided to continue our dialogue regarding ownership. We met with our attorneys to discuss our intentions. Taking direction from our experts in business succession, we established a five-year time limit. We developed a succession plan that included Veronica, our attorney and our CPA. Over that time, I would mentor Betty directly, and then gradually fade away. We also created some points in the timeline that would allow Betty to opt out if that's what she chose to do.

We began to work very closely in training for ownership. Betty Aims is an extremely bright person who understands exactly what must be done to continue our success. She knew packaging. She knew numbers. But she'd never before been the Boss.

Business is funny; people think that big business and high finance are something special, yet they really aren't. It's not all that different from my days as a butcher's helper back during WWII. It's about relationships. People bought meat from me because they trusted that I was fair with my cuts and my weights. Pricing matters, and it always will. I've seen plenty of deals go south over pennies— but it's relationships that seal every deal.

Think back to the last time you purchased a car or a major appliance. You shopped, you met salespeople, and more often than not, if the prices were anywhere in line, you bought from the sales rep that gave you the best vibes. My job was to move myself away from IPC as the giver of the best vibe and have Betty slide seamlessly into my seat.

Betty and I made calls. We made dozens of calls. We walked the floors of our plants together. We walked the floors of our accounts with upper level management. We ate dozens of lunches with high-level customer executives and our bank officials.

I realized that a process of this magnitude takes a great deal of time. I'd built a reputation as a straight shooter, a stand-up guy, and maybe I underestimated the length of time it would take for my reputation to also become Betty Aims's reputation.

I knew the bank would need many months to accept our succession plan. Under my direction, thirty years of IPC had created a strong track record. We met our payroll. Bills were paid on time. We did not seek to renegotiate deals with the bank after the fact. My father raised me that when you shake hands, when you give your word, you are now bound to deliver. As the founder of any business knows, your reputation and your firm's reputation are one and the same. Our bankers could not have been shocked that I was stepping aside, no one works forever, but it took time for them to accept Betty as the new leader. She would need to demonstrate her knowledge and her integrity.

Our customers needed time, too. Many of the men and women I called upon had come to know me well over the years. We raised kids together. We'd gotten married and divorced together. Many of our clients were people who, over the years, I came to sincerely care about as people. I know they felt that way about me, too. When I told them I planned to move on and I would need their support, they responded positively when I told them how the succession plan was structured.

Still, banks and customers do not accept new ownership overnight. They must believe in what you are trying to achieve with a new owner of your company. They must be convinced the company will remain stable and profitable under a new ownership. I realized we needed several years to prove that we were moving in the right direction. We needed to ensure our customer base and the bank we would remain stable and the company would continue to be successful. That's why we devised the succession plan as we did. I'd be very visible early on, right there at Betty's side, and as banks and customers became comfortable with her, I'd fade out of the executive office.

Very quickly, Betty became comfortable in my chair. It did not take long for me to realize that my continued presence in meetings was not needed. In fact, it became a detriment. Aims handled all our meetings, and no matter how damn good she was, people would still look to me. It took away from her authority for me to point at her and say, "Hey, she's in charge. Talk to Aims." As long as I was there to point to her and say, "she's in charge," she was clearly not in charge.

I stopped going to meetings. We'd talk before meetings, and we'd break down meetings afterwards, but I stayed in the office. Betty told me that she noticed the "Where's Willie?" syndrome died quickly. Clients and bankers were so used to me being at her side that when she walked into a conference room, they'd all ask, "Hey, where's Willie?" Ms. Aims would say, "Oh, he's sitting this one out." Pretty quickly, everyone got the idea that she truly was in charge, and that is when the company began to change hands in very real sense. Those were the moments when Betty Aims became a business leader.

As I mentioned earlier, the choice of selling the company to an outsider was made impossible by the business world's perception of Flint and my reliance on local banking.

Yet, I was seventy years old and did not want to operate a company when I reached eighty. That is when I seriously began my discussion with Betty Aims. I had to make sure that she came across as a leader who was ready to manage the company. It was essential that the customers and bank would be on board with us when we were ready for the company to fully change hands. We had to make sure the customers and bank believed in our transition process and the company would continue to be successful under a new owner. It has proven to be one of the best decisions I have ever made in business.

Chapter 52
The Death of B.B. King

While at work on my life's story, I was saddened to hear about the death of B.B. King on May 14, 2015. B.B. passed away in Las Vegas at age of 89. B.B. died from a combination of things. He had Alzheimer's, which caused his organs to shut down. His diabetes caused a series of strokes. He also had congestive heart failure.

I've written about my youthful encounters with B.B. earlier in this book. As an adult, I saw B.B. play many times, frequently in my hometown of Flint and in nearby Saginaw, Michigan. The last time I saw him play was in a Windsor, Ontario casino in 2013. Rhonda and Terence Broussard, our children, treated us to a couple of tickets. I wanted to say hello to B.B. but could not get close enough to the stage.

How times change. As a young teenager, I saw him playing roadhouses and house parties to all-black audiences. As a young man during the 1960s, I saw him playing to integrated audiences in Chicago. But here in Windsor, Canada, the arena was filled with 5000 people, 99% of them white. B.B. built an immense crossover audience since those days in the 1960s. You'd be safe to say that it was B.B. who kept the blues alive for many years.

It was back in the early 1980s when I last spoke with Riley. He was playing a gig in Saginaw. As I walked to my seat, I saw him leaning against a pole backstage while he smoked a cigarette.

"Hey, B.B.! B.B., you remember me?"

Definitely not my best conversation starter.

His eyes slanted closed, and he looked me up and down.

"I know you? Why should I know you?" he said.

"I'm that snot-nosed little kid that used to ride in the back seat of your '47 blue Chevy in Memphis. My brother Howard played in your band for a while..."

I couldn't finish.

"Holy shit, are you *that* kid? Sonuvabitch, how are ya?"

He wrapped me in a hug. Ash from his cigarette fell onto my suit. I didn't care. We tried to catch up a little. His band played a couple tunes solo, just like they always did.

"Hey, dontcha gotta go play?" I asked.

"Hell, no. I'm the guy everyone paid to see."

He laughed.

The band played one more song and I heard an announcer:

"Ladies and gentlemen, let's have a big Saginaw welcome..."

"Gotta go, kid. Thanks for saying hi."

With that, B.B. and I shook hands, he strode out on stage looking like a million bucks, and I made my way to my seat.

Riley B.B. King lived a long time and had a great life. I was sorry to see him pass away.

Chapter 53
The Office is in the Rear-View Mirror

Our succession plan has been intense. As of this writing, we are in Year 4 of our five year succession plan. With over 1000 days of new ownership in my rearview mirror, I can safely say that with Betty Aims in the corner office, the future of IPC is assured. Betty is surrounded by a group of highly qualified executives. Our customer base and the bank are pleased with our succession.

What does Betty do that others might not? Betty has vision and the ability to bring that vision to fruition. She can see beyond the U.S. borders. Here in Michigan, we naturally look towards Canada as a trade partner. After all, the U.S. does about $544 billion in two-way trade with the Maple Leaf. Everyone likes to work with Canada. We share great amounts of culture, history, and of course, language and skin color.

Yet, Betty looked south to Mexico. Betty and company have held discussions with a potential Mexican partner. Mexico is the U.S.'s third largest trade partner at $525 billion. Even in the best of times, trade with Mexico, given the language barrier and the skin color issue, is sometimes seen as less valuable by many here in the U.S. The introduction of a new Mexican trade partner is a high-risk, high-reward activity. However, once it gets up and running, it should prove highly profitable.

I miss the activity. I miss the office. I miss seeing the production line. I miss the game, the sportsmanship, the business buzz, the camaraderie. I miss walking the factory floor and checking in with my people. A handful of those people are children of people I hired when we first launched IPC. For a man whose first thoughts in his morning shower were business, whose last thoughts at night were business, the transition has been difficult. I knew it was time, and that my baby was in good hands, but I still felt a sense of loss. There are moments still when I fight the urge to pick up the phone, give Betty a ring, and see what's what.

Thankfully, I have Veronica. I know she misses the buzz, too. Yet, she seems to cope more easily with retirement than me. We are learning how to live together in retirement. It's not always easy. We were a very busy couple, highly visible at work in the community.

I'll be honest; I find life to be quite dull with nothing to do. I continue to look for something worthwhile to do when I'm at home; a cause, a project, something. Anything. No reasonable offer refused. Email me in care of my agent or publisher.

Writing my life story has been quite a challenge. It's made me feel alive again with every story I got down on paper, er, computer. With 50 years in business behind me, to quote Roy Batty in the movie *Blade Runner*, "I've seen things you people wouldn't believe...All those moments will be lost in time, like tears in the rain." Perhaps that's why I felt so strongly about getting these thoughts down; I'm the last of a generation, a black man who grew from a childhood of Jim Crow to a successful businessman whose firm employed nearly a thousand men and women.

Veronica and I find that life after business is a different world. For forty years, I was involved in decisions that made my life exciting. I met fascinating people—some happened to be the President of the United States and his wife, and some were people I hired to clean our factory floors—and each had stories to tell if you took the time to listen. My business success gave me the power to become a voice for causes I believed in. My business success forced people who would not normally give a black man the time of day to listen to me. My business success allowed me to be a part of our local society. Somehow, I even garnered a little bit of local celebrity. People would sometimes stop me on the street or in a restaurant, "Hey, didn't I see you on the news last night?" I miss that part of life and now, I must learn how to live a much different way of life.

Now that I'm retired, I think back on my time in the segregated South and somehow, I find myself very lonely. Most of my family is deceased. I miss my two older brothers nearly every day. We had a lot of fun while growing up. We didn't understand the horrors of Jim Crow. This was just the way things were. It was up to us to make our lives as good as they could be. We were kids growing up in wartime. The bombs overhead in Europe and the food shortages and the destruction and unfairness were just a fact of life. When we became older, the love, affection, and hijinks lasted until my brothers passed away. I suppose I'm the last Artis standing.

As a child growing up in the South, our lives did not allow for planning ahead. There was no real tomorrow. It was day-to-day. Make a couple bucks. Get some food. Pay the rent. Worry about tomorrow—tomorrow. Ain't no good to worry. You can't change what's going to happen. Keep your eyes down when the cops walk past. And that still might not be enough to keep you from getting the shit beat out of you by a cop on a bad day.

I never knew that one day I would become a successful entrepreneur. I barely gave thought to the idea of owning a business. Maybe I could have a steady job as a butcher. Maybe as a trucker. The world was very small to a black man born in Memphis in 1934. My life as a black person living in Memphis compared to my life today is an anomaly. I cannot say that I understand everything that has occurred in my life over the last forty years.

I find my life today to be surreal when I think of where I came from. I am a black man born in the early 1930s in Memphis, TN. In my eighties here in 2019, I live a luxurious life on a private, privileged golf course in the suburbs in southeast Michigan.

We're at the end of the book. This would be a good place for a list to sum up:

1) You must learn to create your own opportunities in life. You must learn that nothing is given to you. The only way is to earn it.

2) I write this book to encourage a young black person somewhere, or perhaps a Mexican, or a Muslim. You must put forth every effort to better yourself. You do not fail because of your skin color or your religion. I believe with my entire heart and soul that black people do not fail simply because we are black.

3) You will have people throw obstacles in your path. Huge obstacles, placed there with one purpose—to derail your success. Do not allow this to stop you. Those obstacles may impede your progress, yet those people who place them there do not realize that all they've done is given you an opportunity to become smarter, more capable, more determined, more successful.

4) I am the last of my kind. A black man from the Jim Crow South who became a success. My story must be remembered. If not, it will happen again. Maybe not to black people. It might be Hispanics. Or Muslims. But it can happen again.

If you pay attention to my first three points above, you may not become wealthy, but you will create chances—chances for you to grab a better opportunity. I never placed barriers in front of myself, other people did. I always had to be the first guy in line. I had to get the best for myself. I was never satisfied with a "good" second place.

I never tolerated second place. You push me back to second place and you better brace yourself because all Hell is about to break loose. If you are satisfied with second place, then you've missed the point of this book.

This business, you think you finally have a handle on it, and you realize it's always had a handle on you. I never liked losing at anything. Not even when I was a snot-nosed 14-year-old playing dice on Father Coyne's screens in our school's basement in 1948.

Afterword

In May of 2019, the new owner and CEO of the industrial packaging company profiled in this memoir, Jane Worthing ("Betty Aims"), sat down with me (David L. Stanley) for a "state of the company" interview. We walked and talked as she showed me around the company's new facility, one that will be 290,000 square feet when completed. The new plant stands on the shoulders of industrial giants.

At one point in time, AC Spark Plug East sat on the site and oversaw worldwide operations for the manufacture of auto parts. For almost 100 years, the factories on North Dort Highway in Flint produced millions of spark plugs, oil filters, air cleaners, dashboard instruments, fuel pumps, and all the other automotive parts needed to get a car going. The building was purchased by Phoenix Investments, a real estate firm that specializes in the rebirth of industrial operations. With 42-foot-tall ceilings and dozens of semi-truck bays, it was a perfect choice for renovation. With a footprint of five football fields, it will be a monument to the revitalization of industry.

Jane's pride in her company's latest increase in operational size was clear as she showed me around. While not fully up to speed, the shop floor had electric hi-low movers racing around with raw packaging materials like it was Ms. Pac-Man.

DS: This is a thoroughly modern plant. The ventilation is so good I can't even smell the new paint. I saw that (Michigan) Governor (Gretchen) Whitmer was here for a photo op the other day.

JW: This is state-of-the-art. It was an incredibly complex project to put together. We're involved in this with local government partners. We have state and federal input on this. The Phoenix Investors group. A lot of work had to be done to make sure that we were able to take maximum advantage of every legal pathway to get a building that would serve us for many years, yet at minimum cost to everyone involved. The dollars are big, but the payoff is equally big. For everybody: Our company, the people of Flint who will work here, the taxpayers—yes, we pay taxes, the local industry...whenever a plant like this opens up in a community, it opens up a huge set of collateral advantages for everyone.

Governor Whitmer was indeed here. She and her team were great. I showed them around, introduced her to our C-suite, a bunch of our floor employees. She's very bright, asked excellent questions, but still made herself at home, too. I was impressed; she's in touch with both industry and the working folks that are all over Michigan.

I spied loading queues, each with an animal or plant drawing at the end of each queue. Hi-lows were busy filling the queues from one end, and other hi-lows were picking up goods from the queues and rolling them into semi-trailer loading docks.

DS: Can you explain the signage? You've got a rabbit, a deer, a pine tree—a sign at the head of each queue.

JW: Right, the queues. We came up with those. This industry, during my time here, has gotten incredibly complex. There are thousands of different SKUs for our raw products. Every place you see a bar code overhead is a different SKU. All of this product will be shipped to plants where the containers will be assembled.

Ms. Worthing gestured overhead. As far as I could see, a couple hundred yards in any direction, there were bar codes on large signs hanging from the ceiling. It reminded me of the closing scene in the original Raiders of the Lost Ark, where the Ark of the Covenant is rolled into anonymity in a government warehouse.

JW: Our folks go out with the hi-lows and their unique pick tickets. Each load draws from a variety of SKU stops. So they pick the right product and deliver them to a station where they are palleted and wrapped with those giant rolls of Saran Wrap. That generates a shipping load. But which queue does the load go to? It's really hard to match up those load numbers quickly and accurately for humans.

The load numbers are 10-15 digits long. What happens is that the palleted load gets a visual code that tells our drivers which queue is their load drop-off. Meanwhile, our computers keep track precisely of which queue gets which parts and onto which truck we're loading. So, we've removed a possible error spot because our folks no longer have to worry about a "3" looking like an "8."

They could scan it with a device, but this is even quicker. Pick up the squirrel load. Put it in the squirrel queue. And when the squirrel loads are all picked and loaded onto trucks, that job is over. It's timed out to the minute. As far as I know, we're the only packaging company that does this kind of visual coding.

DS: Management is a much different beast in 2019 than it was in 1980, isn't it?

JW: Huge difference. Even though our company has always had good relationships with their workers, it was still a little bit of ruling through intimidation. Willie is a great guy, so I think it was just a product of the era. A Vince Lombardi-style football coach couldn't be successful today in the NFL today, could it? We are just different people these days.

I'm plenty tough, and there is no one that works for me that doesn't know that, but I run this place through engagement. I want people to be able to bring good ideas to the management team, or even straight to me. I want ownership for our folks. When that happens, people work better. They're happier, less likely to take an adversarial position, it makes for a better workplace. A more productive workplace.

Another part of that is every business workplace is much leaner. At our biggest, right before the 2008 crash, we had nearly 400 employees. That's a lot of people. Well, these days, we're around 125, and doing a similar amount of business. Sometimes, we bring in 15 or 20 people for special projects. They're our flextime employees. They're on-call. Those folks are not temps. They work for us. We've trained them and we value that when we have the chance to run a quick project, they can step right in and do a good job for us. They're a crucial part of our workforce and we make sure they know it.

DS: What are you looking for in your salaried employees these days?

JW: In 2019, it is all about analytic skills. We do not have the time to teach analytic skills. You want to work in a future-aimed industrial company today, not just in packaging, you better have strong analytical skills on your resume. You need systems knowledge. You need to have broad operating systems knowledge, the analytic skills to make sense of the data—those are the starting points. Without those, we wouldn't even consider you.

Think about this for a second. We're on a 24-hour cycle these days, right? In the news, in government, in social media? Business, too. Customers insist that things be handled accurately, and with business being a worldwide proposition today, if you can't do that, you're gone. Pftt. Gone.

With us, it's the logistics: How? Where? When? What happened? What do we need to fix and how quickly can we do it? And when nothing goes wrong, how can we make sure that continues? How can be better?

DS: What about the packaging itself? Michigan State University, just forty-five minutes away, graduates about 600-700 packaging science students every year.

JW: We innovate like crazy with our lab. One of our other facilities, not here on this part of campus, is dedicated to just that. New materials are always coming out, new ways of processing and shaping old materials. Corrugated is still the mainstay, has been for 60 years, maybe more, but we are always looking to be lighter, more efficient in our time and our green footprint. Plus, every time our clients innovate with their parts and products, that's a new opportunity for us to create a new container.

When battery packs started to become prevalent, we did some

great stuff with them. They have unique needs, not like anything we handled before with those lithium batteries. They needed to be quite different than our current state of the art. Our lab came through and we now have patents on those products.

DS: We watch TV. We read. Everyone is talking about the global economy. That's a big difference between Willie's day and yours.

JW: Globalization is here to stay and it is real. We have seriously considered a collaboration in Mexico in San Luis Potosi. One thing we've found is that in our industry, there must be an anchor business. We can't simply open a packaging plant and tell everyone in town, "Hey, we're here!" San Luis Potosi is an industrial center. Cummins Diesel is there. GM. The automation firm ABB. BMW is doing a one billion dollar plant there. So, it makes a lot of sense for us to be there. We have expertise. We can produce products those clients need at competitive prices. And if we're not there, someone will be.

Globalization is not without its challenges. When we're closing up for the day here at 6 p.m., someone in Japan is sitting down at the desk because it's 7 a.m. there. The other part of globalization that hit us hard was the crash of 2008.

The year 2008 changed us, changed the face of all industry a lot. It was a rough time. I'm sure Willie told you how difficult it was to keep this place afloat during the Crash. We really were that close. And Willie, God bless him, he was the patriarch. He felt so deeply about his employees. Having to lay off a lot of people was terrible for him, but it was necessary. It wasn't just hourly that lost jobs.

We lost layers of management, too. We made the decision to not rebuild all that management. We're very lean here. You've met my three top people in just the two hours we've been together. That's it. There's us. One of us goes down, well, that's the down side of lean. We don't have any bench strength.

DS: A lot has changed in your tenure, your rise from a just out of high school kid to the CEO of a worldwide corporation. What hasn't changed?

JW: It's cliché, but this is still a people business. We still have to get in front of potential clients and talk with them. Figure out what they need. Show them solutions. It's not like Fortune 500 manufacturers are posting "Hey, we want to buy three million boxes" on our website.

When I first moved into management here, it was a little. different. There was a lot of entertaining. We had to wine and dine our clients and potential clients. The folks who supplied us with our raw product had to wine and dine us. Tickets. Travel. All of that is gone now, and that's a good thing.

It's still the face-to-face that sells. Our reputation helps, too. People know we do business fairly, aboveboard. Our numbers are spot-on. Our products are always, 100% always, the best possible.

We prevent client headaches. If we can't do a project properly, we'll pass on it. Better that someone else gets the business than we get a black eye. We generate fair profits back into our company and charge a fair price to the client. That's a win-win. We deliver.

That's how Willie always did business. That's how I learned how to do business. And that's how it's always going to be here at our company.

About the Author

Willie E. Artis was born in Memphis, Tennessee. He is the founder of an industrial packaging company headquartered in Flint, Michigan. Now retired, Willie and his wife Veronica are philanthropists mentoring the next generation of black business owners.